Porgy and Bess

The Sequel

Published in the United States by Sainte Colombe Press

Disclaimer

Porgy and Bess – The Sequel is a work of fiction. All incidents, dialogue, and all characters, with the exception of the characters and events from the novel and play *Porgy* by DuBose and Dorothy Heyward, and any well-known historical figures and well-known historical events, are products of the authors' imagination and not intended to be construed as real. Where real-life historical persons appear in the work, the situations, incidents, events, and dialogues concerning those persons are entirely fictional and are not intended to depict actual events or to change the entirely fictional nature of the work. In all other respects, any resemblance to persons living or dead is entirely coincidental, and not intended otherwise by the authors.

Paperback ISBN: 9798893795288

Hardcover ISBN: 9798893795271

Porgy and Bess

The Sequel

Denisha Hardeman

Harold Goldberg

Frada Goldberg

Sainte Colombe Press

2024

Acknowledgement

The authors wish to thank the Lomax Digital Archive (www.archive.culturalequity.org) for the use of "Times is getting harder" lyrics.

Contents

CHAPTER ONE

Phillip Johnson, the maintenance supervisor at the Old Charleston Jail on Magazine Street, is shouting at a group of Negro inmates in the courtyard. "If'n y'all don't move faster and clean up these tree branches and broken glass and tiles, y'all gonna miss lunch!"

Alonzo Washington pauses his sweeping and, under his breath, says to the inmate nearest him, "Like jailhouse lunch be such a great prize! But dis sho' bin de mos' scary harricane I ebbuh seen een Sout' Carolina."

The hurricane has added insult to the injury already caused by the Great Depression in Charleston, one of the poorest cities in the country, with thirty percent unemployment. Only half the homes have indoor plumbing and twenty-five percent have no electricity. South Carolina was especially hard hit because the price of cotton had dropped to six cents a pound from twenty. Thousands of plantations closed down resulting in many Negroes losing their jobs. The hurricane just made things worse. Even though it came through weeks before, many of the wards in the city were still partly under water, including the area where the Charleston jail was.

Now that the roof and windows of the jail were finally repaired, Johnson was under a lot of pressure to make sure the courtyard was cleaned up and drained in a timely fashion. He was a burly white man who had worked at the jail for most of his life. He had seen dozens of storms and many hurricanes over the years but this was the worst damage he had ever experienced. From across the courtyard he heard the familiar menacing voice of his boss, "Mr. Johnson, come ovuh to mah office right now."

Going through Johnson's mind as he walked toward the warden's office was: *What does that bastard want from me now?* "I'll be right ovuh, warden," Johnson yells back.

Warden Edwin Plunkett ruled his domain like a medieval lord. He was especially harsh with the Negroes, and wished the authorities would put them back on the chain gangs and keep them out of his prison. He was always concerned about them causing problems with his white prisoners, who would harass the Negroes at every chance they got.

Plunkett was seated behind a large mahogany desk in a light airy modern office, decorated with silk brocade draperies and plush carpeting. "Johnson, I need you to set up a work gang to fix up the property of a frien' of mine ovuh on Hugar Street. Maybe you know the Leonard's big white house? Well, the hurricane destroyed the columns supportin' the porch roof an' it collapsed, an' branches from their Magnolia an' Elm trees are scattered around their lawn. Go get some of your niggahs ovuh there to clean it all up right away."

Johnson is used to taking inmates outside the jail for various chores but is worried about the warden's request. "Warden, I'm not sure this is a good idea. One of the guards tol' me the prisonahs are res'less an' unnerved 'cause of the hurricane's effect on their own homes an' families. If'n they git outside, I caint guarantee they might not try to escape."

Plunkett slams his fist down on his desk and yells, "Jus' take extra men witchew. I caint be bothered by the details of your clean-up crews. I've got a meetin' with one of those niggah's lawyers this afternoon to git ready for!"

Without delay Johnson and four guards climb the iron stairs to the third floor of the jail. Johnson picks out the Negroes to make up the crew to take to the Leonard house. He passes by one of the cells where Porgy, a Negro beggar from Charleston's Catfish Row neighborhood, is sitting on his cot.

Porgy yells in a pleading voice. "Mistah Johnson, please tek' me fuh de clean-up!"

Johnson laughs, wags his finger at Porgy, mocking, and says, "What Porgy? Did your 'Jedus' come an' heal you while we wasn't lookin'?" The guards join in the laughter and they move along.

Porgy's faith is powerful, but he knows nothing can fix his crippled legs that dangle uselessly off the side of the cot, not strong enough to support him without the aid of crutches. Unlike his legs, his shoulders and arms are very strong. Porgy is of an indeterminate age. His ancestry had not been muddled by white plantation owners and his skin is as black as obsidian.

Porgy turns to his cellmate and asks, "Bookah, how come Johnson ain't pick yuh fuh de clean-up crew?"

"Well, he ain't no dummy, yuh know. He know Bookah T. Millah would be off an' runnin' at de fust chance he git. Dey t'ink dey kin scare we intah stayin' put by jailin' we up heah en dese dingy cells next tuh all dose white murderers an' thieves." Flailing his arms angrily toward the cells farther down the hall he shouts, "Eben de worse ob dem white prisonah hab it bettah den we! All us git are dese moth-eaten cot, a du'tty blanket, rusty sink an' a share piss-pot. But dey dunno de powah ob we wantin' we freedom."

Porgy hangs his head. "I hab tuh git out ob heah too. All I do eb'ryday is worry 'bout muh woman, Bess. I ain't heah f'om she, so I don' know ef her eben survive de harricane. Befo' I meet Bess it would nebbuh hab madduh tuh me wedduh I bin' lock'up heah or on de street beggin' fuh a few coin eb'ryday. Back den I would jis' put on a big grin fuh da white folks an' mumble a t'ank yuh. But now I en a frenzy tuh git out."

"Porgy, I feel jis' like yuh. I wonda wuh is goin' on outside too. I don' heah enny cars honkin' der horns, no trolleys clatterin' 'long de tracks, an' no Good Humor truck clangin' its bell. I kin see Magazine Street an' it is berry empty. Der be down telephone poles, some damaged autos, an' mountains ob glass f'om all de brok'n windahs. Dey is nobody down der. Ef I hab bin pick fuh dat clean-up crew, I would hab bin gone en a flash."

Booker moves away from the window, allowing a ray of sunlight to beam down on Porgy's face through the bars. The warmth and comfort of the sun momentarily reminds him of his happy life before he was jailed. He closes his eyes and a vision of Bess's smiling face appears. He remembers that smile from when he would return from his daily trip to beg near the stately buildings in Charleston's business district. But he also remembers Bess's cries as the police took him away. The sun's warmth can't erase the chill and the cold in the confines of the prison cell nor the hopelessness he felt when he first entered the jail.

Approaching the jail for the first time, Porgy cringed at the dark and menacing arched façade with twin towers which made the place look like a dismal old castle. Porgy turns to Booker and asks, "Bookah, yuh know 'bout Lavinia Fisher bein' executed heah, right? Do yuh t'ink her really poison all dose men at she Wayfarer Inn an' dat she ghost haunt dis jail?"

"I don' know Porgy, but Hoodoo High John a few cells down de hall say him kin conjure up Lavinia, but jis' tuh scare de guards, so us don' hab tuh worry. I mo' worried 'bout bein' heng en de courtyaa'd, like dey did tuh de slabes when der revolts fail. I only stole some chicken cuz I lost muh job pickin' cotton when de plantation close. But, de white justice hab not change en de last hundrud yeah."

4

Porgy's normally ramrod straight back and shoulders are slumped in defeat. He contemplates the reason he is in the jail and what it will take for him to be free of this horrible place, if ever that could happen. He turns toward Booker. "Yuh know Bookah, I be usually purty smart 'bout dealin' wid dey white lawman, so I guess I should hab done wuh dey wan' me tuh do. But I din't, an' dat's how I landed en jail. I hab always bin able tuh survive en der worl' as a beggah cuz I could smile an' mek frien's wid de people who drop der few pennies intah muh cup, eben when de lawman hus'le muh tuh move on. But, like I tol' yuh, dis time dey wan' me tuh do somet'ing dat chill me tuh de bone, an' I jis' couldn' bring muhself tuh do it. So now I gots no one tuh help me an' not 'nuff money tuh pay de bail tuh buy muh way out ob heah."

Porgy scrutinizes his filthy threadbare shirt, which was once clean and white, and closes his eyes as he tries to remember the good life he once had. His bare feet are a constant reminder that his shoes were the first thing taken from him when he entered the jail. He thinks, *As ef habin' shoes would mek a diffrunce. Do dey t'ink dat wid dem I would sudd'nly be able tuh 'scape de bars on de door an' windahs? Jailahs be stupid.*

With his back to his cellmate, Porgy reaches inside a tear in the mattress where he has hidden the small wad of money he has won playing craps in the prison yard. He is extraordinarily good at it and wins considerably more times than he loses. He counts it again but realizes it is still not enough to pay the bail.

Finished with his counting, he watches a blue jay that has landed on the window sill. Gazing at it longingly, Porgy wishes he had wings, so he could fly away. He starts talking out loud to console himself and help sustain his love for his woman, Bess, and their adopted baby. His words fill the jail cell, "Bess, purty soon I comin' home tuh yuh an' de baby. Us will hab a great life. Jis' wait fuh me. I comin'." Porgy sighs as he worries about her being alone in Catfish Row, caring for a baby by herself, and also having to deal with the devastation of the hurricane. He now understands better the charges against him but still doesn't have any idea about how to defend himself in order to gain his release.

Booker can't help overhearing Porgy's lament. "Porgy, I hab a woman like dat once an' I know how yuh feel."

"Bookah, I sorry tuh trouble yuh tuh heah muh worries. But befo' I foun' Bess, muh life bin trap en a kind ob unendin' jail sentence cuz ob dese useless legs. I could nebbuh earn a real wukin' man's libbin' on de docks or ennywheah else. All I could do bin beg on de streets like some stray dog lukkin' fuh he next meal. But her be de one t'ing dat change all ob dat fuh me. Fuh she, it don' mattah ef I be a cripple beggah. Her warm an' carin' an' now I almos' don' care 'bout muh legs or bein' a beggah. Her mek me feel like a whole man. No woman ebbuh lub me like her do . . . an' wid de addition ob us baby, us is a real fambly."

The sound of footsteps coming toward his cell gets him to quickly stuff the money back into the mattress.

CHAPTER TWO

Perspiration glistens on the bodies of the Negroes who live in New York's Harlem as the summer sun beats down on them. This is the same heat and humidity that has now worked its way north to New York from Charleston, minus the winds and rain of the hurricane. New Yorkers are used to this weather so the streets are filled with people rushing to their destinations to escape the hot weather. Some of them, who have a few coins to spare, are going to the air-conditioned Harlem Grand Theater to see *Harlem Rides the Range*, billed as an "all-colored Western" starring Herbert Jeffrey.

Others are going to or from work, if they still have a job, since so many businesses have closed because of the Depression. Only essential establishments, like beauty parlors, groceries, and undertakers, mostly owned by local Negroes, are still open. The majority of the white-owned Harlem businesses, like Blumstein's Department Store, are shuttered.

On the ledge of a window in a run-down hotel in Harlem, a vibrant blue jay flutters to a landing. Sitting in a chair next to the window is a Negro woman named Bess. Her hair is matted and tangled. Her eyes are dull, lifeless and have lost their shine. Bess's body languishes in total despair, but she is still a beautiful woman. She gently taps her fingers on the windowsill and the bird stares at her. Her almond-shaped eyes, the same color as cinnamon, gaze back, and she wishes she were as free as this bird.

Her forehead is creased from a life of stress but her skin doesn't show any blemishes. It has the color of light brown sugar. Bess's hair curls around the loosely pinned bun. Her cheeks are sunken from cocaine use, but her bone structure is perfect, like that of a model. Her pink lips are full and plump. Chipped, red polish covers her nails. Her slim figure makes her look younger than her years. Her long legs are curled up into her chest as she listlessly eyes the blue jay.

Ironically, the blue jay very much resembles the one that landed on Porgy's jail-house windowsill in Charleston. The chirping of the blue jay reminds Bess of Catfish Row and her love, Porgy. She watches as the bird walks back and forth along the ledge as if he doesn't know where to go. Bess begins to hum as the bird sings, and she smiles. She puts her hand on the window, longing to touch something to give meaning to her life. The blue jay flies away as she thinks, *Be Free, li'l one.*

Bess slides her hand down the window, but she is sluggish and moves slowly. *I so weak an' I miss de strengk dat Porgy gib me when us bin tuhgedduh en Catfish Row . . . I bin so strong den, an' helt'y. I hab eben gib up cocaine aftuh us hab jis' 'dopted Clara's baby orphan' by de harricane. I know dat I couldn' hab done all ob dat wid'out Porgy en muh life.*

"Hey, girl, you were mighty fine" says the man from across the room.

Bess turns around to look at a heavyset Negro man who is pulling up his pants behind her in the sleazy hotel room. The room is dismal and depressing. The bed is unmade and there is a table covered with half-filled liquor bottles and leftover food on chipped plates. The man walks over to the chair where Bess is sitting. Striding over, he throws a dollar bill onto the table in front of her and heads toward the door.

Bess jumps up from the chair. She is wearing a long, black and pink flowered dress with long sleeves. The sun reflects off her brown-sugar complexion, and the man can't help taking in her beauty. "My, my, yo shuh were worth it." The john laughs as he starts to leave the room.

"It's pose to be two dolla," she yells as the man opens the door to go.

"Listen you li'l slut." He swings around to face her. "Dat's all yo' finna get. Dat's all I gots!"

Bess hesitates, struggling to understand the dialect of the Negro people here. The word "finna" was especially hard to figure out until Sportin' Life told her it meant "fixin' to" or "going to."

"Well, den, yuh shouldn' hab ax fuh muh serbises! An' yuh did a line ob cocaine wid me. I need muh money." She is shaking with anger.

The man lunges toward Bess and puts his hands around her throat. She struggles to scream, as the man shouts, "Who is yo talkin' ta girl?" As he tightens his grip around Bess' neck, she claws at him, but he just squeezes tighter. "I could break yo inta two pieces if I wanted."

Hearing the shouting, Bess's pimp, Sportin' Life, crashes the door open and rushes in. Seeing the john choking Bess, he searches around for a weapon, and picks up a heavy glass ashtray. Running up behind him, he screams, "What the hell are you doing? Have you lost your mind?" He hits him hard on the back of the head. The john lets go of Bess, and she drops to the floor, gasping for air. He pulls out a knife to defend himself, but before he can act, Sportin' Life punches him in the face. The knife falls out of his hand, and he howls in pain. Bess's pimp grabs the man by his shirt and shoves him out of the room.

Sportin' Life is a tall, skinny man. He was not as muscular as the john, but he was quickly able to overcome the man with speed, agility, and surprise. The piercing glare of his hazel eyes and the outrage on his face fill the john with fear. "Don't you ever put your hands on her like that again! Get out of here before I kill you!" The john gathers himself up and runs down the hall.

Sportin' Life turns from the doorway and looks around the room, his chest heaving. Bess is still on the floor trying to catch her breath. She stares up at him and tries to understand why she lets him run her life. But in her drug haze, no answer comes.

He steps over to her, kneels down and turns her face so she can see him. She is hurt and angry and at the same time resigned, because this has happened to her many times before. Bess gazes at him with her empty eyes and cries the tears of every abused woman. With a falsely compassionate tone, he asks, "Are you okay? I am so sorry this happened." Sportin' Life is cunning and charismatic, and he knows how to control Bess, who he believes does not have a will of her own. She is wholly dependent upon him for her survival.

Sportin' Life is an octoroon; a Negro who is extremely light skinned, and is able to "pass" as a white man at first glance. His teeth are perfect and white. His cheeks are a little sunken, not unlike Bess's facial structure. He is wearing khaki pants, an expensive red silk shirt and a brown fedora. When he has the money, he spends it on showy clothing, which is how he got the nickname "Sportin' Life."

Before he met Bess, he was the maitre d' in the fancy restaurant in an upscale hotel in New York. They employed him because of his light skin. Because he has a "white" New York accent, different from Bess's southern Gullah dialect, he was able to converse easily with the hotel's customers. And, as is typical of white people who hired Negroes, they also didn't have to pay him as much as they would a white employee.

The restaurant, however, didn't pay enough for the lifestyle Sportin' Life wanted to live. He realized in order to gain the wealth he desired he had to resort to less-than-honest activities. So, while working there, he was also able to use the rooms at the hotel to pimp girls out. The prostitutes would meet him after his work ended and use the rooms for meeting with the johns. Many of his customers were guests in the hotel. Then, after the government outlawed the use of cocaine, anyone who wanted a special "high" had to buy it from a local drug dealer, and Sportin' Life saw an opportunity. He started supplying the johns and the prostitutes with cocaine. Cocaine use had become so popular you could even hear the hotel maids singing the Maple Leaf Jug Band's song, "Cocaine Bill."

> *Cocaine's for horses, not for men,*
> *Doctor says it'll kill me, but he don't say when,*
> *Hey hey honey take a whiff on me.*

Kneeling next to Bess, Sportin' Life takes out an envelope of cocaine and places some on his long fingernail for her. He only pretends to care at this moment because she is an important part of his livelihood. She makes him a good deal of money, and he wants her focused and well-taken care of at all times. He will do anything and say anything to keep her from refusing to service the men he arranges to meet her.

While he holds her in his arms, she thinks, *I know yuh don' really care 'bout me, so holdin' me en yuh arms don' mek t'ings right. I know t'ings will nebbuh change. Muh life will be like dis 'til I die, unless I fin' a way tuh 'scape.*

CHAPTER THREE

Edwin Plunkett, along with his deputy, stops in front of Porgy's cell, pulls out his baton, and runs it across the bars. The warden rarely visits the third floor and the noise from the baton brings all the inmates to the bars of their cells to watch. "Hey boy! Stand up!" he shouts at Porgy.

Porgy lifts himself off the cot and lowers his body onto his knees to the floor. His arms are muscular, the opposite of his crippled legs. Plunkett glares at him menacingly when he doesn't get up on his feet.

"I said stand up, boy!" Plunkett shouts again.

Porgy's chest heaves anxiously. Raising his head, he looks the warden in the eye and says defiantly, "I be standin', Suh." Most of the people in Catfish Row, and around the streets of Charleston where he begs, didn't make fun of his legs. Porgy refuses to let the warden humiliate him due to his physical condition. While Plunkett continues to yell at him, Porgy decides he needs to be eye-to-eye with his tormentor and slides over to where his crutches are leaning against the wall.

Plunkett smirks at him. "Oh yeah. You the cripple who didn't wanna identify the body of that murdered niggah, an' was charged with contempt of court." The warden shakes his head. "Niggahs out there killing niggahs," and adds sarcastically, "what a shame. Did he make you crippled? Did you stick the cotton hook intah him? Why didn't you wanna identify the body, boy?" He cackles at the insults he is throwing at Porgy who is unbothered by the name calling and doesn't answer. Plunkett is now annoyed with Porgy, and asks again, "Why wouldn't you do that, boy?!"

He isn't sure if he is being tested. "I hab nebbuh met de man in muh life."

Plunkett glances through the court file paperwork about Porgy. "The man was known as Crown. He was wanted for murderin'. . . a man named . . . Robbins. Foun' dead in your part of town, an' you don't know anythin' at all?" He doesn't believe Porgy's denial for a minute.

Porgy doesn't move as he responds. "I din't know anyt'ing, Suh."

Still, not believing him, Plunkett surveys Porgy with the same sense of superiority his forbears had when they looked upon their slaves. "Come closah, boy." Porgy makes his way to the bars on his crutches. "How'd your legs git like that, boy?"

Porgy's legs aren't strong enough to let him stand on his own without crutches. They don't move or work as well as those of other people who can walk, dance, and stand freely. His condition has never hindered him before, and he refuses to allow the warden to shame him. But, while he is used to being asked this question, it always stings his heart having to explain his handicap. He tells the warden, "I reck'n I bin bawn dis way."

"You reckon?" Plunkett asks. "Either you was born that way or you wasn't."

"I bin bawn like dis, Suh. Muh legs don' wuk like dem s'ppose tuh. I learn tuh lib wid it." Porgy doesn't understand why the warden is picking on him, and again begins to think he will never be released from this jail.

Ignoring Porgy's explanation, Plunkett interrupts him to say, "Well, somebody believes in you." Unlocking the cell door, he snarls, "You're bein' released! The court ordered me to sign the paperwork. I'm okay with one less niggah in mah jail! You're free to go!"

Thinking he is just baiting him, Porgy is not sure if he can trust him. He turns to Booker for help, but his cellmate puts both hands up, shrugs his shoulders, and shakes his head in uncertainty. Porgy moves back as the warden opens the cell door and warily asks, "Who release me, Suh?"

Plunkett hesitates before he answers. "The lawyer, Alan Archdale, know him?"

At this moment Porgy's thoughts recap the trauma of his jail time, starting with his refusal to identify Crown's body, his arrest and sentencing by the judge, and the miserable conditions of the jail cell. He is afraid to show any emotions to the warden, thinking perhaps it is his way of making a cruel joke about being freed.

Plunkett repeats his question. "Didja hear what I asked? How do you know that niggah-lover Archdale!?"

"Mistah Archdale see me all de time beggin' en front ob de apot'ecary on King Charles Street," Porgy answers.

Most of the police and judiciary in Charleston have come up against Archdale in the past. Alan Archdale was one of the few white attorneys who abhorred the racism of the South. He was a partner with Julius Waties Waring in a law firm that regularly took on Negro civil rights cases.

The deputy turns to Plunkett and asks, "Warden, ain't Archdale a partner of Waring, the lawyah who represented that niggah who couldn't git intah the state law school?"

Plunkett turns his back on Porgy's cell and whispers to the deputy, "Yeah, an' the Klan burned a cross on the lawn of his home. Well, we've gottah handle Archdale with kid gloves. I met him in mah office this aftahnoon, an' he reminded me he handles legal affairs for the Rutledge family. They own half the city. Archdale tol' me Rutledge an' his family employ many of Catfish Row's '*Negro citizens*', that's what *he* calls them, as housekeepers, cooks, an' caretakers. He said he helps out the people in Catfish Row whenever he is needed, and that's how he learned this one was in jail."

Plunkett is a little more conciliatory now that he remembers his conversation with Archdale. "O.K. Porgy, pull your things togethah an' the guard will help you down the stairs."

Porgy is still a little concerned about whether to trust the warden, but he hobbles out of the cell and into the hallway. Booker, seeing an opportunity, yells to the deputy, "Hey, Mistah. Sandahs, kin I gib yuh a hand helpin' he down tuh de gate on Magazine?"

Sanders closes the cell door, shakes his head. "Booker, right, you git outah the front gate an' skip, an' I lose mah job. No thanks for the help!"

Sanders helps Porgy into the hallway, then down the stairs, and escorts him to the first floor of the jailhouse. Alan Archdale is waiting for Porgy at the exit door of the jail, and Porgy can't help but to break into a wide grin. He is happy at last to be getting out of this hell hole and back to his true love, Bess.

Before arriving at the jail, Archdale had stopped at the Court House and paid Porgy's bail for the contempt of court charge. The court documents he read over reminded him Porgy was the Catfish Row denizen who had originally told him the details about Crown's murder of Robbins. Porgy said Crown and Robbins were both drunk on corn liquor and Crown was losing at craps. He thought Robbins was cheating and during a ferocious fight killed him with his stevedore cotton hook.

Archdale had asked one of Porgy's neighbors to bring along Porgy's goat and cart. While Porgy was able to move around on crutches, for longer distances he had fabricated a cart to sit in. It was constructed of an inverted packing-case with two wheels, and had improvised shafts with a rope harness for his elderly goat, Sam, to pull the cart.

As he leaves the jail, Porgy squints as the sun shines blindingly into his eyes. He hasn't been out in the open air for weeks. The summer breeze hits his face, and he takes in a deep breath of the fresh salt air blowing across from the bay. He goes over to where Archdale and the goat are waiting, they shake hands, and Archdale puts his arm around Porgy's shoulder.

Passersby on Magazine Street stop to look at the unusual scene of an unkempt Negro on crutches being embraced by an elegantly-dressed white man. Archdale is in his sixties, with dark brown hair and craggy features. His appearance and demeanor have been compared to his contemporary, Clarence Darrow.

The lawyer steps back from Porgy and asks, "How was it in there?"

He tries to sound grateful. "I lib in mo' bettah places." He puts his crutches on the back of his goat cart and slowly lowers himself into it. Porgy looks at Archdale and asks, "So, how yuh know I bin in der?"

"One of my maids shops with your Maria from Catfish Row."

"Her is one ob de bes' people yuh can hab on yo' side," replies Porgy as he smiles at the thought of help to come from Maria. "Her be like de grammah ob Catfish Row, tekkin' care ob eb'ryone. Her bin de oldes' ob many chillun, so tekkin' care ob odduhs come naturally tuh she. Her allus hab a willin' ear tuh listen tuh people's problems. Her treat me like a son, so I be not surprise dat her done eb'ryt'ing her could tuh git me out ob jail."

Alan Archdale turns to Porgy. "Yes, yes she is wonderful. My maid told me you were in jail, and so I came here as soon as I got the chance." Archdale stops Porgy. "Look, Porgy, you can't leave Catfish Row until all of this is sorted out. We may have to come back to court to deal with the contempt of court charge. You should have just identified Crown's body at the morgue and you wouldn't have had to spend time in jail."

Porgy grimaces as he thinks about the outcome of having to come back to court and possibly going back to jail. "Mistah Archdale, I caint tell yuh why, but I jis' couldn' luk at Crown's body."

Archdale notices his sigh and gently pats him on the back. "I'll help you with this, but don't get into any more trouble until we sort this out. I'll keep in touch. You go on home. I heard you and Bess have a baby to take care of."

Porgy nods his head and says with a smile that lights up his face, "Us do." Archdale shakes Porgy's hand before walking off.

A familiar voice shouts his name as he is leaving. He turns his head up to the third floor, where Booker is yelling at him through the bars of his window. Waving back to his cellmate, he wonders if Booker will someday have his chance at freedom. Porgy ponders whether the white man's justice will keep him there for an indefinite time for a few stolen chickens. He makes a clicking sound in his cheek to tell the goat to start walking and heads toward his home in Catfish Row.

CHAPTER FOUR

Porgy has been dreaming about Bess since he was first jailed, and he feels an immense sense of joy as Sam pulls him along Magazine Street toward his home. He hasn't felt this way since the first time she showed up in Catfish Row, and he took her in. Her husband, Crown, had abandoned her, and was on the run from the law after killing Robbins. They immediately saw in each other a loving companion. Before Bess, the closest thing to love for Porgy had been Sam nuzzling him at feeding time.

He smiles as he sees his reflection in the few unbroken store windows. Porgy has a cheery greeting for the strangers he passes and for everyone he sees who gave him coins in the past. Porgy thinks, *Ef I could, I would be dancin' down de street.* He stops at the market on the way home to bring back gifts for his Catfish Row family and friends.

It is market day in Charleston. Because of the recent hurricane, the weather is even hotter and steamier than usual. Near the market stalls, in a previously affluent section of Charleston, is a building on Church Street called Catfish Row. It is in a predominantly Negro neighborhood and is comprised of a three-story residence built around a courtyard, paved with colorful flagstones.

The entry to the building from the street is through an arched Italianate wrought-iron gate. It was constructed before the Revolutionary War and, until the Great Depression, had been the elegant home of one of Charleston's formerly wealthy white families.

Banks in South Carolina had foreclosed on thousands of homes, including the Catfish Row building. The Farmers National Bank now owns it and rents it out to its current Negro tenants, like Porgy, at a small fraction of its former value. While the building has seen better times, the residents have tried to maintain it as best they can without any help from the bank.

As Porgy turns into Church Street, he anticipates with joy seeing the Catfish Row window sills with planters filled with pretty geraniums that add a festive spirit to the courtyard.

People who live in Catfish Row say the name comes from the work they do, fishing off the Charleston coast and around the Sea Islands. But, it could just as well have been named Cabbage Row because of all the vegetables sold there along with the fish on market day. The vegetables for sale come in to Catfish Row from local farms and include cabbages, Irish potatoes, asparagus, turnips, string beans, and lettuce.

However, this is not a normal happy market day. The residents of Catfish Row are starting to take down the barricades after the ferocious storm swept through the vibrant city. The hurricane came up from Florida with a hundred and fifty mile an hour winds and first made land fall on Edisto Island, one of the Sea Islands off the coast of Charleston.

In Catfish Row, Maria finishes preparing the day's meals and is out in the courtyard. She says to Serena, Robbins' widow, "Serena, kin yuh roun'up sum ob yuh frien's tuh sweep up de leabes and glass? Git Annie an' Lily... an' Nelson for de heaby brok'n up roof tiles."

Serena sits down on a bench and looks up at Maria. With a plaintive voice she says, "T'ings be en such bad shape fuh me, I jis' dunno ef I kin go on wid'out Robbins by muh side."

"All ob us hab our spirits down, but us gone t'rough bad times befo' . . . us like fambly dat kin mek it t'rough anyt'ing."

Outside Catfish Row on Church Street, fallen trees and broken window glass cover the cocoa-colored ground. Many boats had been lost at sea and the wives of the missing seafaring husbands are in mourning. The vessels still docked during the storm were upended and many of the wharves at the Charleston Harbor had been destroyed.

The residents of Catfish Row are used to dealing with the ravages of hurricanes. They are the resilient descendants of slaves who were captured on the Western Coast of Africa and brought to Charleston to work on the cotton and rice plantations. They speak a language called Gullah, a mixture of African languages, Creole, and English. The Gullah culture of Charleston's peninsula and the Sea Islands also sets them apart from other Negro communities in the South.

The heat of the day is still stifling as the setting sun lowers over Catfish Row. Denizens in the community sweat as they continue to work, enduring humidity almost as high as when the hurricane was raging through. They are waiting for the sunset to give them some relief from the searing heat.

As Porgy rounds the corner leading to Catfish Row, some of his neighbors and friends spot him and begin to scream out his name. "Porgy! Porgy! Porgy's home!" they yell as they race to his side. The children jump on Porgy and all the adults hug him. Jim, a neighbor, leans down to the cart to give him a handshake. "Man, us t'awt yuh bin a gonnah."

He turns to Jim and hugs him. "Gawd knows wheah muh haa't be. I hab tuh come back home." He has tears in his eyes as he relates his ordeal in the jail. "Yuh know why I couldn' luk on

Crown, but I din't t'ink dey would t'row me en jail, but dey did ennyway. I be so happy tuh be home an' be wid Bess an' de baby finally. An' I brought prezunts! Fuh eb'ryone!"

Dropping his bag on the ground, he begins handing out trinkets: toys for the kids, hats for the women, and pipes for the men. The townspeople accept the gifts but are wondering about Porgy's newfound wealth. Jim laughs, jokingly. "Porgy, I din't know dey allow beggin' en de jail!"

Porgy smiles and addresses his friends, "Right. I got lucky at craps en de prison yaa'd."

Catfish Row's huge cook proprietress, Maria, presses her way through the crowd holding a baby. Porgy sets his eyes on her and the baby. He sees the guardian angel that brought him and Bess together and got the lawyer to free him from jail. Tears of happiness roll down his face as he makes his way to meet her.

"Maria! I be so unb'lieb'ly happy tuh see yuh! I hab miss yuh!" He cries as the crowd watches.

Smiling, Maria gazes into Porgy's eyes. "I bin prayin' fuh yuh so haa'd." She hands him the baby. "Somebody wan' tuh see yuh!"

Porgy cradles his newly adopted son in his arms. He kisses the boy tenderly on his head. His son looks up at him with his big, brown eyes. "Hi, son! I miss yuh so much." Porgy kisses him again as the child responds with a cute baby giggle.

Porgy's mind recalls the night when all the tenants of the building were huddled on the second floor during the hurricane. He can still remember Clara, the baby's mother, when she looked out the window and saw her husband Jake's wrecked fishing boat and realized he was missing. She had a wild-eyed, terrified look on her face, and thrust her baby into Bess's arms, and then ran out into the storm. Her last words were, "Keep muh baby safe till I retu'n!"

Lily and Nelson stop their cleanup work in the courtyard and move close to Porgy and the baby. They kneel down next to the cart and Lily says, "Porgy, us bin' on us knees jis' like dis prayin' fuh yo' retu'n an' now Gawd hab warm all us haa'ts."

Porgy searches around but doesn't see the one face he really wants to. He yells out, "Bess! Bess, honey, I back! Bess wheah yuh is?! Bess!" If Porgy had been a seagull, his plaintive cry would have reached his flock at the harbor a few blocks away, and they would have flown to console him. But, the people gathered around are silent and bow their heads in despair as they listen to him call out for Bess.

Porgy keeps looking around, but there is no Bess in sight. Maria avoids Porgy's eyes. She pokes him in the stomach. "Whew, chile! Wuh were dey feedin' yuh en der? Yuh luk like yuh lost t'irty pound. Leh me fix yuh a good ole' plate ob gumbo." Maria takes the baby back from Porgy and starts to walk off.

Taking hold of her hand in desperation, he implores, "Maria, wheah be Bess?" His tears turn from happiness to fear as he suddenly realizes it is Maria who is taking care of his son and not Bess.

No one in the crowd says anything. She motions for him to follow her. "Leh's go intah muh kitchen, chile. Us need tuh talk." Turning back to the people watching, she commands, "Eb'rybody back tuh wuk. Us need dis town tuh be back up an' runnin' like befo'. G'won!"

Maria signals Porgy to follow her and walks toward her kitchen. Porgy picks up his crutches and hobbles behind her. His handicap doesn't stop him from keeping up with her.

He takes a look around the area as they walk to Maria's kitchen. The hurricane has caused much more damage and destruction than he remembered before he was arrested. Some nearby buildings were totally destroyed. Others had lost their roofs or walls. Porgy has to maneuver his way around tree branches and other debris scattered in the street. Serena and her helpers are still cleaning up as the sun starts to set.

A hot wind blows through Catfish Row like a ghost making a woosh sound as it swishes through the broken windows. They enter Maria's kitchen where large, fresh catfish cover the chopping board. The delicious aromas of onions and freshly cooked cabbage fill the room. On the table there is warm bread and freshly churned golden butter. A huge kettle of gumbo is simmering on the stove next to a steaming pot of white rice. Porgy's mouth begins to water. The aromas remind Porgy of what he missed after spending weeks eating what he named "mystery-meat" at the jailhouse.

Maria carries the baby over to his cradle and places him in it. She puts a pacifier in his mouth, rocks the cradle, and then makes her way over to the stove to stir the gumbo. "Aftuh de harricane, eb'rybody needs tuh eat an' eat well."

Porgy is getting impatient. He desperately wants to know where Bess is. "Maria I . . ." Avoiding his question, Maria rambles on to forestall answering. "An' I hab tuh be de one tuh feed'um. Ef I don' feed'um, which will?"

She takes a bowl out of her pantry and sets it on the stove next to the pot of gumbo. She fills the bowl with hot white rice and covers it with her famous gumbo filled with chicken, shrimp, okra, crawfish, and crab legs, all in a thick creamy sauce. Setting the gumbo in front of Porgy, Maria cuts a piece of bread, and spreads it with her homemade butter. "Eat up now. Yuh need tuh eat. Yuh luk like yuh din't eat en days. Please. Eat it all 'til der none lef' en de bowl."

"Maria, please!" Porgy stands and raises his voice, which startles the baby, who begins to cry. Maria runs over to pick him up. Porgy realizes he was yelling and is instantly apologetic. "I be so sorry. I ain't mean tuh shout. I jis' . . . please tell me. Wheah be Bess?"

23

She picks up the child and rocks him in her arms as she seats herself next to Porgy. Closing her eyes, she vividly remembers when she rescued a drunken, drug-addled girl who showed up in Catfish Row. That was the girl Porgy took in and who brought him the only true love he had ever known. She struggles to find the courage to say the words she is sure will devastate him. "Her gone, Porgy."

CHAPTER FIVE

For a second, Porgy is shocked into silence and falls back into his chair at the news Bess is gone. In a voice registering panic and fear, he shouts, "Gone? Gone wheah? Wheah her be, Wheah?'

"Us all bin worried 'bout yuh, Porgy. Us bin all feah'full dat yuh goin' be in jail 'til de end ob yuh time on dis heah Eart'. Us din't know wuh tuh do."

Porgy is regretful about everything that has happened, but defends himself. "I din't wan' tuh go tuh jail. I jis' war tryin' tuh protec' muhself, muh fambly."

Maria pulls the baby tighter to her chest and holds Porgy's hand to comfort him. "No one blame yuh, Porgy. No one. An' don' yuh dare blame yo'self'. Us sho' yuh did de right t'ing by not 'dentifyin' Crown body."

They share a moment of understanding, but at this moment she wishes she didn't have to tell Porgy the rest of the bad news about Bess's departure. "Bess din't know how tuh tek it aftah yuh gone 'way. Her be wid de newly 'dopted baby an' 'lone. Her miss yuh. Yuh 'membuh her bin wid Crown fuh five yeahs befo' her met yuh, an' wid he dead, an' aftah' yuh gone 'way, her bin torn. Her git drunk one night an' . . ." Maria pauses. She questions herself, wondering if she should really tell Porgy the whole story.

Porgy leans in when Maria suddenly goes silent, trying to take in all this new information. He squeezes her hand tightly. "An' wuh, Maria? Wuh happ'n'?"

The tears are falling from Maria's eyes onto the baby's blanket. She clutches the child as she rocks him. "One night Bess gone down tuh de docks. Some ob de stevedore dockwukahs got she drunk. An' dey kidnap she."

Porgy's heart skips a beat. He springs out of his chair using his powerful arms, leans heavily on the table, knocking his plate of bread to the floor. The noise startles the baby who once again begins to cry. Now he is truly afraid for Bess. "Kidnap'? Why ain't ennybody tell me dat when I bin en jail?" Porgy sadly realizes being jailed for his reluctance to identify Crown's body has led to losing Bess. Falling back into the chair, he cries, "I caint bear de pain ob losin' she. I won't be able tuh go on libbin' wid'out she."

"'Cuz, Porgy . . . us dunno how tuh tell yo! An' I din't wan' yuh tuh worry 'bout de baby."

"Wheah dey tek she? Yuh know?" Maria tries to calm him down, but he is nearly hysterical. "Maria, I hab tuh go git she an' bring she back."

"Dey tek she tuh Savannah . . . but . . . last us heah . . . dat pimpin' drug dealer Sportin' Life mek fuh Savannah an' sweep she off tuh New Yawk City. I dunno how him eben fin' out 'bout Bess bein' en Savannah. I kick he outa Catfish Row befo' yuh fust meet Bess so him couldn' sell she enny mo' cocaine." Maria treated Bess like a daughter. After Crown ran away and abandoned her, Bess had shown up on Maria's doorstep, drunk and drug-addled. She felt sorry for her, took her in and helped her to get sober.

Soon after, Bess met Porgy, and they fell in love. They were destined to be with each other. Bess needed Porgy's strength and stability, and he needed her warmth and caring. In their past lives, neither of them had had any true love in any of their relationships. Porgy's life as a cripple and a beggar had been a solitary one, and she made a loving home for him, something he never had before. And, until she met Porgy, her life had been one of being used by men, and Porgy's sincere love for her also made it easy to stop using cocaine.

"New Yawk City?" Porgy is staggered. "Why did him tek she der? How did dey git der? Why would her go wid he? I jis' don' undahstan'. I t'awt her lub me an' would wait fuh me 'til I git out ob jail."

Maria shakes her head and wipes away her tears. "Us dunno. Us jis' git word dat Sportin' Life got she back on dat happy dus' an' took she wid he tuh New Yawk. Him paid off dem dockwukahs an' dem gib he Bess in retu'n. Dat all us know."

Porgy feels like his heart is beating out of his chest. His mind is in a frenzy, zigzagging back and forth from one solution to the next. *How kin I... wat kin I... wuh happ'n tuh Bess? How will I fine' she?* He grips the table and tries to catch his breath. Looking at the baby, his mind darts off to the last time he heard Bess's voice the day he was taken away in handcuffs. "Prommus me dat yuh will come back tuh me, an' dat us will spen' de rest ob us lives happ'ly tuhgeddah."

As he was being led away then, he had called over his shoulder, "Us will be a fambly ag'in!" He remembers the beautiful glow on Bess's face when they agreed to adopt the orphaned baby. He is torn. He doesn't want to leave his son, but he can't bear the thought of Bess being with Sportin' Life.

"Maria, I know her bin a pros'tute befo' her bin wid me, sellin' she body en order tuh mek money fuh Sportin' Life. Muh lub fuh she war so deep dat I bin willin' tuh tek she as her bin. I worshup she as a goddess. I scare now dat Sportin' Life hab she strung out on de drugs ag'in an' back sellin' she body tuh earn money fuh he. Dat t'awt mek muh stomach tu'n. Ef I ebbuh git hol' ob Sportin' Life I will kill he." He becomes light headed, loses his grip on the table, and falls.

27

Maria puts the baby back into the cradle and runs over to help Porgy up. "I tol' yuh dat yuh need tuh eat. Yuh weak."

"No, I ain't weak! I haa'tbrok'n," Porgy yells. His thoughts begin to clarify. He looks at Maria and the baby. "I hab tuh go git she. I don' know how I will do it, but I mus' do it."

"Do yuh hab enny idea how far dat New Yawk City be? It be a whole diff'ren' world out der. An' wid yuh legs . . ."

"I nebbuh leh muh legs git in de way! I wuk an' move 'roun dis town jis' like a man who be not handicap'. I caint leabe Bess in New Yawk wid Sportin' Life an' yuh know dat."

Taking the baby out of the cradle, she caresses his face and gently hands him over to Porgy. "But wuh 'bout yuh baby? Dis be yuh life now. Yuh tek on de 'spons'bility ob raisin' dis boy tuh be a man . . . tuh be a good man. Yuh caint go 'way when him need yuh. Him 'ready lost him real mama an' him papa . . . him eben lost him new mama when Bess lef'. Don' leabe he too."

Porgy hugs the baby close to his chest. "One day, him goin' tuh grow up. An' him goin' tuh come tuh muh room an' ax me, 'Pa, weh be muh Ma.' Wuh kind ob man would I be ef I lukked 'um en de eyes an' tell 'um her bin gone . . . an' I did nutt'n' 'bout dat? I caint do dat Maria." Raising his head, he turns back to her. "I jis' caint."

Fearful that if Porgy fails to make it to New York, she is worried she will have lost both him and Bess. Her worry about what might happen is as much for herself, trying to take care of a helpless baby. Knowing she can't win the argument to convince him to stay, she says, "Well, I will watch'um fuh yuh now. Prommus me yuh come back tuh he." She grips his hand.

Half smiling, he nods, realizing the burden he is putting on her. "I prommus." They both look at each other, realizing neither of them honestly can be sure whether he will make it back alive, with or without Bess.

Maria takes the baby from him. "Eat yuh dinnah, Porgy. You goin' tuh need yo' strengk'. New Yawk be a long way f'om heah. Yuh hab enny idea 'bout how yuh goin' tuh git der?"

"By boat, I reck'n." Porgy downs the gumbo as if he hasn't eaten in days.

The hot gumbo burns his tongue, and he hastily drinks a glass of water, making Maria laugh. She rocks the baby to sleep and says, "Do yuh 'membuh de name Jake an' Clara christen' dis chile?"

Porgy picks his head up from the gumbo. "Wid eb'ryt'ing dat hab happ'n tuh me, goin' tuh jail, learnin' 'bout Bess bein' kidnap, I caint b'lieb I almos' fo'git muh son name. I t'ink . . . Jonah. Yaas. Jonah. Like en de Bible story wheah him git swalluh up by de big fish an' den sabe de people ob Nin'bah. Jonah will be muh insp'ration tuh sabe Bess." Porgy smiles at the name.

Maria has a delighted look on her face. "I lub dat name too. Come back home tuh Jonah. An' bring Bess back wid yuh."

"I will, Maria. I will!" Porgy grins reassuringly, and continues to feed himself as Maria sways the baby back and forth until he is fast asleep.

CHAPTER SIX

Bess and Sportin' Life are sitting at their table in the hotel room talking about what happened earlier with the john. Bess is trying to calm down from the ordeal. Her hands are shaking and fear still shows in her eyes. Sportin' Life takes her hands in his.

She looks down at the floor as she speaks, "I tell he dat him owe me mo' money an' him got mad." She touches her neck, where the mean red marks from the john's hands are still visible.

Sportin' Life lifts her chin to see the bruises. "This is why I'm always close by. I will always be there to save you." To help calm her, he speaks softly with Bess in perfect English rather than in Gullah. When she first got to New York, she had a hard time understanding him, but over time she has gotten used to it.

"But, I don' wan' tuh ebbuh need sabin', Sportin' Life."

"Perhaps you won't, but . . . I'm still never too far away."

Bess takes Sportin' Life's hand. "I know der be odduh t'ings dat I good at. Maybe I can wuk somewheah. I bin allus good at cookin' an' creatin' t'ings. I kin fin' a job doin' dat. An' I kin read an' write an' do figgas, so mebbe I could be a sales gal en a shop. Wuh yuh t'ink?"

"Listen to me, you're beautiful. This is what you're good at. Just do what I tell you, and let me handle the thinking."

Instead of comforting her, the words hurt her. She wants to be more than just a prostitute for New York men. *No one wants tuh*

see me fuh ennyt'ing mo' den muh luks. Ef only I hab some money
ob muh own, I could buy some real city clothes, fin' a job an' kick de
happy dus' . . . an' not be trap' by Sportin' Life plan.

Flashing his pearly white smile, he grins at Bess. "I have a
surprise for you. It will put you in a much better mood and both
of us in a better situation."

Bess is curious. "Wuh be dat?"

"Do you trust me? I can tell from the look on your face you
don't. I want you to trust me. What happened today was terrible,
but . . ."

"It happ'n mo' den once Sportin' Life," she says warily.

"That's because these low-class New York men are more
aggressive, and they think you are a weak country girl. We are
going to move to a new place that will bring in a classier, higher-
paying clientele."

In her mind, Bess questions what Sportin' Life has up his
sleeve, but at this point she has no choice but to trust him. "I trus'
you, Sportin' Life." She swallows her anxiety as she speaks the
words.

Sportin' Life gives her a charming smile. "Okay. Let's pack up
our belongings. Where we're going is ready now. First, a treat."
Pulling out a small bag of cocaine, he adds to the lines already on
the table and cuts it for Bess, who stares at him for a second. *Gawd,*
I need tuh kick dis happy dus'.

The dollar bill the john gave Bess earlier is sitting on table,
and he rolls it up and hands it to her. "Today, we start a new day."
He holds Bess' hand as she takes the dollar bill, dips down and
snorts the cocaine. Almost instantly, her pupils dilate as it is
quickly absorbed into her blood stream, and she gets a fast burst
of energy.

Sportin' Life glances around the room. "Let's get our stuff and
head out. Pack our things, Bess." He stands up and goes into the
bathroom to retrieve his stash of cocaine from the vanity cabinet

where it was hidden. Taking hold of the dollar bill again, Bess does another line and wipes her nose. She gets up, finds the suitcases in the closet, and begins packing up her and Sportin' Life's belongings.

They carry their suitcases and leave the seedy hotel. At the curb, Sportin' Life flags down a taxi, and they drive off along the busy Harlem streets. Bess gazes out the taxi's window in wonder at all the lively activity going on by the largely Negro population of Harlem.

While Harlem is over seventy percent populated by Negroes, it wasn't always like that. The migration of Negroes in substantial numbers began in the early 1900s when real estate values crashed. Philip Payton and his Afro-American Realty Company lured Negroes to now-affordable Harlem, and the Negro churches soon followed them.

Negroes also moved there because of their fear of a resurgence of anti-Negro riots, like the one in 1900 in Midtown Manhattan. That riot began when a Negro man killed a white police officer who was trying to arrest the man's girlfriend. A result of the killing was that white mobs attacked the Negro residents in the neighborhood, and many rioters were injured or arrested.

The taxi stops at a red light, and she can hear jazz playing from the doorway of the Harlem Music Shop. The sights and sounds of the bustling Harlem streets fascinate Bess. Women who are passing by attract her attention. Even though her mind is clouded by cocaine, she can tell they are nicely dressed and well put together. Bess is jealous of them. *I wan' tuh be like dat someday.*

CHAPTER SEVEN

The taxi drops them off on 160th Street and she notices the women on the street are staring at her and whispering to each other. Bess has on a small hat, and she is still wearing her long-sleeved black and pink dress. The combination of the heat and the cocaine is making her perspire profusely. Bess grips Sportin' Life by the arm. "Eb'ryone be starin' at me."

Much of Sportin' Life's control over Bess is based on her insecurity. "Not at all. They are noticing how beautiful you are."

"No," she says in a sad voice, "Dey be starin' 'cause dey know wuh kin' ob woman I be."

Bess is breathless and in awe of the fancy cars going by and all the activity on the sidewalks. The Depression hit Harlem harder than the rest of New York, so the vast majority of the predominantly white-owned store-front shops have been shuttered. They have been replaced by people with push-carts and stands set up on the sidewalks and in the streets. Some are selling food and others books and children's toys. *I wonda' ef I will ebbuh hab de chance tuh buy a toy fuh muh son.*

After getting out of the taxi, Sportin' Life and Bess continue to walk a few steps along West 160th Street to the corner and then turn into Edgecombe Avenue. The two- and three-story brick buildings on this street, called brownstones, are much bigger and nicer than those on other streets in Harlem. A man is sitting outside on the steps of one of these buildings, painting the banisters. He smiles at Bess as she walks by. Now calmed down a bit, she smiles back.

Bess has never seen buildings this elegant in her life. She has spent most of her time staying inside their hotel since arriving in Harlem, even during the daytime hours, and mostly in a drugged state. The view from her window was of old and dilapidated tenements. Here, these beautiful brownstones are attached to one another, each with its own entrance and distinctive architectural details. Staircases leading up to their doors are bordered by ornate banisters. The doorways are trimmed with unique carvings, and many have small gardens with stone flower pots.

In the middle of the block, Sportin' Life stops at a tall apartment building. He turns to Bess and grins, "Welcome home." The building they are standing in front of is in a neighborhood in Harlem known as Sugar Hill.

Sugar Hill got its name in the 1920s when the neighborhood became a "sweet" spot for wealthy Negroes who had "sugar," or money. They moved into the area during the early years of what people are calling the "Harlem Renaissance." This is the neighborhood where the "who's who" of the Harlem elite live. Bess is stunned at the beauty of the building. She has never seen anything like it before.

The neighborhood name came to represent an opulent and swanky lifestyle. Living here meant "you had arrived" and Sportin' Life wanted to show everyone he was a man to be reckoned with. He didn't want to be associated any longer with the run-down hotel where he and Bess had lived when they first moved to Harlem.

People on "The Hill" looked down on the people on the other side of Harlem in "the valley", where Negro families lived in overcrowded and cramped apartments. Sportin' Life has become wealthier, and he wants to live a flamboyant, bigger and better lifestyle than anyone else, and Sugar Hill is the perfect place to flaunt it. It is exclusive, expensive, and classy.

Across the street from the apartment building is a beautiful park, and Bess turns to watch the people strolling along the pathways. She envies the women and men and exclaims to Sportin' Life, "Jis' luk at all de bootiful, expensive lukkin' dresses an' shoes dose women be wearin'. Yuh kin heah der high heels clickin' as dey walk 'long de pavement. An' dose men, dressed en purty colored t'ree-piece suits mek ob fine-lukkin materials." She watches some women pushing baby carriages. However, her excitement is dampened by thoughts of her adopted baby, who is so far away.

In front of their elegant apartment building, a sign reads "555 Edgecombe Ave." The building is thirteen stories tall, and she tilts her head back to see the top. She is mesmerized by the brick building that towers in front of her. The entrance is two-stories high, with a rounded archway, and a beautiful awning. "Home?" She questions Sportin' Life.

He extends his hand to help her up the stairs to the entrance. A doorman in a fancy uniform with epaulettes on his shoulders is standing outside the front door and, when he opens it, he smiles at Bess.

"Welcome, ma'am." At this tiny show of respect, Bess's shoulders straighten, her head is held higher, and her fragile ego gets a boost almost immediately. Suddenly, she feels valued and important in this big city. No one ever called her "ma'am" before. A warm sensation begins in her tummy and makes its way up to her heart and head.

They walk into the huge lobby of the apartment building, where she is dazzled by sparkling crystal chandeliers hanging from the stained glass and art deco ceiling. The marble floors are highly polished, and mirrors in beautiful gold frames hang on the walls.

Bess touches the frame of one of the mirrors, sees her reflection, and tries to convince herself she is not dreaming. If someone had asked her what she felt, she would say, "It be brea'takin'.'" Looking around the lobby, she is enchanted by the walls which are painted with cherubs playing flutes for dancing goats. For an instant Bess's thoughts sadly return to Porgy and his goat, Sam. *Will I ebbuh see Porgy an' Sam come home en time fuh dinna en Catfish Row ag'in?*

Sportin' Life leads Bess down a hallway to the elevator. The operator opens the door for them, and they step inside. He turns to them and asks, "What floor, sir?"

Bess is confused by this tiny room she has entered. Sportin' Life is amused by her perplexed look and laughs at her confusion. "It's an elevator. It will take us up to our apartment." He turns to the operator and says, "Nine." The elevator operator closes the gate and door and moves the handle to number nine. It begins to rise, and the expression on Bess's face is one of pure exhilaration.

The elevator reaches the ninth floor and jerks as it makes its final stop. Bess almost falls as the momentum of her body doesn't stop at the same time as the elevator. Sportin' Life grabs her as she loses her balance, and he steadies her. "See, I told you I will always protect you." He puts his arm around her as he kisses her on the forehead. Sportin'Life helps restore her balance, and the elevator operator opens the door to their floor.

Sportin' Life leads the way and Bess follows him down the hallway. The doors are painted red and have apartment numbers engraved on plaques next to them. The amber lights along the hallway make her brown-sugar skin glow. Paintings of Negroes involved in everyday family life decorate the walls. The scent of sugar and cinnamon fills the air, and the aroma makes her wish it could take the place of cocaine's sickening flowery smell in her life. "Dis place sho' be bettuh den dat' du'tty ol' hotel us bin libbin' en."

In front of apartment 9D Sportin' Life stops, reaches in his pocket for the key and opens the door. Bess walks in and drops her suitcase, her mouth agape, "Whoah!" She has never seen any place so beautiful. The foyer alone is larger than their run-down hotel room.

Sportin' Life flips a switch on the wall, turning on a crystal chandelier that illuminates the foyer as Bess moves a little further into the apartment. It is beautifully furnished, and she guesses there must be room for more than a hundred people to stand around and talk all at one time.

Maids are in the apartment, cleaning and getting food ready for the day's meals. They smile at Bess as she walks into the living room. Smiling back at them, she turns to Sportin' Life. "Who be all dese people?"

"They're our maids. They will come here every day to take care of the apartment. They will do the cooking and laundry and the cleaning."

She goes farther into the living room. Three white couches are separated by marble tables. The hardwood floors glisten with a fresh coat of wax. "Sportin' Life, dis whole place smell like labendah an' dis sunny room remin' me ob sunflowahs bloomin' en Charleston."

Walking into the kitchen, a gleaming white stove with four burners and a large oven capture her attention. She runs her hand over the sink which is cold and smooth under her fingertips. There is a shiny white cabinet, taller than she is, and she stands in front of it, not knowing what it is or how to open it. Anna, one of the maids, opens it for her. "It's an electric ice box, called a refrigerator. Yo put da food in der ta keep it cold."

Refrigerators cooled by a new liquid called Freon are now being introduced into the market and Sportin' Life bought the latest General Electric Company model. In Harlem, very few of the apartments have a refrigerator and so it is a true sign of wealth.

"Wow. Dat's amazin' . . . I Bess."

"My name be Anna." She is a plump, Negro woman in her mid thirties. Her hair is short in a marcelled style, and her skin is dark. She smiles shyly at Bess. "Let me know if yo need anythin', Miss Bess."

"T'ank yuh. I be fine fuh now. Yuh don' hab tuh . . ."

Sportin' Life comes up behind Bess and gives Anna a dismissive wave. "She will let you know if she needs something. Get back to work." Anna nods her head and walks away. He continues to show Bess the apartment, taking her down a long hallway toward the bedrooms.

Bess makes her way into one of the bedrooms. The double doors open wide to a full-sized bed draped with a white silk canopy. Covers on the bed are also made of silk and remind her of white fluffy clouds. Under the east window, next to a bookshelf, there is also a loveseat.

She stands in front of the windows facing the Harlem River nearby. *Dat daa'k ribbuh choke' me up an' mek me t'ink ob dose filt'y dockwukah who git me drunk an' tek me down de ribbuh tuh Savannah an' rape me.* With a quick shrug of her shoulders, she tries to make those memories fade from her mind.

Bess is enchanted and glides into the bathroom. The marble "his and her" sinks have shiny brass faucets. The bathtub is so huge it can fit two full grown people. She can't resist the novelty and climbs into the empty bathtub. A French design vanity sits across from the bathtub. Bess closes her eyes and smiles, never having experienced this kind of luxury before.

Sportin' Life goes into the bathroom and bends down next to her. "Do you like it?" He removes her hat and runs his fingers through her hair. She struggles not to flinch at his touch while marveling at the wonders of the apartment.

"How did yuh git all dis?" Bess honestly doesn't know if she wants to hear the answer to her question, but she asks it anyway.

He laughs at Bess's question. "No need to worry your pretty self on how a man gets all of this. Since we arrived in Harlem, I've been working really hard. I'm important here now. I just had to find the right place for us, and this is it. This shows New York City how big I really am."

Sportin' Life grins broadly as he surveys the room. *This is just the beginning of what I am going to do. I will become a man to reckon with in Harlem.*

Bess gets out of the tub, steps back into the bedroom and, relaxed and relieved, gleefully hops on top of the luxurious bed. *I feel like I hab die an' gwone tuh hebbin.* At this moment, she doesn't have to think about her depressing life. Sportin' Life follows her to the bed. He lies down next to her, interrupting her peaceful reverie. She is smiling but her eyes are still sad with knowing what she will have to do on this bed to make money for him.

He caresses her face, "I'm going to take care of you. Now we can get high-class higher paying johns and I will be confident you will be safe." Sportin' Life believes he has it all figured out.

I don' wan' tuh be a pros'tute ennymo', but dats all Sportin' Life says I know how tuh do. But, him de only one heah who tek care ob me. Reluctantly, she nods her head in agreement with him. He gets off of the bed and straightens his clothes. "There are four bedrooms in the apartment, three bathrooms, and lots more rooms to explore here. You can spend all day looking around and moving things as you wish."

Bess sits up in the bed, reaches out toward Sportin' Life as he walks toward the bedroom door. "Yuh goin' out?" She tries not to sound clingy or afraid. "Please don' leabe me heah 'lone. I be scared."

"Hey, no one is going to hurt you anymore. We've moved up. I have to go out now, but I'll be back soon." Sportin' Life kisses Bess on the forehead. "I left you some treats in the front room. Go easy. Also, you can find food in the refrigerator." He walks out of the bedroom and closes the double doors.

Once Sportin' Life leaves, Bess lies back, admires the silken canopy, and closes her eyes. She daydreams about her true love, Porgy and her adopted baby. She cries as she worries about him being alone and who is caring for him. She whispers to herself, "I so sorry, li'l one." Warm tears fall down her cheeks, and she hopes her words will travel to Catfish Row if she says them out loud, "I lub yuh Porgy."

The last happy night they spent together before the police took Porgy away enters her mind, and she reminisces about how happy they were in the small room they called home. She visualizes how small Catfish Row is compared to Harlem. It seems to her that the whole neighborhood could fit inside this apartment. She also remembers how much happier she was in Catfish Row. After she met Porgy she stopped being a prostitute and quit using cocaine, and he nursed her back to health once when she was sick with a fever. In the short time they were together, they had learned to care deeply for one another. Porgy loved Bess and she loved him.

Her crying becomes more intense as she imagines him in jail, reminding herself he doesn't know she is no longer in Catfish Row. "Porgy, I be sorry fuh leabin yuh." She buries her head in the pillow as she silently prays, "Gawd, please protek me. Sabe me. Lub me." Bess closes her eyes tighter, and she falls asleep, dreaming of her life in Catfish Row.

CHAPTER EIGHT

Porgy is surrounded by his friends, the residents of Catfish Row. His bags are packed and his goat and cart are ready for the journey to New York. Sam the goat gets a pat on the head and Porgy turns to Maria who is holding baby Jonah. He takes Jonah from her and hugs him. He looks into the baby's big brown eyes, and Jonah returns the gaze with a smile. His baby laugh warms Porgy's heart. Porgy doesn't want to let him go, but he must. "I goin' fin' yuh mammy. An' den I come back." He kisses him on the forehead and in return he kicks his feet and giggles.

It makes Porgy smile to hear the baby giggle, though he realizes sadly he might not hear it again for a long time. He hands Jonah back to Maria, tears streaming down his face as he reluctantly lets the child go. Maria touches Porgy's hand and her eyes meet his. "I goin' tuh come back. Wid Bess. I prommus," he says, trying to reassure Maria, and himself, that he will succeed in his quest.

Maria is still doubtful that Porgy can really get to New York and find Bess. "New Yawk is so far 'way, an' I jis' don' know how him kin do it wid dem cripple legs. Yuh be careful. Ef yuh don' fin' she, yuh retu'n home tuh Jonah." She squeezes his hand.

Porgy hugs Maria in a powerful embrace, "I prommus. I come home tuh muh baby wid muh lub." He leans backs in the cart and turns to face everyone. "T'ank y'all fuh eb'ryt'ing. Be back soon"

He starts off in his cart and makes his way out of Catfish Row. The residents run alongside him. "Bye, Porgy! Bye, Porgy!" They wave and scream after him, hoping for the best, but all carrying the same doubts in their hearts. Maria holds on to Jonah as Porgy drives away toward the docks.

Porgy and Sam finally arrive at the docks. At the far end, a huge white ship is moored at Union Pier. The pier stretches 2,500 feet from the waterfront to its end in the harbor. The ship is the *S.S Virginia*, a steamship owned by the Panama Pacific Lines. It is a luxury cruise liner with two giant funnels, one red and one blue.

White men and women dressed in elegant attire are walking toward the ramp leading onto the ship. Approaching the ramp, they hand their bags to the Negro ship workers. Many more passengers are lingering on the dock, saying their farewells to friends and family.

A band seated on the deck between the two funnels is playing the popular song, "I'm Coming Virginia." The cruise passengers, moving up the ramp, know this song from the Bing Crosby and Paul Whiteman phonograph recording. Many hum along or sing the lyrics as they board the ship. They would be surprised to find it had been written by the Negro composer Donald Heywood about his longing to return to his home in Virginia.

The cruise ship has a sunning deck where passengers can swim in the pool or recline on canvas chaise lounge chairs. Inside, there is a library with hundreds of books, including popular fiction such as F. Scott Fitzgerald's *The Great Gatsby* and Ernest Hemingway's *A Farewell to Arms*. There is also a children's section with books like *Little House in the Big Woods* by Laura Wilder.

The ship has a steam room, a smoking room, and a parlor with gambling games going on all day and night. In the evening the ship's entertainment crew hosts parties with an orchestra in a ballroom with a dance floor.

The *S. S Virginia* is outfitted for elegant travel with some cabins connecting to private bathrooms. There are 184 first class cabins and another 365 for tourist class passengers. Fifty-two of the first-class cabins are two-room suites.

Porgy reaches the pier and is confronted by the seemingly frantic activity and hustle and bustle alongside the ship as the crew and passengers arrive. Lifting himself out of the cart, he uses his crutches to hobble down the pier, pulling Sam along with him. He tries to sneak past the passengers as they walk up the large sloped ramp. Porgy pulls Sam with the cart to a place nearby where he spots two of the ship workers putting the passengers' bags into the ship's hold.

"Pssst! Pssst!" Porgy tries to attract their attention and one of the crew members is drawn to the sound he is making.

He turns to Porgy. "What's yo doin' here, brotha? Yo workin' on dis ship?" He walks over to Porgy, curious. "I nevah seen yo heah befo'."

Porgy moves as close to the dock worker as he can on his crutches. Never having seen anything this large up close before, he is overwhelmed by the massive white ship. Porgy is very familiar with the small fishing boats, called the Mosquito Fleet in the Charleston harbor. The Mosquito Fleet includes a few motor boats and sailboats and employs many of the men of Catfish Row. They are a familiar sight as they sail out from the wharves on the Cooper River out to the ocean each morning, returning each afternoon with their catch.

Hoping the ship is heading north, he asks the dock worker, "Wuh be dis boat?"

The dock worker points at the ship and then back to Porgy. "This heah is a cruise ship fo' passengers an' entertainment." He is trying to figure out what Porgy wants. He needs to hurry back to work to avoid a reprimand from his boss.

"Weh be her goin'?"

The worker responds, "New Yawk," now more interested as to why Porgy is asking so many questions.

Porgy's eyes grow wide and his heart skips a beat when he hears the words "New York." He knows this is a perfect chance for him to make his way there to Bess. *I know dat dis ain't goin' tuh be easy, but I mus' fin' muh woman no mattah wuh it tek.* Moving closer to the worker, he checks all around to make sure he is not being overheard. "Do yuh t'ink I could sto'way?"

He shakes his head. "No, brotha. I can't help yo. Me an' mah brothas can't get caught wit' yo on board in no uniform. They would fire me. This job is how I feed mah fam'ly. Sorry." He turns around and continues loading the suitcases onto the ship.

Another worker yells at Porgy, "Come on, brotha, move along! What is yo doin'?" Looking at the man who was talking to Porgy, he points to Porgy and the goat. "What dat guy is doin' heah?"

The worker who was talking to Porgy points at him as well. "He wants to stowaway. Tol' him no." He moves away from Porgy and goes back to what he was doing. In order to avoid trouble from their boss, they try to work quickly. The passengers continue boarding until the area is nearly empty.

Porgy turns back to the first ship worker, grabs his arm and the man whips around. The dock worker can tell that he is desperate to get on the ship. "Muh wife bin tek f'om me up tuh New Yawk, an' I hab tuh bring she back tuh be wid me. Please, bruddah. Dis be de only way I kin keep muh fambly tuhgedduh." Tears well up for the second time that day, and he squeezes the worker's arm harder.

The worker, studying the goat and cart, sighs with sympathy at Porgy's plea and the look of despair in his eyes. "Do yo have ta brin' da goat?" He glances again at the goat and then back to Porgy.

Nodding his head, he says. "Him is how I git 'roun fast. I be a cripple. I don' hab legs like normal mens." With that explanation, Porgy slaps his legs. "De goat an' muh cart mek it easiah fuh me tuh git 'roun on de streets. I do need he. Please." He closes his eyes, praying for a positive answer.

The worker, now finished loading the luggage, takes Porgy's arm. "Okay. Come on, let's go." Having a family of his own, and feeling sorry for Porgy, he helps him up the ramp and onto the ship. The other worker follows, not wanting to be left out of anything. They throw a tarp over Sam and the cart and help Porgy sneak past the few passengers who are still boarding. This is really an unnecessary endeavor, as they are so involved with their own activities, they barely notice them.

They continue down to the end of a hallway where there are stairs to the lower level of the ship. Taking the tarp off the goat, the two men help Porgy and Sam down the steep and narrow stairs. They attach a pulley to the cart and ease it down the stairwell. One of the workers nearly falls as he loses his balance trying to work the pulley down. "Woah! Dat was close! I don' want ta die helpin' a goat ta stow away."

They lead Porgy down the windowless hallway of the lower deck where he can see doors on the left and right. Small electric lights are lit along the walls so the hallway isn't completely dark. Rusty brown water drips from the ceiling and make puddles on the hard metal floor. The hallway is musty and smells of sweat and engine oil. This is where the workers sleep. The three men stop in the middle of the hallway and one of them opens a door to a cabin.

Inside the cabin there are two sets of bunk beds that essentially fill the whole room. They are uncomfortable looking, each covered only by a thin blanket. The first worker Porgy was talking with points to a bottom bunk near one wall. "Heah, no one be sleepin' on this bed. Yo can definitely sleep heah. By da way, mah name is Jonathan." He shakes Porgy's hand.

45

The other ship worker turns to Porgy and shakes his hand. "An' I'm William." He gives Porgy a friendly pat on the back.

"I be Porgy. T'ank yo so much." He points down at his goat Sam. "Will Sam be okay in heah?" Sam makes a bleating sound as he moves around the small room. The goat cart takes up almost the entire area.

Jonathan takes hold of Sam, "I will go put him somewhere he will be safe at da end of da hallway. Me and mah brothas will only be on da ship fo' about two days. He will be fine, as long as no one fin' him and tries ta cook him." Jonathan and William laugh. Porgy grimaces, frightened by that possibility, but Jonathan just laughs seeing the expression on his face. "It's alright, man. We will make shuh no one eats him."

William is studying Porgy's appearance. "Me and mah frien's have to figga out what we're finna do wit' yo. It will be hard ta keep yo hidden, so me an' mah brothas will have ta fin' yo a real job onboard. No one would believe a cripple could be a waitah or cook, or a cabin cleanah. But, he can try ta pose as a . . ." William thinks on it more. "Maybe he can be a busboy in da dinin' room." Jonathan nods his head approvingly. Jonathan and William are part of the typical Negro work crew on luxury ships. They are the cooks and stewards, butlers and maids, steam-fitters, and men who keep the engines running. They work sixteen-hour days and could be penalized for the slightest offense and have their wages docked.

Jonathan assesses Porgy's grubby clothes. "I think one of da guys down da hall might have an extra pair of clean pants and a shirt so he can dress up like da busboys in da dinin' room. All he has ta do is push da dinin' room cart aroun' cuz it has wheels, and he best be able to manage it wit' his crutches. I think dis makes sense." William contemplates this idea for a moment, and nods his head again at the plan.

While listening to them talk about getting him clothing for a job onboard, Porgy notices they are both wearing black pants and white shirts. He can tell they are neat and clean in their uniforms in spite of the fact that the area they sleep in is dim and dingy. Porgy questions them, not quite understanding. "Busboy?" He isn't too sure what they are talking about.

William steps up and says, "A busboy. Aftuh ev'ryone is done eatin', yo clean up da tables, put da dirty dishes in da cart, and roll it back into da kitchen. I don' think anyone would question someone on crutches cleanin' up da tables. If anyone asks, we'll say he sprained his ankles gettin' onboard, rathah than say he is a cripple. Hope I ain't offendin' yo."

Porgy grins and pats his heart, "Yuh din't. I know I be a strong man inside an' out. Muh weak legs don' keep me f'om doin' anyt'ing I need tuh do. Dey jis' mek me stronger eb'ryweh else."

An alarm goes off in the lower deck and a red light starts blinking in the room. Porgy jumps, frightened. "Wuh dat be?" *I bettah calm down so dat I kin do dis busboy job right. I hope dat red light don' mean I bin discovered.* Turning to his new friends, he asks, "Did dey fin' out I be a stowaway? Do I hab tuh hide?"

William, looking at the light, grabs Sam and the cart. "No, that jus' means we have ta go now. I will get yo some fresh clothin'. Aftuh yo get dressed, I will take Sam ta a room wheah he will be safe. When we go to da uppah deck, we all stand in line. Da officers will come talk ta us. If dey asks, say yo is workin' as a busboy. Jonathan, make shuh he get his clothes on right."

After Porgy is freshly attired in a white shirt and black pants, the uniform of a busboy, William takes Sam and walks out of the room. Jonathan assists Porgy, and they hurry out of the room as well. At the stairwell, Jonathan anxiously asks Porgy, "How the heck are yo goin' ta get up them stairs?"

Porgy hands his crutches to Jonathan, "Jis' watch!" He then proceeds to pull himself up the narrow staircase one step at a time using just his powerful arms and shoulders, his weak legs dragging behind.

CHAPTER NINE

All the ship's service workers are standing in line on the main deck of the ship, dressed in their uniforms. Porgy stands in the line with them, wearing his newly acquired white shirt and black pants. Except for the fact he is on crutches, he fits in. He is standing between William and Jonathan, hoping not to be easily noticed, or make any trouble for his new friends.

The white officers are standing facing the Negro ship workers. The sun is beginning to set and a cool breeze blows gently across the deck. One of the officers steps out in front of the others and sweeps his eyes down the line. He walks to one end and begins working his way slowly past each worker. His ramrod straight back and the fierce expression on his face make him appear intense, and as he gets ready to speak, he does not have a smile on his face.

"Good evening. My name is Captain Frederick E. Cross. I will be addressed by you as Captain Cross." He is wearing a white uniform and has on a white hat with a black visor embroidered with gold piping. "I have been a captain for thirty years. I have a Master's Degree in Marine Engineering from the U.S. Coast Guard Academy and I have been the captain of the S.S. *Virginia* since it was first commissioned."

When it comes to dealing with Negroes, his philosophy is to use fear and intimidation. Cross glares piercingly at the men in front of him as he moves down the line. "I am the commander of this ship. Many of you have worked under me before and know I do not tolerate any nonsense. Our passengers' safety is in our hands. I demand a clean ship. Cleanliness is next to Godliness. I need a crew that is committed to that belief. Wake up time is 4 AM. Breakfast, lunch, and dinner will be served on time according to the posted schedule. Every request by our passengers must be met. If there is a complaint from any passenger, it is your duty to make sure the problem is fixed promptly."

Cross stops in front of Porgy, noticing he is on crutches. William and Jonathan become nervous as Captain Cross stares at Porgy with a menacing look in his eyes. Porgy, avoiding eye contact, gazes past him out into the harbor. Jonathan and William had already warned Porgy not to make eye contact with him unless prompted to do so. "Look at me, boy!" Cross glares at Porgy.

"Yaas Captain?" He tries to position himself as upright as possible on his crutches. *I hope him don' kick me off de ship now dat I hab got dis far.*

Captain Cross inspects him up and down. "I haven't seen you anywhere before. I would have remembered if I did. You new here?" Saliva sprays out of his mouth as he talks.

Porgy makes every effort to stay as calm and relaxed as he possibly can. "Yaas Suh. I be a busboy," forcing his breathing to stay steady as he faces the captain.

"Busboy, huh? Why aren't you standing up straight? Something wrong with your legs, boy?" He moves closer to Porgy.

Refusing to be intimidated, he thinks, *I mus' git tuh New Yawk enny way I kin. I hab tuh come up wid all de right ansahs, so I bettah act like I respec' white mens who t'ink dey be bettah den me.* "Yaas Suh. Muh legs don' wuk normal, so. But, eb'ryt'ing else wuks, so. I be def'nitely mek sho' eb'ryt'ing be clean an' propa' en de dinin' room." He turns his eyes away toward the side of the ship.

Captain Cross nods his head. "You better. Don't cause any problems, boy. You understand?" Cross stands perfectly still, waiting for an answer.

Porgy smiles at him, putting on his most subservient face possible, "Yaas, Suh," nodding his head.

Addressing the crew, he says, "I don't want any trouble from any of you, understood?" All the ship workers yell in unison, "Yes, sir!" and continue looking straight ahead.

Captain Cross turns to face one of his officers on the upper deck and signals him to tell the engineer to start the ship's engines. Moments later, a loud rumbling noise comes from deep down in the lowest level of the ship, which then starts to move slowly away from the dock. Watching the Charleston shoreline recede, Porgy breathes a sigh of relief. *Bess, I be comin'!*

The passengers are at the railings of the decks waving to their families and friends back at the pier who are watching them leave. Captain Cross turns back to the workers and claps his hands. "Alright, everyone get to work!" He watches as they move off to their various work stations.

Jonathan and William guide Porgy as they walk together over to the kitchen. Many Negro sous-chefs are broiling steaks on the grills. Flour is being sifted all over the metal counter as bread is being made ready for baking. The dishwashers splash hot soapy water in the sinks as they prepare to clean all the plates, bowls, utensils, and cups the busboys bring in from the dining room. The chefs are running back and forth preparing the evening's courses for dinner.

It is hot in the kitchen as the fires from the stove-top burners and ovens heat up the air in the jammed, tightly packed area. The only kitchen Porgy has ever seen is like Maria's in Catfish Row. He is bewildered by all the frenetic activity, and asks Jonathan and William, "How do ennyt'ing ebbuh git done wid all dese people runnin' 'round en dis kitchen? How do ennyone know which plates ob food go wheah?"

"Don' yo worry about dat, Porgy. All yo need ta do is jus' get da dirty plates off da tables." William laughs.

Jonathan and William take him to a corner of the busy kitchen and introduce him to the other busboys. Jonathan touches Porgy's shoulder. "Hang wit' these guys. They are mah frien's, and they will show yo what ta do. See yo tonight." They walk off and Porgy remains with his fellow busboys. They all introduce themselves and shake Porgy's hand.

The lead busboy gets up onto a milk crate. His skin is as dark as night. He is very serious about his job. "My name is George. Our job is to make shuh all these tables is squeaky clean and all da dirty dishes is taken away quickly. I do not want Captain Cross ta evah have ta come in heah ta complain. Do . . . yo' . . . jobs." George points at Porgy and asks, "Are yo shuh yo can really do dis?"

Porgy assures George. "Yaas Suh, I knows I kin." All the busboys go over to the rolling carts and Porgy nervously follows them, taking one, as they hurry into the dining room. *I know I kin do dis busboy job. I jis' hab tuh 'membuh tuh keep one hand on de cart, so I don' lose muh balance.*

CHAPTER TEN

More than three months have gone by since Sportin' Life and Bess moved into their new apartment. Bess usually wakes up late and, on a typical morning, she is lying in bed daydreaming, longing for her days in Catfish Row. She remembers Porgy making his way around, cleaning their home, while she cradled their new son in her arms. She smiles as she fondly recalls him bringing her a flower and kissing her passionately on the lips. A tear falls from her eye as she relives being held in Porgy's loving arms.

A knock on the door interrupts Bess's reverie. Anna walks in with a couple of the other maids, and bows her head as she enters. "Sorry, Miss Bess, but Mistah Big wanted us ta come in heah and clean da apartment early today." They have been instructed not to bother her, so they rarely have the opportunity to converse with her.

Bess wipes the tears from her eyes, and motions them to step inside the room. "'It be alright, I guess, fuh yuh tuh clean now. Come on en. Mistuh Big? Dat's wuh yuh call he, right?"

The maids come in and tell Bess that is what they were told to call him. They begin tidying up the room while Bess sits in a chair by the window. As Anna makes the bed, she turns to Bess and asks, "How yo likin' Harlem?"

"I reck'n it be good. Diff'rent, I guess. I don' really know ennyt'ing 'bout Harlem since I hab nebbuh bin out en de neighborhood berry much."

"Where is yo from? If yo don' mind me axin'."

"Charleston. Yuh could fit de whole town en dis bedroom." Bess giggles as she makes the comparison. "But it bin home. Muh home. One day, I wan' tuh go back an' git muh son."

"Wow!" Anna says, dropping her broom and dustpan in amazement. "You gots a son! Why din't yo bring him?"

Elizabeth, one of the other maids, hits Anna on the shoulder. "Shut yo mouth girl an' stop axin' questions."

Before Bess answers, she hesitates and then and raises her hand. "No, it be alright. It be . . . nice . . . habin' someone tuh talk tuh." Looking down, she takes a deep breath and continues, "I hab a husban', a stevedore, name Crown. Him bin a mean man, but him bin all I hab at de time. Him . . . kill somebody."

Bess raises her eyes from the floor. Anna and Elizabeth are listening intently to the story, with shocked expressions on their faces. "Yaas, him did kill anuddah man. An' him fled 'way fom de town. I war 'lone 'til a wondah'ful woman, Maria, tek me in. An' dat be how I met . . . Porgy."

Thinking for a moment she should probably not be sharing all this information with them, Bess fidgets and rubs her legs, but it is such a relief for her to tell her story. "Porgy lib der right 'cross fom Maria kitchen. Her bin de cook in Catfish Row, a paa't ob Charleston. I would see he all de time. Us fall en lub. He tek care ob me. An' den, de harricane hit, 'stroyin' mos' ob Charleston. A neighbor name Clara bin kill en de bad storm."

Taking a shaky breath, she continues. "I tek in she son, an' Porgy an' I 'dopt de baby. An' den . . . Porgy bin 'rrested, an' dey tek he 'way tuh jail. I try tuh stay on de right track, but I git en wid some real bad people. Dey kidnap me, 'way fom Charleston. 'Way fom Porgy an' muh son . . . Mistah Big sabe me an' convince me

53

tuh come tuh New Yawk. So, heah I be." Bess holds back tears as she shares how she came to be in New York.

Anna walks to Bess and takes her hand. "What's da baby's name?"

For the first time in her conversations with the maids, she smiles sweetly. "Jonah."

The maid encourages her with a positive tone of voice, "I jus' know dat one day, yo will get ta go back to Charleston. Yo will."

Elizabeth gives Anna a warning look. "I hope she can, but I think Mistah Big will wan' ta stay in New York."

Bess's conversation with the maids is interrupted by a loud knocking at the front door. She tip-toes to the bedroom door and sees Sportin' Life with a young, good-looking Negro in the foyer. He is neatly dressed in khaki pants, a white shirt, a blue blazer, and a tweed newsboy cap. Bess has never seen this man before. Assuming he is a john, she runs to a table in her bedroom and pulls out a small canister with cocaine in it. *De happy dus' will help me serbis de man de way Sport in' Life like me tuh.* The maids watch what she is doing, but pretend to be busy cleaning up.

Bess puts a small amount of the powder on the back of her hand and sniffs it up. She quickly pats her nose with a handkerchief and starts to brush her hair and fix her makeup. Once her hair and makeup are finished, she goes to the window, gets down on her knees and closes her eyes. With her hands clasped together, she quietly begins to pray. "Gawd, please protek me. Please leh dis go fas'. Please fuhgib me fuh all muh sins. Please . . . continue tuh luk ober me. Amen." Bess finally opens her eyes, walks back to the bedroom door, and peeks out. The man and Sportin' Life are sitting at the table talking and counting money.

Bess turns to Anna and waves her hand indicating she should come over to her. Anna peers through the doorway as Bess asks, "Who dat?"

Squinting, she peeks through the doorway. "I think he might be one of Mistah Big's numbahs managers."

"Numbahs? Wuh be de numbahs?"

"It's da business Mistah Big runs. It's a . . . money game. Dat's how he makes all his money."

In the other room, Sportin' Life turns to the man, and stops adding up the money. "This is looking good, Joshua. Do you have any more betting slips and cash to pick up?"

Joshua has only had a few meetings with Sportin' Life in his apartment, instead of in his office, and its opulence always impresses him. "Yes, but most of our othah customahs said they will make their bets tonight at yo' party, Mistah Big. They all know yo is pullin' da numbah t'morrow at da theater."

Sportin' Life nods his head approvingly and smiles. "Tonight will be great. Make sure you collect from everyone. For those who need a little extra . . ." Walking over to a painting on the living room wall, he removes it to reveal a safe. He dials the combination and the safe makes a clicking sound as it opens. Inside is a brick of cocaine, which he removes, and then places the betting slips and the money he counted so far into the safe.

He walks back over to Joshua, sits down, and hands him the cocaine. "We need to have this broken down by tonight for the party."

Joshua is concerned. "Dat's a lot ta break down in so little time. The whole brick, Mistah Big? I gots ta also get da othah bettin' slips." He grimaces at the look on Sportin' Life's face, knowing his boss is not pleased with his comment.

Sportin' Life stops counting the rest of the money and stares at Joshua. His demeanor changes, and his voice rises. "Is it too much for you, Joshua? Huh? Because I can find someone else to do this job, if you can't handle it!"

Still peeking from the bedroom door with Anna, Bess recognizes the change in Sportin' Life's voice. The high pitch reminds her she needs to stay away from him when he is angry. She clutches the door knob and feels her palms become sweaty, and tries not to make a sound.

Joshua, realizing he should not have complained about getting the cocaine cut, mumbles. "No, Mistah Big. Not at all." He gazes down at his feet, sweat beading on his forehead, and doesn't move a muscle. Sportin' Life can be dangerous when he doesn't get his way. Joshua is paid well for this unique job and doesn't want to lose it in these tough times.

Sportin' Life puts down the remaining money. "Don't you have help? Didn't I get you more runners and helpers? Isn't that what you asked for? And now you're telling me you still can't handle the job?" He leans forward in his seat as if he is about to stand up. The room is silent for a moment.

Finally, Joshua speaks, "No Mistah Big. I will get it done." Joshua fearfully bites his bottom lip.

Sportin' Life doesn't say anything for a minute, then smiles and laughs. Joshua nervously joins in on the laughter. Sportin' Life gets up out of chair. "Well, I guess you better go and get to work then, right?" Suddenly, Sportin' Life lunges and grabs him by the shirt, lifting him out of the chair. Grasping the brick of cocaine, he slams it into Joshua's chest. He shoves Joshua hard toward the door, making Joshua's hat fall off. He opens the front door and pushes Joshua toward the opening. "Remember. I want all of that done for the party. Be here at 7:30." He picks up Joshua's hat from the floor and holds it out to him.

"Yes, Mistah Big." Joshua holds onto his hat and juggles the cocaine so it doesn't drop from his hands, steps through the doorway, and leaves the apartment.

Bess is bewildered by the scene she just witnessed. *Who dat man? Wheah do all de money come fom? Why do Sportin' Life git so mad wid he? Wuh kin' ob paa'ty be him habin' t'night.*

CHAPTER ELEVEN

Sportin' Life bangs the apartment door shut and sighs in exasperation. His head and shoulders ache when he has to deal with numbers managers or runners who don't follow orders. He keeps an eye on the other numbers operations in Harlem, and is always worried about his employees' loyalty. Sportin' Life uses fear, intimidation and the benefit of getting of cheap cocaine, which he hopes will keep them in line.

Looking toward the bedroom, he spots Bess peeking through the doorway. When she sees him staring at her, she closes the door and runs to the bathroom, fearing he will be angry they have been eavesdropping. She tells Anna and Elizabeth to continue to clean the room. Sitting in front of the mirror, Bess takes out her hair brush and begins brushing her hair, pretending she hadn't been listening in on Sportin' Life and his conversation with Joshua.

Sportin' Life walks into the bedroom and observes the maids cleaning the room. In an annoyed tone, he orders them, "You ladies go start lunch, now!" After they leave the room, he goes into the bathroom, where he sees Bess brushing her hair, and comes up behind her.

Bess looks anxiously at Sportin' Life. She is still nervously brushing her hair. "Who bin dat en de odduh room wid yuh?"

He puts his hand on Bess's shoulder and kisses her on the cheek. The kiss sends chills down Bess's spine because a kiss from

Sportin' Life just reminds her that he owns her and can do whatever he wants. His kiss is so different from the kisses she cherished from Porgy, filled with love and respect. A kiss from Sportin' Life, on the other hand, always reinforces his power over her. With no money and no friends, she feels there is no way to escape from her life with him.

He snatches the brush from her, and holds it above his shoulder like a hammer. "Were you spying on me Bess?" He glares at her in the mirror.

Staring back, she responds haltingly, "No. Not at all! I jis'. . . I t'awt . . . I t'awt him bin someone yuh had come tuh de apa'tment fuh me." She watches him in the mirror, hoping the cocaine in her system will calm her and make her sound truthful. Since they have been living in this exclusive neighborhood for a while, she discovered, unlike what Sportin' Life told her, all johns are the same. The ones in Sugar Hill don't treat her any nicer than the johns in the seedy hotel, but they dress better and don't smell.

Sportin' Life laughs, then lowers the brush and begins brushing her hair. "No. His name is Joshua, and he wasn't for you. He was here for me. I will always tell you when to come out of the room and meet my guests. Don't spy on me." He continues watching Bess as he brushes her hair.

Bess is still shaking, but relieved he is now calmed down. "I din't. I prommus. I jis' wan' tuh prepare muhself dat be all. I din't tryin' tuh spy on yuh or ennyt'ing." She forces a smile, hoping to further alleviate the tension.

Running his fingers through Bess's hair, he says, "I'm always going to take care of you, better than what that crippled Porgy could do. Everything I do is for the best." He smoothes Bess's hair behind her shoulders and brushes some more.

Timidly, Bess asks, "I be jis' wondahrin', why do de maids an' dat man call yuh Mistah Big? Dey say yuh run somet'ing call a numbahs game. Wuh be dat? How do it wuk?" She is curious about how Sportin' Life can afford this apartment and their lifestyle, "Wuh do dat man do?"

Sportin' Life brags, "Honey, the numbers game is what brings us all our money. My customers make bets with me, kind of like in craps when players try to guess which numbers the roll of the dice will turn up. Here, they can choose any number they want between 0 and 999 and make a bet with one of my numbers people, hoping it will turn out to be the winning number for the day."

"How do de playahs know wuh de winnin' numbah be?"

"Well, at the end of the day at my office in the Apollo Theater, I spin a wheel three times to come up with the winning number. There are a thousand possible numbers, so, if their number comes up, they can win a lot of money. It's just a game of chance and very few people ever win . . . and I get to keep the money that isn't paid out to the winners. People love the rush and the chance to win lots of money without even doing anything, and I can make money off their laziness." Sportin' Life laughs at the thought of all the people who believe they're going to win.

Bess looks up at him and asks, "How did yuh eben git intah dis numbahs game? I t'awt it bin . . . sellin' de happy dus' an' me dat git we dis place."

Walking to the window, he gazes out at the river. "Before I arrived in Charleston and found you, I lived here in Harlem, and used to work in a hotel here. I also sold cocaine to the rich and famous people at the hotel. White, Colored, orange people . . . no color mattered to me except the color of money, green. Because there was a law that cocaine could only be used for medical reasons, I became the man with the 'medical' supply and the right prices in Harlem." He chuckles at his tongue-in-cheek explanation.

"But, I had lots of competition, and it was a hard-scrabble life with never enough money. Unfortunately, when the hotel found out what I was doing, they kicked me out. Bumpy Johnson, the man I got my cocaine from, was from Charleston and thought maybe I could do better in that town. That's how I ended up in Catfish Row.

"After you were kidnapped, and I found you in Savannah, I realized there weren't ever going to be enough happy dust customers for me in Charleston. I was trying to figure out what to do and where to go, so I got back in touch with Bumpy. Besides dealing in cocaine, he was also now a big shot in the numbers game in Harlem, and he set me up with my own territory. I started by connecting with my old happy dust customers and got them to start making bets. We had to live in that seedy hotel until my operation got going. I even lend money to my managers, charging them interest, of course. Now, everything is running smoothly, and here you are, sitting in front of this fancy gold-plated mirror, brushing your beautiful hair."

Thinking he still did not answer her question, Bess cautiously asks, "But yuh din't tell me, why do dey call yuh Mistah Big?"

Sportin' Life flashes a dazzling movie-star smile at Bess. "Because I am Mr. Big. I now run the biggest numbers racket on the streets in our neighborhood."

Sportin Life is indeed now the main numbers "bank" in his part of Harlem. If a lucky customer picks a winning 3-digit number, the bank pays off at 600 to 1. The runners earn a twenty-five percent commission on the money bet. Most of the rest of the money goes to Sportin' Life, out of which he pays his managers, like Joshua.

Bess doesn't fully comprehend what he's talking about with the numbers, but she understands it brings in a lot of money and surmises, *Mebbe now I won' hab tuh serbis enny mo' johns.*

"I tell you about this because I trust you, and I don't want anyone to know my real name is Sportin' Life. In this business, secrecy is essential." He stops brushing Bess's hair. "By the way, you will see a lot of my numbers customers and other important people I deal with at a party here tonight."

"Yuh goin' tuh leh me come out t'night, at a paa'ty?"

"Yes. I want them all to see what I have on my arm." He fixes Bess's hair on either side of her face and massages her shoulders. "You are the most beautiful woman in the world and worth every penny."

Bess is uneasy about the "worth every penny" remark, but she keeps smiling so as not to let him see she is bothered. "So, yuh de man? Be it safe fuh people tuh know wheah us lib? I mean wid de cocaine an' all ob de money an' stuff . . ."

Sportin' Life interrupts her. "No one would dare steal from me or harm you. I am untouchable, and we also have bodyguards watching out for us all the time. I supply to the best of the best. You're protected, no matter what." Leaning down so that his face is right next to Bess's face, he says, "Wear your hair like this tonight."

Bess admires herself in the mirror. "I like it dis way too." Her face is lovely, but her eyes seem sad. She is always distressed when Sportin' Life touches her, and remembers when Porgy kissed her, and how tender he would be. *Ef I ain't git drunk an' gone down tuh de dock aftuh Porgy bin 'rrested, I would nebbuh hab bin kidnap, an' wouldn' be heah now.* Her eyes fill with tears, but she holds them back. She smoothes back her hair and flashes the radiant smile she knows always pleases Sportin' Life.

He takes a cellophane bag out of his pocket. There are a few grams of cocaine in it, and he takes a little out with his elongated pinky fingernail. "I will always protect you." He raises his finger next to Bess's nose. She turns to face him, hesitates, and then sniffs it in. Bess fights the urge to cry and run out of the apartment, but then loses herself in a haze as the drug takes possession of her body.

CHAPTER TWELVE

As the S.S. *Virginia* steams out from Charleston's harbor and begins its journey north, the first-class passengers enter the dining room for the ship's first seating for dinner. During the meal, Harry J. Dooley, the tour director for the Gray Line Company, walks to the microphone on the stage at one end of the room.

Dooley is telling the passengers about Harlem, part of their tour package in New York City. "Yes, Harlem is a vibrant and growing section of the city with lots of night life. Not quite as exciting as what we do here . . ." The audience laughs at the joke. "But you will have great fun once we dock. There is a lot of entertainment to be found in Harlem, like at the Lafayette Theater, where we can catch a show with Bill "Bojangles" Robinson. We know Bojangles is a world-famous tap dancer, so you will really receive an authentic taste of Harlem. We will go to the Friday midnight show.

"Most Negro revues begin and end here, but we will have an extra special treat. We will go to the Savoy Ballroom to see Earl Tucker perform his famous "Snake-hips" dance. We will also visit Monroe's Uptown House and Minton's Playhouse to hear the latest jazz music!" This announcement is met with excited applause.

The tour director waits for them to settle before continuing." Of course, for our most anticipated stop, we will go to the world-renown Cotton Club on 142nd Street to see Bessie Smith and

Count Basie. On Sunday night when they have "Celebrity Nights," we might see . . . Sophie Tucker!" The audience stamps their feet, yells, and screams in excitement. "We thank you for travelling with us on the *S. S. Virginia*. Now, let's enjoy some music!" The passengers chat animatedly about the program as they continue to eat their dinner.

Their attention is now again directed to the stage at the front of the room where a white man in "blackface" goes up to the microphone. His lips are painted grossly oversized, and in a glowing bright red. His black greasepaint makeup covers his face and neck, and he begins to sing a "coon song" called, "All Coons Look Alike To Me." He sings with head and body movements he knows the audience will see as a comical caricature that makes fun of Negroes. The song is popular in minstrel shows.

> *Talk about a coon a having trouble.*
> *I have enough of ma own.*
> *It's all about ma Lucy Jamey Stubbles*
> *and she has caused my heart to mourn.*
> *There's another coon barber from Virginia.*
> *In society, he's the leader of the day.*
> *And now ma honey gal is goin' to quit me.*
> *Yes, she's gonna drive this coon away.*
> *She'd no excuse to turn me loose.*
> *I've been abused.*
> *I'm all confused.*
> *Cause these words she did say.*
> *All coons look alike to me.*
> *I've got another beau you see.*
> *And he's just as good to me*
> *as you nigger ever to be.*
> *He spends his money free.*
> *I know we can't agree.*
> *So, I don't like you.*
> *All coons look alike to me.*

The singer continues to belt out the song through his red-painted lips as the audience laughs and sings along.

Porgy is cleaning off a table when he hears the lyrics. He is used to white prejudice against Negroes, turns in disgust to the blackface performer, and wonders if it will ever end. The song also make him think about his Bess with Sportin' Life, and he worries whether she thinks about him that way, like in the song. He is upset about the entire scene and is momentarily distracted.

Porgy turns around with the dirty plates in one hand, and the other hand on the cart, but accidentally bumps into one of the white passengers. He loses his balance and falls to the floor as his dishes go flying. The passenger is tall with a dark brown beard so long it covers half of his dinner jacket. His blue eyes are the color of the ocean, and they pierce through Porgy like the eye of a hurricane.

The silence in the room is almost immediate as everyone becomes aware of the incident. The performer on the stage stops singing, and the attention of the guests in the dining room is drawn over to where Porgy is lying on the floor. The man he collided with steps over him, angrily leans down, and pulls him up by his shirt. "Are you outah your mind, boy? Huh?" He shakes Porgy.

Porgy is wary of he white man and grits his teeth. He is not cowed, but realizes he must pull himself together quickly. When the man stops shaking him, Porgy tries to stand using the handle of the cart for support, "I be so sorry Suh. I din't mean tuh . . ."

The passenger interrupts him. "You should be whupped for this, boy. Git on your feet." Using his arms, Porgy straightens up and balances himself on his knees. His crippled condition is now apparent to his tormentor. He looks him up and down and continues to taunt him, "You caint stand up, boy?" The passenger again grabs Porgy by the shirt and shakes him.

"No, Suh. I kin not. Muh legs don' wuk well, Suh." Porgy lifts his head, not ashamed. The passenger laughs. The rest of the dinner guests find the situation amusing and burst into laughter, too. Negro waiters and cooks are watching from afar, afraid of what is about to happen to Porgy.

Captain Cross has been having his dinner on the other side of the dining room and rushes over. "What is going on here?" He runs up to the passenger and Porgy. He looks at Porgy and then at the man with the beard. "What happened here, Mr. Chatham?" Cross glances down at Porgy, who is now more nervous than when he was being shaken.

Mr. Chatham points to Porgy. "This boy caint walk straight. Ran right intah me. A monkey in the flesh. Walkin' on all fours. Fascinatin'." Mr. Chatham eyes Porgy again, this time more closely examining his legs. "Was you born like this, boy?" He prods Porgy's legs with his foot.

"Yaas, Suh. Bawn a cripple." Porgy grits his teeth again, and clenches his fists. He'd like Mr. Chatham to keep his hands off of him and feels like he is being put on show for the whole dining room full of white people. Rather than looking up at Cross, he shifts his gaze across the room toward the Negro cooks, busboys, and chefs, hoping they will rescue him. But they are all waiting to see how this will end, and are fearful of becoming involved.

Cross is furious. "I am sorry, Mr. Chatham. I will take care of this immediately! He will be punished." He reaches down to drag Porgy out of the middle of the dining room.

Mr. Chatham stops him. "No. No, it's fine. He's a fascinatin' one. Legs that don't work. They sure are made different." He laughs at his cynical joke. "Jus' git him outah here," Mr. Chatham says as he smiles and casually walks away.

Captain Cross seizes Porgy by his shirt collar and drags him along the floor into the kitchen. He pushes Porgy against the wall, causing him to slump down in pain. Cross bends down, puts his face right up into Porgy's, and glares at him. "You are lucky, boy. If we were on land, I would have had you lynched already. Don't let this happen again."

The captain kicks Porgy in the ribs. Even though he is in pain, Porgy silently rolls over onto his back, wondering if the ordeal is now over. Cross turns to the other workers as he stomps out of the kitchen, and yells. "Get back to work! Now!"

Porgy sits up in the corner to catch his breath and let the pain subside. He is embarrassed and humiliated. He hopes he can make it to New York without getting thrown overboard.

CHAPTER THIRTEEN

Later that night, Porgy returns to the cabin he shares with Jonathan and William. They are both lying on their beds already and Porgy lies down on the bunk below Jonathan's. Jonathan peers down at him in the darkness. "Weah were yo? Were yo gettin' somethin' ta eat?"

"No. I bin feedin' muh goat Sam. I tek some scrap f'om de kitchen an' feed he." Porgy lays his head down on the pillow and sighs, relieved his first day on the trip is over.

William is sympathetic to the defeat he senses in Porgy's deep sigh. "What happen' t'day Porgy? Is yo okay?"

He shrugs his shoulders. "I bin distracted by dat song." The words that upset him during dinner pop back into his mind. Using the slang word for a white person, he says, "Dat buckruh git in us face, singin' 'bout us troubles. Him distract me." Closing his eyes, he grudgingly realizes he must learn to ignore the racist comments by the passengers and crew on board the ship.

William responds, "That's how they is, man. They don' respect us. Captain Cross took away yo pay fo' da day?"

"Yaas, him did. But I din't 'spect nutt'n else. All I be is a joke. A monkey man tuh dem."

Jonathan looks from William to Porgy and questions, "Were yo really born like dat, Porgy? Were yo born wit' yo legs not working?" Jonathan and William become silent as they wait for Porgy to respond.

Porgy opens his eyes, and pauses before speaking. He has never told this story to anyone, not even to his love, Bess. His gratitude is heartfelt toward these two men who have befriended him, and put their own livelihood on the line. He begins, "When I bin younga, I bin wukin' at de Snee Faa'm in de town ob Mount Pleasant. It bin on de coast ob Sout' Carolina. De plantation bin own by Osgood Hamlin an' him fambly." Just uttering the man's name makes Porgy shiver with a cold sweat. He inhales deeply again, grimaces, and goes on with his story. "Muh legs were wukin' jis' fine. Dey bin bawn . . . jis' fine . . ."

Choking on his words, he has trouble speaking as he relates what happened. "An' I bin pick cotton fuh Mastuh Hamlin. Muh sistuh wuk in him house. One aftuhnoon I heah she scream. I could recognize she scream f'om all de odduh screams on dat plantation. I run enside de house. lukkin' fuh she, searchin' fuh she. I fin' she in one ob de upstairs bedroom. An' de Mastuh son on top ob she." Porgy starts to cry as he talks about his past. "Him is tryin tuh rape she. An' I couldn' leh dat happ'n. I jis' couldn'. De luk on she face, haunt me 'til dis day. I grab he by de neck an' punch he as haa'd as I could. Him cry out en pain. Him nose gush blood. An' I grab muh sistuh . . . an' us jis' run."

Jonathan and William are listening intently, but they are not surprised or shocked. They have heard the same kind of story many times before. In the South, white men grow up believing they can do whatever they want to Negro women and not get punished. In South Carolina, the Governor has said he doubted whether a white man could even be indicted for the crime of rape if committed on a Negro woman.

Porgy continues. "Us run out intah de field wid no dest'nation en mind. I jis' know us hab tuh git out ob der. I could heah de hoof beats ob de horses an' de howl ob de dog on we tail. I could sense de fear in muh sistuh breat'in'. Us hide behin' a tree. I hol' she face b'tween muh hand an' say, 'I will protek yuh. Her luk at me an' cry. Sudd'nly, dey catch up wid us an' dey tackle me f'om b'hin' an' trow me tuh de ground. Dey tek hol' muh sistuh an' tie she hand b'hin' she back. I t'awt us was goin' tuh be lynch. I know us bin close to deat' an' it bin muh fau't."

The tears run down Porgy's face. "An' de Mastuh ob de house walk ober tuh me wid he son who be holdin' he bloody nose. De son hit me in de face. Muh sistuh scream out. De Mastuh say, 'Porgy. Niggah. You will pay fuh dis!' Dey grab muh arm a hol' me down. I kickin' an' screamin'. Muh sistuh is kickin' an' screamin'. De Mastuh bring out dis big sledgehammah. Him hand it tuh he son. De mens hol' me down on de ground! An' dey stretch out muh legs an' dey break dem. An' now I caint walk ennymo' wid'out de crutches." Porgy is yelling as he visualizes how his legs were injured so badly they won't ever support him again without the help of crutches.

He is sobbing and clutching the blanket on his bed. The memory of the pain of the sledgehammer blows is still with him today after all these years. Putting his hands to his eyes, he slowly wipes the tears from his face once more. From the look on their faces, Porgy can tell Jonathan and William are heartbroken to hear his terrible tale. Porgy finishes his story. "Muh legs couldn' be sabe. An' needuh could muh sistuh. Dey sold she peonage wuk contract tuh annodah plantation! Sold she off, jis' like her bin a slabe!"

"An' dey mek me a cripple . . . I spen' de next few yeahs at dat plantation. Dey gimme crutches an' hab me do de job ob cleanin' de bolls an' leabes off de cotton aftuh' dey bin har'bisted' But I bin deb'stated wid'out muh sistuh. Wid'out muh blood, muh sistuh . . . her bin de only t'ing I hab lef'. An' den, cuz ob muh legs, der war no way I could try ta sabe she!"

Porgy is in such anguish that he can barely finish. "An' den one horr'ble day I heah dat her walk intah de ribbuh an' din't come out. An' I bin fuh'ebbuh a cripple. Dis freak! Jis' like dat Mistah Chatham say, a monkey man! But der be a woman who lub me! An' one time I sabe she! An' now I hab tuh sabe she a'gin!"

Taking a few shaky deep breaths, Porgy calms himself down as he completes telling his story. "De boll weev'l destroy mos' ob de cotton crop, so when I done muh peonage contract at de plantation, I decide tuh go tuh Charleston an' try tuh git a bettah job. Aftuh I lef', I keep en touch wid muh ol' wuk-mates at de Snee Fa'am. A few yeahs ago dey tell me dat Mastuh Hamlin son git ketch up in de cotton gin an' los' boff ob him legs." Porgy adds, with a rueful smile, "Funny t'ing, no one know how dat happ'n."

William asks, "What da hell is a peonage contract?"

"It bin a bad papuh yuh bin made tuh sign tuh git a job. When yuh staa't wukin' de boss would gib yuh a advance on yuh wage so yuh kin eat an' lib. Den dey mek de job haa'da an' haa'da en hope dat yuh would quit wid'out payin' de loan back. Dat way, de sherruf could bring yuh back tuh de job cuz yuh bin still ondah contrac'. Yuh would mos' likely hab some jail-time too. Yuh would be force tuh wuk 'til yuh pay off de debt wit' intres'. An' dat wuh happ'n tuh me an' muh sistuh at de Snee faa'm. Us hab a huge amount us owe an' hab tuh wuk it off 'til it be pay."

"Dat's really unfair," states Jonathan, from the bunk above.

"Yaas, it bin. When I got tuh Charleston, I hab nutt'n lef'. De town bin fill wid good people like me. I t'awt I would jis' wuk der in peace, but der bin no job fuh a cripple, so I bin force tuh be a beggar. I also mek some money cuz I bin real good at craps an' I b'come known fuh dat. Den I met muh woman." With a determined voice, Porgy says, "Her bin tek tuh New Yawk an' I goin' tuh fin' she."

Jonathan and William now see why Porgy has to get to New York to find Bess. They understand that since he couldn't save his sister, he was determined to rescue the love of his life. William rolls over on his cot facing Porgy and says encouragingly, "You tried to save yo sistuh, but it wasn't yo fault. That buckruh in the dining room called yo a monkey. Yo' not a monkey! Yo' not a freak! Yo' a man! An' we will help yo da best way we can. Yo' finna be fine." Jonathan nods his head in agreement.

Porgy, grateful for their support, smiles tentatively. "I will fin' she. I will fin' muh woman."

Both his friends smile, and Jonathan says, "I'm sorry dat happened ta yo, Porgy. Things will get bettah. God would nevah let yo down." They jump out of their cots, sit next to Porgy and comfort him with brotherly pats on the back.

William adds, "We understand yo tryin' to get yo woman back an' make a bettah life. Me an' Jonathan is tryin' to do da same thin' and make it up North permanently aftuh our tour on dis ship is ovah."

"Wuh up North dat be so good?"

"A bettah life than where we are now," exclaims Jonathan.

William says, "Porgy, we heah from our friends about how much bettah they is doin' in New York. Definitely a bettah life. Da farm where we worked was lost durin' da Depression. Der was less an' less work ta do. An' da farm ownah use da Jim Crow laws all da time to keep us in line. We were afraid . . . we were afraid we was finna get lynched. Just fo' bein' Negroes."

"Me and Jonathan were friends wit' Claude Neal, who was accused of killin' a white woman down in Jackson County, Florida." Angrily, he continues," Ev'ryone knew he din't do it. Anyway, a mob dragged him out of jail and tortured him and then hang'em from a tree on da courthouse lawn. Maybe they don' do dat in Charleston, but regular white folks, not jus' da Ku Klux Klan, lynch Negroes all da time. They even do it in front of Sunday picnickers fo' somethin' as simple as not callin' a white person ma'am or suh."

Jonathan says, "That's why we took jobs on dis ship. We is hopin' getting' work up North can give us more wages an' bettah schoolin' fo' our kids. Down south our chil'n can only go ta Jim Crow schools. At dose schools da only thing they is taught is how ta work on a farm or be someone's maid."

"Wheah yuh guys' chil'n now?"

"Wit' fam'ly, down in Atlanta . . . fo' now. Until we get 'nuff money to get them up North. It will work out." William forces a smile, trying to convince Porgy as well as himself.

"I know it will, I know it" Porgy says.

They all look at each other with hope in their eyes for their dreams, and lie down again on their beds. Porgy lays his head on his pillow and covers himself with his blanket. He rubs his aching legs and looks at the ceiling, thinking about his son Jonah and Bess. He can't wait to hold them again. As he closes his eyes and tries to fall asleep, he becomes aware of some singing coming from down the hallway.

> *Money's gettin' scarce.*
> *Soon as I gather my cotton and corn,*
> *I'm bound to leave this place.*
> *White folks sittin' in the parlor,*
> *Eatin' that cake and cream,*
> *Nigger's way down to the kitchen,*
> *Squabblin' over turnip greens.*
> *Times is gettin' harder,*
> *Money's gettin' scarce.*
> *Soon as I gather my cotton and corn,*
> *I'm bound to leave this place.*
> *Me and my brother was out.*
> *Thought we'd have some fun.*
> *He stole three chickens*
> *We began to run.*
> *Times is gettin' harder,*
> *Money's gettin' scarce.*
> *Soon as I gather my cotton and corn*
> *I'm bound to leave this place.*

"Who be dat singin'?" Porgy asks as he sits up in his bed.

Jonathan lifts his head. "Prob'ly some of da kitchen workers. Sometimes they get tagethah and shoot some craps late at night." Suddenly, an idea pops into Jonathan's head and excitedly he says to Porgy, "Yo said yo were good at craps, right?"

The three men walk down the hallway to where Jim and Junior, kitchen helpers, Titus, a cook, and Patrick, head of the cleaning crew are playing craps. William and Jonathan introduce Porgy to the group and ask if he can join the game. Titus laughs. "We gots all played craps tagethah on dis ship befo', an' we is more than happy ta take money from a new playah." As the game progresses it is clear that Porgy has the knack and when he rolls the dice and makes his bets, he is on a lucky streak.

Junior exclaims, "Man, ya'll din't tell us how good he was at craps."

"Bawn wid it, I guess. Dis skill mus' hab replace muh legs," Porgy laughs.

"What do yo mean, yo guess'?" Patrick asks in an angry tone.

"Leave da man alone, Pat. Yo is jus' mad b'cause yo is losing," Titus says as they laugh.

They all continue to play and Porgy continues to win. Patrick pushes some money toward Porgy. "Yeah, yo finna do great in Harlem if yo can shoot craps like dat."

"I need all de help I kin git. Wheah Harlem?"

"So, yo nevah been ta Harlem? Evah? It's da place ta be . . . fo' some brothahs, that is," he growls.

"Yeah, not so much fo' us, unless yo got money. Da Depression hit Harlem hard too," Junior says. "I heah half da people der is out of work."

William replies, "It's bettah than bein' down South. At least da peoples in Harlem gots some friendly churches they can turn ta when they needs help."

"Wuh dat 'bout de chu'ches?" Porgy looks at them, curious, wanting to learn all he can about Harlem.

"Der's a church der that I know helps those in need called da Aby . . . da Abyss . . ." Jim tries to remember the name.

"The Abyssinian Baptist Church! Get it out!" yells Jonathan jokingly. They all laugh. "The pastor der, Adam Clayton Powell, helps feed and clothe da Harlem poor. Some church leadahs organized da Harlem Cooperatin' Committee on Relief and Unemployment. We go der if we need anythin'."

"Well dat's good. It don' sound dat bad at all . . . what else do dey do?"

"The churches all ovah Harlem is places where people can make friends and get help fo' whatevah they need."

"Yeah, well, Harlem's okay if yo don' count da smell of da poor and constant hungah," Junior exclaims as he throws the dice.

Patrick says, "Yes, but Harlem's got da dance clubs! Da music! Yo finna love it, Porgy. Yo will have a really fun time!" He points to Porgy's legs. "Can yo dance wit' those . . . leg things?"

Titus hits Patrick on the arm. "Don't ask stupid questions. If he can shoot craps like dis, he can win lots of money, and do anythin', and even figga out how ta get da legs fix."

Patrick adds, "Okay. But da women der is ev'rything!"

"Porgy already got a woman." Jonathan smiles and nudges Porgy in the ribs, "Ain't that right Porgy?"

"Yes, her de one. Muh woman bin kidnap up heah an' I goin' tuh fin' she no mattah wuh."

"In New York? Well, good luck. We will be rootin' fo' yo. I'm finna fin' me a dancah girl who works at da Cotton Club. Yes, I am!" Patrick says.

"De Cotton Club? Dey grows cotton up der in New Yawk?"

"Yo gots a lot ta learn Porgy. A lot ta learn!"

They all laugh and keep shooting craps as the ship sails silently into the night toward New York.

CHAPTER FOURTEEN

After two and half uneventful days, Porgy has managed to do the job of busboy with no further notice paid to him by the passengers or the officers. Sam, however, nearly became dinner when one of the chefs discovered him. Fortunately, when the word of his find got around, Jonathan and William quickly stopped his plans, explained the goat's presence, and rescued Sam.

At the end of its voyage the S.S. *Virginia* pulls into the dock in New York. The waves churn against the side of the ship and the anchor drops into the water making a great splash. The dock is at the 129th Street pier on the Hudson River, in a neighborhood called Manhattanville.

The pier is between the picturesque bluffs of Morningside Heights and Washington Heights. It is highly ornate, featuring ornamental ironwork and a canopy with a bright red roof. Cruises to the Catskills Mountain recreation area dock here, too. The pier also offers weekly summer concerts and dancing.

Mr. Dooley, the Gray Line tour operator, accompanies the first-class passengers as they disembark. Waiting at the dock is a bus he arranged to take them to the Hotel Belleclaire, the finest Upper Westside hotel, near Harlem. The Belleclaire dates from 1903 and is a typical example of the blending of Art Nouveau architecture and Beaux Arts style.

The building rises ten stories and gives the impression of an elegant Parisian apartment, somehow transported to New York.

Dooley tells the passengers, "This fine hotel has three hundred rooms, and on the street level is the very fashionable Grubers Ladies' Clothing Store, and a French brasserie-style restaurant. You can catch the cooling breezes on the roof garden while you look at the boats cruise by on the Hudson River."

The Negro workers are loading the white passengers' suitcases and trunks onto the Gray Line tour bus that is taking them to their hotel. Porgy makes his way next to William and Jonathan who are working with the luggage. He tries to help without getting in the passengers' way, having learned this lesson very painfully in the first few hours of the passage. Turning to William he asks, "Do yuh t'ink us l be pay a lot mo' fuh helpin' wid dis?"

William laughs under his breath, "Yeah. Pennies." William and Jonathan hit each other and laugh.

While he helps the passengers with their bags, Porgy says to Jonathan, "I only hab a li'l bit ob money lef' f'om Catfish Row an' muh gamblin' winnin's. I need somewheah tuh lib dat I kin afford."

Jonathan turns to him, "We will help yo fin' somethin', but yo will gots ta fin' some work ta pay fo' da rent an' food. William an' me is only here fo' a week befo' da ship leaves." They continue handling the passengers' luggage and trunks.

After all the luggage and trunks are loaded into the storage area of the bus, William and Jonathan help Porgy gather his bags, and William brings Sam and the cart down the ramp. He gets in and sets up the reins so Sam can pull him. They wait in line at the bottom of the ramp for their money, and Mr. Dooley hands each of them two quarters, and sends them on their way.

Porgy stares at his two quarters, and sees Jonathan shrug his shoulders." At least it's not pennies." They all shake their heads in disgust, and move away from the ship toward the streets of

Harlem. Approaching the front of the pier, the sound of loud music reaches them.

The music gets louder and louder as they make their way closer to where the pier meets the street. "Wuh be goin' on ober der?" Porgy asks the guys.

"It's a parade! I've seen dis befo'! Da Marcus Garvey parade! Let's go!" Jonathan speeds up his walking as they get near, with William close behind. Porgy urges Sam on as he hurries to keep up with his friends.

They reach the street where the parade is taking place and see a large crowd of people milling around it. Marcus Garvey's organization, The Universal Negro Improvement Association, represents the largest mass movement in the Negro community, preaching a nationalist "Back to Africa" message. Garvey owns an auditorium in Harlem, named Liberty Hall, where he holds nightly meetings to get his beliefs out to the people.

The brass bands and floats excite Porgy. Jonathan points out the high-level Harlem community dignitaries riding automobiles festooned with gorgeous flags and insignias. "Look! der's Marcus Garvey in dat beautiful open limousine." Garvey is using a loudspeaker to exhort the crowd to come to his next meeting, when he will once again promote his philosophy.

The colors on the floats give Porgy the feeling that someone has painted the streets of New York with vibrant blues, greens, yellows and reds. The people on the floats are smiling and throwing beaded necklaces to the crowd. Marchers hold banners proclaiming, "We want a Black Civilization." Surprised by the boldness of the banners and signs, he tells his friends, "Yuh know, dis would nebbuh be allowed en Charleston. Dey would 'mediately be 'rrested."

The hundred-degree heat has made everyone's skin glisten with sweat, but the people on the street don't seem to mind. No one appears to have a care in the world as they dance in the street to the jazzy music.

The band going by reminds Porgy of parades he saw in Charleston, organized by The Jenkins Orphanage Bands. The orphanage didn't have much money, so they got their musical instruments from donations. Mr. Jenkins hired two local Charleston musicians, P.M "Hatsie" Logan and Francis Eugene Mikell, to tutor the orphan boys. The Jenkins Orphanage Bands, when first established, was the only organized Negro instrumental group in South Carolina. The band was an amazing sight to see, with dozens of Negro children in colorful uniforms, marching down the main street playing musical instruments.

Porgy, William, and Jonathan squeeze to the front of the crowd. They haven't had a chance to enjoy a good time in days, having been either cramped into the tiny sleeping area, or tending to the passengers' needs. The music gets their bodies swaying and they wave as the brass bands pass by. Sam is agitated by the loud noise, and Porgy holds on tightly to his reins. Leaning over, he whispers, "Easy, boy. Yuh hab bin at parades like dis befo' . . . well, mebbe not quite like dis." He daydreams about the small parades they used to have near Catfish Row. There were fewer people in them, but they were just as spirited and created as much excitement among the residents.

The brass bands and floats are followed by some colorfully-decorated automobiles. Behind the cars are some double-deck buses with people on top throwing brochures about Marcus Garvey's organization down to the watching crowd. This is a beautiful event, and Porgy can feel the pride and love of the Negro community flowing through the crowd.

Porgy pulls on William's arm, and he bends down to listen to him... "Wheah be us at?" He looks around, hoping to figure out which part of New York he is in, and tries to remember the conversation he had with the ship workers about different neighborhoods in the city.

"Harlem. Yo remembah we tol' yo about it on da ship." William laughs at Porgy's lack of New York knowledge.

"I ain't dumb, yuh know." Then, realizing he is being a little harsh, laughs and says, "Sho', I 'membuh. Sorry fuh bein' defensive. I seen dese type ob parade wheah I lib en Charleston. But dis be grand! De smells. De sounds. Mistah Garvey speech 'bout Black freedom. De boot'ful bannahs." They keep on watching the passing cars and floats. To get a better view, Porgy tries to stand up using his crutches but gets bumped left and right by the throng. William tries not to laugh. The people on the float shout out, "Welcome to Harlem. If you can make it here . . ." Boom! The band hits the drums and confetti suddenly flies out over the crowd. Porgy watches in amazement.

After about thirty minutes of listening to the speaker, Jonathan turns to William and Porgy and points down the street. "Hey guys. Let's get out of here. We gots ta go that way. We still gots ta fin' a place fo' Porgy ta stay."

"Wheah us goin'?" Porgy shouts over the music.

"A frien' of mine said der might be some roomin' houses available wheah yo can live down in Morningside Heights. Dey is probably not much, but dey may be somewheah yo can stay fo' da time bein'. Let's go check it out." They follow Jonathan toward Amsterdam Avenue and begin their search for a place for Porgy to live.

Along Amsterdam Avenue, Porgy sees the devastating results of the Depression, and remembers what the men were telling him about Harlem while they were on the cruise ship. Putting his hand in his pocket, he realizes how little money he has left, and worries about how he is going to survive in Harlem until he finds Bess.

"I habn' 'sperience dese bad times berry much en Charleston cuz I nebbuh hab lot ob money tuh b'gin wid. Der I lib en a community wheah people care 'bout an' help one annodah. Now, I b'ginnin' tuh ondahstan' wuh de Depression really luk like en New Yawk. Somehow de beggahs heah seem mo' po' and mo' desp'rate."

Jonathan says, "Yo right, Porgy. And us Negroes are hit da hardest. I read in da newspaper we gots fifty percent outta work, way more than da white folk.

Moving down the street, the reality of the Depression becomes even more apparent to Porgy and his friends. The stench of rotting garbage and the droppings of peddlers' horses is overwhelming. The three men instinctively put their hands over their noses and mouths to block out at least some of the fetid odors.

Seeing the poorest side of New York's Harlem where the beggars are camped out on the streets, Porgy is saddened. *Eben when I be a beggah en Charleston, I hab a place tuh lib an' a woman who change muh life.*

Suddenly, he spots a woman down the street who appears from the back to look very much like Bess. Her body shape is like Bess's and her hair is flowing down her back. On her head is a pretty hat, similar to the kind Bess always wears. She is wearing nice clothes and the rhythmic way she walks signals she might be a certain kind of woman. Watching her, Porgy's anger builds as he thinks about what Sportin'Life may have Bess doing again to make him money. Her youthful appearance and smooth brown skin makes him think she might be Bess.

His heart skips a beat. In his excitement, he prays it will turn out to be Bess. He stops Sam and the cart in its tracks to stare at her. In his heart, he wants it to be her more than anything. Then he frantically urges Sam on so he can catch up to her.

"Porgy!? Porgy!? Where is yo goin'?" They run after him.

Porgy desperately tries to get Sam to move faster, and as he approaches the woman, yells "Bess, Bess, be dat yuh?" Catching up to her, he lunges for her skirt, causing her to spin around in fright.

"Hey what is yo doin'?! What da hell is yo doin'?!" she screams.

It's not Bess. Porgy is crestfallen and embarrassed. With all his heart he wanted it to be her, hoping beyond hope it would be. He was so anxious to take her back home to resume their happy life in Catfish Row.

The woman is screaming and pushing Porgy away, afraid he is trying to attack her or rob her. "Why is yo tryin' ta harm me?" she yells.

Porgy is near tears, and struggles to find the words. "No! I not tryin' tuh hurt yuh. I t'awt . . . I . . ." He is confused himself about what he has just done. His heart is breaking.

William and Jonathan jump between the woman and Porgy. Jonathan turns to the woman. "He din't mean no harm. We're sorry." He tries to push Porgy away, so they can leave.

As they are walking away, the woman picks up a can from the street and throws it at Porgy and his friends. "Get da hell away from me!" she hollers after them.

A small crowd begins to gather and William, Jonathan and Porgy move away from the commotion as quickly as possible. Puzzled, William asks, "Hey man, what was dat all about?"

"I t'awt . . . dat bin muh woman. I t'awt dat no-good who kidnap she hab put she out tuh walk de streets, an' I git intah a rage. I hab tuh fin' she." He sighs and tries to erase from his memory the embarrassing incident he was just responsible for.

Jonathan pats Porgy on the back. "We'll do ev'rythin' we can ta try ta help yo fin' her, Porgy," he reassures him. Actually doubtful himself, he wants to make Porgy feel better.

William exclaims, "Well, let us fin' a house fo' yo first, please." Porgy is silent, now worried he might never find Bess.

CHAPTER FIFTEEN

Night has fallen on New York, but the activity on the streets is as busy as during the daytime. The moon shines brightly through Harlem's beautiful trees, illuminating the people going about their business. Outside Sportin' Life and Bess's apartment building, taxicabs and limousines are pulling up as guests arrive for their party.

Inside the apartment, people holding cocktails are gathered in small groups around the living room. Everyone is dressed in the classiest attire from head to toe. Negroes and whites mingle together, as if no history had ever existed between them. They reach for the caviar on toast, crackers with smoked salmon, and other hors d'oeuvres being served by the waiters in white jackets circulating around the room. Other waiters are serving champagne and cocktails.

With Prohibition having ended, lavish parties like this one have now become popular again among the cultural elite and the wealthy. Champagne and hard liquor flow freely with food, bright lights, and fashionable clothing. These are the things that have attracted people to Sportin' Life's "Gatsbyesque" party tonight, and some have come even though they see him as just a social-climber. It is Sportin' Life's goal to make this party the flashiest of the season.

Many of those invited are numbers customers of Sportin' Life, here to make bets and hoping to win big. These high rollers help him keep his business going strong and pay for the luxurious life he leads.

Tonight's social gathering has taken on a new dimension. Sportin' Life sent invitations to some special white men and women, prominent in the New York arts community. He hopes they will be able to further the careers of the Negro artists and writers also in attendance. In his mind, he believes they will not have a chance for advancement without the support of the white establishment.

Sportin' Life had met many of the white guests and the Negro writers and artists when he catered A'Leila Walker's "Dark Tower" 'salons,' the first time he lived in Harlem. At Walker's grandiose apartment, these elegant functions became the ultimate gathering place for the cream of Harlem's intellectuals. He wants desperately to fit into that circle and be seen as much more than just "Mr. Big," the drug dealer and numbers banker.

The white guests are excited to be at the party because they want to meet and support the Negro artists and writers of Harlem. They are interested in becoming financially involved in Negro culture and what they, condescendingly, call "racial uplift." The rise of what journalists are calling "The Harlem Renaissance" drives their interest in the kind of art and literature that can't be found within their white society.

A Negro jazz band is playing in the center of the room. They have encouraged everyone to dance to the music blaring throughout the rooms of the apartment. The beat of the drums and the sound of the horns shake the windows.

Leading the band and playing a saxophone is Benny Carter, a charming young musician with a handsome face distinguished by a nicely trimmed mustache. As he plays the saxophone, his body sways to the music. He is dressed in a dark suit with a white shirt and tie, his face glistening with perspiration. The music sounds as though it comes right up from his very soul. Carter smiles as he looks out into the crowd, pleased everyone is enjoying the music.

Benny Carter is a popular saxophonist and composer hoping to impress some key white people at the party. He is one of the originators of the music style called "Swing." Sportin' Life invited him so he can finalize a performance arrangement with Sidney Cohen, the owner of the Apollo Theater.

The invited guests also include a group of wealthy Negro residents of Sugar Hill. The men are dressed fashionably in their hand-tailored suits and the women in their dresses from Bergdorf's, with their hair done up in the latest fashion. They are neighbors of Sportin' Life and are at the party to associate with the white "liberal" guests, and be seen as what W.E.B. DuBois has called "The Talented Tenth," the elite of Negro society.

Standing in one corner of the room, near the apartment's balcony, is the painter Romare Bearden. He is young and full of energy, dressed in a black suit, a mauve shirt, and a black bow tie. He brought some of his paintings to the party, artwork depicting the Negro community in scenes of everyday life in the South. His beautiful paintings are in both oils and watercolors, and they light up the area where he is displaying them.

Sportin Life' had purchased a few of Romare Bearden's paintings and invited him to the party, so he can meet Gertrude Whitney, the owner of The Whitney Studio Club. Emerging artists show their work there and Sportin' Life bought artwork from the gallery as well. Gertrude accepted the invitation, so she could learn more about Bearden and another artist, the sculptor Richmond Barthé. She is contemplating the possibility of exhibiting their artwork at her gallery in Greenwich Village.

Whitney is the daughter of Cornelius Vanderbilt, one of the wealthiest men in America. She stands out among the elite guests in the apartment, exquisitely dressed in her long black Schiaparelli silk dress accessorized with a black fur collar. Her lustrous pearls hang gracefully around her neck and glisten in the moonlight shining through the balcony's huge glass doors. Whitney looks much younger than her actual mid fifties age.

Whitney approaches the lovely paintings and Romare introduces himself, "How do you do. My name is Romare Bearden, and these are my paintings."

"Hello, it's nice to make your acquaintance. I'm Gertrude Whitney." She gives Romare her business card. "Yes, Mr. Big said you would be here tonight. Tell me about your work."

"My art depict the American South so people will understand the hardship and hard work my family, peers, and all of us Negroes endure. I was born in Charlotte, North Carolina so my roots are there."

Pointing to one of the paintings, he says, "This depicts a Negro jazz band on a stage. They are wearing traditional striped suits. I want people to sense that the band is ready to bring the house down with the smooth sounds of the drums, trombone, bass fiddle and the horn. This is one of my favorites. I think the colors and shapes capture the atmosphere in a beautiful light. I hope you can feel the music through this painting."

Gertrude Whitney points to the band playing at the party. "Louder than this band?"

Romare chuckles as he nods his head. "Yes, even louder than this band," making her smile.

He puts his painting called "Jazz Village" against the wall with the others. "So Mrs. Whitney, what do you think?" He raises his arm and makes a sweeping motion across the air above all of his work.

A server walks by with champagne. "Champagne sir? Madam?" The server lifts the tray toward Gertrude and Romare.

They each take a glass of the amber bubbly. Gertrude sips slowly, noting that Sportin' Life is serving Dom Perignon. "Aren't we glad prohibition is over?" They both laugh. Taking another sip of champagne, she appraises the paintings and smiles. "I do love them. My first reaction is that these are the kind of things I would like to show in my gallery. Just what I was looking for!"

They clink glasses and Gertrude reminisces. "When I visited Europe some years ago, I discovered the art of Picasso and Matisse in the Montmartre section of Paris. I was so impressed so when I came home I opened my own gallery in New York. Now I want to show works by Negro artists and help financially if necessary. Please do come and visit me." Romare can hardly believe his good fortune and excitedly shakes her hand as she turns toward the other guests at the party.

Sidney Cohen is seated near the apartment balcony's glass doors. He is a well-known movie theater owner who recently bought the Apollo Theater, a live entertainment venue. Sportin' Life runs his numbers operation out of a small backstage office there. It would normally be risky for him to allow an illegal numbers game to be run out of his theater. However, Sportin' Life helped finance the purchase of the Apollo and said he would bring in big-spending customers so Cohen felt he had no choice. Cohen's partner, Morris Sussman, did not trust Sportin' Life and warned Cohen about dealing with him, but went along with the arrangement anyway.

Sidney Cohen decided to make the Apollo a club where Negroes and whites can watch shows together. Cohen believes great entertainment will get white customers to put aside their concerns about mingling with Negroes. Hearing and seeing Carter's band at the party has convinced him to open the Apollo with the show "Jazz a la Carte." The show will be headlined by Benny Carter and his Orchestra, with Ralph Cooper as Master of Ceremonies and Aida Ward as the featured singer.

Sportin' Life is drinking champagne and talking to Sidney Cohen when Joshua joins them. Sportin' Life turns away from

Sidney Cohen, and quietly asks, "Did you bring the betting slips?" He takes a sip of his drink and puts a hand on Joshua's shoulder. Joshua takes out an envelope with the slips and a wad of money. Smiling, he hopes he has made up for his tiff with Mr. Big earlier in the day. Sportin' Life takes both bundles and nods his head approvingly. He turns to Sidney who is also smiling. "See, Sidney! We are booming even more than last month. The new office is going to need to expand."

Cohen looks at Sportin' Life and says cautiously, "Yes. You are doing very well. Morris was doubtful, but our share of this money changed his mind. I want to bring changes to the Apollo, and this extra cash will help me do that. I think it would be good public relations if I donate some of that money to the Harlem Childrens Fresh Air Fund."

"Yes. That would be a nice way to encourage people to come to the Apollo."

Sidney turns back to watch the band. From across the room he waves to Carter. "You were right about Carter. I want to hold auditions to find new talent, too. We will have an 'Amateur Night,' where we can find new acts. Let's become the best entertainment spot in New York." He clinks glasses with Sportin' Life.

Sportin' Life smiles, and turns to Joshua. "Did you take care of our other chore for this evening?" He gives him a slick smile and Joshua nods his head. He instructs him to walk around the room, discreetly take bets, and give "powdered party favors" to any of guests who want them.

The party continues, with everyone enjoying themselves listening to the music and chatting. Sportin' Life excuses himself from Sidney and walks off to the bedroom.

CHAPTER SIXTEEN

Inside the bedroom, Sportin' Life sees Bess sitting on the bed. She is wearing a beautiful long red silk dress, and pearl earrings hang from her ears. Her hair is flowing down over her shoulders the way he likes it. On her feet are very high heeled red satin pumps, the exact matching color of the dress. Her red lipstick covers her full lips and the pale dusting of pink blusher brings out the color of her light brown eyes. "Bess, you look wonderful, like a glamorous movie star!"

Even though she is, in fact, stunning, she still projects an aura of sadness about her. Bess hates being dressed up like a doll for Sportin' Life's guests.

He walks further into the room and, ignoring Bess, proceeds to remove a painting from the wall, revealing another safe. He opens it and places the money and number slips inside, closing it firmly when he's done. Bess watches while he does this. She never knew there was another secret safe in the bedroom, and looks up at Sportin' Life. "So, us hab one in heah too?"

Sportin' Life spins the combination dial to lock it, and after replacing the painting, turns and grins. "I have them everywhere. Can't be too careful, and I don't want to put anything in the one in the other room while the party is going on. Speaking of the party, tonight's going to be your debut. I want you come out and mingle with the people I invited here." He sits on the bed next to Bess, putting his arm gently around her. She resists flinching in distaste at his touch.

Bess shrugs. "I dunno. I nevah bin ta a fansee paa'ty like dis. I eben dunno if mah lipstick look right. I dunno wuh ta say. I dunno how ta ak'. I eben dunno wuh e'rybody der will say ta me. I dunno . . ." She is trying to learn how to speak like a New Yorker by listening to the maids. Still a little unsure about how she speaks, she is worried her Gullah dialect is too pronounced, and some of her words won't be understood by the guests.

Sportin' Life, annoyed, interrupts her. "I want you to join the party now! You're going to be okay. You're a beautiful woman, and everyone will love you. And, you are good for business."

Bess puts her hand on Sportin' Life's arm, frowning. "Wuh do 'good fo' business' mean?" She doesn't like being put on display.

He gets up abruptly, irritated at Bess questioning him. "Haven't I looked out for you? Haven't I taken care of you, no matter what? Everything I do is for you. Everything! I picked out this apartment just for you, for us. I rescued you from that dump of a place when those ship workers kidnapped you. I do all I can for you and you question how I take care of you?"

Sportin' Life's injured tone is designed to manipulate Bess, and it works. She doesn't realize he is trying to make her feel guilty. "Yo right. I is sorry. I be out in a minute."

"Good, see you when you come out. You look beautiful, don't worry." He strides out of the bedroom.

I hope I don' do enny't'ing dat will embarrass Sportin' Life an' mek he angry. She walks to the table in her room, finds her canister of cocaine, and quickly sniffs a line. When she hears clapping from the living room, she walks nervously to the door, opens it just a crack and peeks out toward the brightly lit and crowded room at the end of the hall.

The sheer number of people in the room gives her pause about leaving the sanctuary of the bedroom. Dozens of beautifully dressed men and women are milling around the room, talking and laughing and drinking champagne. Terrific jazz music is making the room vibrate. Then, the cocaine kicks in, and a false sense of security buoys her courage.

CHAPTER SEVENTEEN

After the band takes a break, Sportin' Life finds a place in front of his party guests and begins a speech he prepared for the evening. "Thank you everyone for being here. Tonight I am doing my small part to promote the artists and writers of the Harlem community." His ego can't resist, and he says, "A hundred years from now people will remember this as the greatest cultural event of our time." The guests begin to applaud. As they settle down, Sportin' Life continues. "I hope you all are meeting new people and helping your careers and businesses. The band is great. Let's hope we don't wake the neighbors." The crowd laughs.

Sportin' Life beckons to a handsome young Negro who has a sparkle in his eyes and a smile on his face. "I want to introduce a good friend of mine, a writer and a major voice of our time. Ladies and gentleman, please meet Langston Hughes." There is respectful applause for him. Bess listens from the bedroom doorway as Hughes walks to the center of the living room.

Hughes is thirty years-old. He is regarded by many as an extraordinary poet, and he is also an activist for the rights of the Negroes. Known for writing "revolutionary" poetry, he is now a prominent figure in the Harlem Renaissance scene. His poems, fiction, and plays depict the lives of the working-class Negroes in America. Hughes portrays life full of love and struggle.

Sportin' Life puts his arm around Hughes' shoulder, trying to imply a close friendship. "His first novel, *Not Without Laughter*, was published by one of tonight's guests, Blanche Knopf. It is based on his own life, about a young Negro growing up in the Midwest. The book won the Harmon Gold Medal of Literature award. Langston writes in this new 'jazz-poetry' style, which I just love! His beliefs are strong and he sticks to them!"

Langston Hughes smiles as he looks out at the party goers. His well-tailored suit fits his body like a glove. Hughes is confident and self-assured, with a radiant smile. He is clean-shaven with smooth skin the color of brown sugar. He is one of the new Negro poets and novelists who are being sought out by publishers. Everyone is very attentive, even Bess from behind the bedroom door, as Langston Hughes begins to speak,

Peering out at the guests, he says, "I have a short poem I want to recite. I think it relates to everyone here as lovers of art, and dreamers too. We are all here to broaden the awareness of our art and become the voices of our generation."

The guests all nod their heads in anticipation. Bess continues to peek out, and opens the door a little more, not wanting to be seen.

"This poem is called 'Dreams.'" He stands very tall, and begins to recite.

> *Hold fast to Dreams*
> *For if Dreams die*
> *Life is a broken winged bird that cannot fly*
> *Hold fast to Dreams*
> *For when Dreams go*
> *Life is a barren field frozen . . . with snow.*

Everyone begins to applaud. They are awed by his convictions and command of the poetry medium. Hughes thanks them and begins reciting another poem as Bess closes the door.

The "Dreams" poem resonates with her. She slides to the floor against the door and cries, thinking about all the dreams she's ever had. Her love, Porgy, floats into her mind. She closes her eyes and whispers, "Hol' on tuh yo' dreams Bess. Hol' on tuh yo' dreams."

She goes to the vanity mirror and fixes her face as the guests listen to more of Langston Hughes' work. After Hughes finishes, the band starts up again. The ambient sounds in the room slowly escalate as people return to their conversations. Sportin' Life's party is a success with everyone circulating, talking, drinking and discussing art, literature and business.

Bess finally gets up her cocaine-induced courage and walks out of the bedroom into the living room. With the damage done to her makeup from crying now fixed, she searches around the room to spot Sportin' Life. As she continues her entrance into the room, her striking presence is immediately noticed by many of the party guests. Her figure is stunning and her face glows with renewed vitality from the effect on her from Langston Hughes' poem, "Hold Fast to Your Dreams."

Sportin' Life is across the room talking to Bearden, Hughes, and some other guests, and she makes her way through the crowd over to him. She taps him on the shoulder, and he turns around and smiles. "Baby! I'm glad you are here so I can introduce you to some of my friends." Sportin' Life kisses Bess on the cheek as she demurely nods her head. The people surrounding Sportin' Life look at Bess and smile. He is beaming as he introduces her. "Bess, this is Romare Bearden. The painter of Black beauties."

Romare can't take his eyes off Bess as he shakes her hand. "A pleasure to meet you."

"Hello. Nice ta meet yo, too." *I wondah why he be starin' at me like dat.*

Sportin' Life is happy Bess is getting a lot of attention. With his huge ego and his control over her, he feels it is a further reflection of his importance. He continues introducing her around to his other guests. "This is Benny Carter, the man behind the saxophone. This is Mr. Langston Hughes, the writer and poet of our people, Richmond Barthé, who is a sculptor, Gertrude Whitney, who owns an art gallery. And Sidney Cohen, the owner of the Apollo Theater."

Sportin' Life puts his arm around Bess as she greets everyone. She looks at all the Negro and white attendees and is excited to meet them. She has never been in this close a space with white people before and suddenly realizes she is on equal terms with them. It's a very heady experience for her, and one that boosts her confidence even more than the cocaine does. She is beginning to enjoy herself.

Sportin' Life sees Zora Neale Hurston across the room and ushers Bess over to meet her, "This is Zora Neale Hurston, one of the greatest authors of our time." After graduating with a degree in anthropology from Barnard, she became an influential author of books about the experiences of Negroes. They portray the Negro racial struggles in the American South during the early years of the current century. Another book she wrote was about Haitian voodoo.

Zora Neale stares at Bess with admiration. "My, my, my Mr. Big, where have you been keeping this beauty? She is absolutely stunning, and makes you look a whole lot better than we know you really are." People around them all giggle at her witticism.

Hurston decided to show up, hoping to find a publisher for her latest work, *Barracoon: The Story of the Last 'Black Cargo'*. It is a book about Kossula, the last Negro survivor of slavery. It describes his kidnapping in Africa, his years as a slave in Alabama, and his life after Abraham Lincoln's Emancipation Proclamation.

Hurston is a close friend of Langston Hughes. They have both been supported by Charlotte Osgood Mason, the white literary patron who funded Hurston's travels for research in the South. Mason's money for her support of Negro artists came from her own family's wealth and from the fortune she inherited from her deceased husband. She is sitting quietly on a couch across the room, observing the artists she mentored.

Charlotte Mason is around seventy-five years old, the oldest guest there. She is the only one present who had actually lived through the Civil War and the Reconstruction period. Familiar first-hand with the plight of the Negro community, she feels strongly about helping young talent to succeed. Mason is a petite woman, wearing a lilac dress with a lace collar that, along with her white hair, gives her a serene appearance. However, she is known to be far from serene in her championing of the writers she has helped.

Zora Neale Hurston is in high spirits. Earlier in the evening Charlotte had told her, "If you are interested in a new project, travel back down South and do a study of Negro folklore and culture. I'll buy you a car and a camera, and foot the bill for your expenses." She didn't have to think twice before accepting the offer.

Since her arrival in New York Bess has been trying to learn the way people in Harlem speak, a dialect quite different from her native Gullah. She has listened intently to the maids' conversations, in an effort to pick up words and phrases to help her understand the differences in the dialects. She also noticed the Negro artists and writers speak like the white guests and not in any dialect at all. So, with some hesitation she asks Zora Neale, "Uh . . . . What hab yo write Miz Hurston?"

Hurston smiles as she discusses her novels. "I'm working on a new novel called, *Their Eyes Were Watching God.* It's about a young woman in the South, who suffers through a bad marriage, but in the end her husband is killed and somehow she comes through it all."

Hearing about Hurston's book gets Bess to reflect on her marriage to Crown and his being killed. *I wondah if I will come t'rough it all.* "I would like ta read da book when it be finished."

"I also just wrote a comedy called *De Turkey and De Law.* The way you talk reminds me a little of one of my characters whose name is Lindsay. I'll read some of it for you." Zora Neale pulls out a small folder of typewritten pages, and begins to read.

> *You see dat gal shakin' herself at her mammy?*
> *De sassy li'l bitch needs her guts stomped out.*
> *Run! I'm comin' on down there an' tell yo ma how 'omanish*
> *you is, shakin' yo'self at grown folks.*
> *You must smell yo'self!*
> *Now de rest of you Haitians scatter way from in fron' dis*
> *store.*
> *Dis ain't no place for chillen, nohow.*
> *Gwan! Thin out!*
> *Every time a grown person open they mouf y'all right dere to*
> *gaze down they throat.*
> *Git!*

The group near Zora Neale starts clapping and laughing as she finishes reading the small excerpt from her play. Bess enjoyed hearing the Gullah dialect. "I lub it. Do it hab music an' songs in it like "Shuffle 'Long"? Bess was familiar with this popular Broadway musical show since the maids were always singing songs from it while they worked.

Zora Neale shakes her head, "Just a play, first. Hopefully, I'm going to find a backer and put this on the stage . . . Bess, do you sing? Will you sing for us tonight?"

Fearful of what his reaction might be, she looks at Sportin' Life and then back to Zora Neale. "Ummm . . . yes, I kin sing. I hab, back in Charleston where I came f'om. I mean . . ." She is a little nervous and trembles slightly at the prospect of singing in front of strangers.

Zora Neale senses Bess' fear, and changes the subject. "It's okay, beautiful. You're among friends. How did Mr. Big talk you into coming all the way up from Charleston, anyway?"

Bess hesitates. "I . . . was . . . in wit' a bad crowd back der an' he . . ."

Langston Hughes suspects what keeps her shackled to him, and before she can finish, he interrupts her story. "Bess, If you want to sing, then we want to hear you sing! Mr. Big here is creating opportunities for all of us, especially to show off our art tonight. So maybe this will start you off on a new career. I'm excited. "

Bess looks back at Sportin' Life, who nods his head in agreement. Bess takes in a deep breath. She is uncomfortable being the center of attention. But she knows this is her chance to prove to herself, and to everyone in the room, she is more than just Sportin' Life's "good for business" woman. Bess begins to sing "Down Hearted Blues" by Bessie Smith, a song she heard the maids singing while they were cleaning the apartment.

> *Gee, but it's hard to love someone*
> *When that someone don't love you*
> *I'm so disgusted, heartbroken, too*
> *I've got those down-hearted blues*
> *Once I was crazy 'bout a man*
> *He mistreated me all the time*
> *The next man I get has got*
> *To promise to be mine, all mine*
> *Trouble, trouble, I've had it all my days*
> *I ain't never loved but three men in my life*
> *My Father, my brother and the man that wrecked my life*
> *It may be a week, it may be a month or two*
> *But the day you quit me honey, it's coming home to you*
> *I got the world in a jug, the stopper's in my hand*
> *I'm going to hold it until you didn't come under my command*

Bess's voice is a little shaky because she is nervous, but all in all, her performance is well-received. The people at the party smile and applaud, surprised at the sweetness of her voice. She grins and is impressed with herself. Her face is flushed, and she has goose bumps all over from singing in front of all of these people. A tear runs down her cheek as the words remind her of Porgy and touch her deep down in her very soul.

After hearing her performance, Benny Carter comes over to Bess, "Wow! We may need you to join our band and sing at the Apollo Theater."

"Oh, I would like dat a lot!"

Carter turns to Sidney, who takes a sip of his drink. "Maybe. I was just telling Mr. Big we are going to have both Negroes and whites as customers in the theater, and we will be having an Amateur Night. We will see what the future holds."

Bess is disappointed in Sidney Cohen's lukewarm response to Carter's suggestion, but she is determined to enjoy the company of the artists and musicians she is meeting.

CHAPTER EIGHTEEN

She turns and finds herself next to Richmond Barthé. He is a sculptor and has brought some photos and a few of his sculptures for Gertrude Whitney to see. He hopes he can convince her to show his sculptures at her gallery. Barthé attended the Art Institute of Chicago and most of his sculptures are of African themes. He uses predominantly male nudes to express his artistic ideas.

Bess stares at his work in admiration. "Dis is booty'ful."

Barthé smiles at her. "Thank you so much. You're Bess, right?"

She points to one of the sculptures. "Yes. Dey are mek of metal, right? How do yo mek dese sculpcha?"

"Right, they are bronze. First I make a clay model and a mold. I do this at my studio in Greenwich Village, way downtown from here. After that, a foundry employs a technique called lost-wax and fills the mold with hot liquid bronze. I just had a show at the Caz-Delbo Gallery in Rockefeller Center. Have you ever been?" Bess shakes her head, embarrassed. She doesn't even know what a gallery is, or Rockefeller Center.

Barthé picks up a sculpture depicting a handsome Negro emerging from a black stone. With a little bit of his ego showing, he says, "The Caz-Delbo Gallery is a prestigious showcase where I showed this one. The figure's head is modeled deeply to give the impression of alternating light and shadow. This intensifies his emotion and personality. I wanted to capture a brief moment in time of a young man in mid-thought expressing the aspirations of our entire race."

"It be very detail', like a real person." She reaches over to touch it but stops herself.

Barthé laughs. "It's okay, you can put your hands on it."

Bess runs her hands over the sculpture. "'An' smooth, too."

"I call this *The Negro Looks Ahead.* It's one of my favorite pieces."

"Why did yo call it dat?" Bess is curious.

"Because there is no point in looking back. You can't get anywhere if you're always worried about the past. You have to know things will better if you, you know, look ahead. As Negroes, we have to look to the future to make a better life. Dream ahead and move forward. That's what the man in this sculpture is doing, getting ready for the future."

Bess is comfortable talking with Barthé, and dreamily gazes around the room. *It mek me wondah wuh de future might hol' fuh me.*

She walks over to where a group of people are gathered around one of the guests, Carl Van Vechten. He is a writer, and is talking about how he is trying to promote Negro artists to the public. "I think everyone should have the opportunity to share their art and get it out there. I'm from Iowa, a Midwesterner like Fitzgerald, Sinclair Lewis and Sherwood Anderson. We didn't grow up knowing any Negroes back there. When I first moved here I got a job as arts critic for the *New York Times* and became fascinated with their culture."

Unlike many whites in the arts community, Van Vechten and his wife, Fania Marinoff, don't merely admire the works of the Negro artists; they are famous for flouting society norms by inviting them into their home.

As Bess approaches, he introduces himself, telling her he is an author. She asks him what he has written, and he mentions his latest book, "The name of the book is *Nigger Heaven.* It's a novel about two young people who are in love. The young girl is a librarian, and he is a writer, and the story is about the conflicts they face living in Harlem." He sees Bess grimace at the title of the book and smiles. "Yes, I know the title will be controversial. 'Nigger Heaven' is actually a slang term referring to the balcony in theaters, the only place where you Negroes are allowed to sit."

"Oh, I see," Bess responds, trying not to seem lacking in sophistication for not knowing about these types of books.

At the other end of the room is Blanche Knopf, the president of Alfred Knopf Publishing. Van Vecten brought her to the party as his guest. She has fallen under his influence and is always looking for books by Negro authors to publish. Knopf is in her mid-thirties and relishes the glamorous side of the book business, the lavish parties and public relations meetings where she meets writers and literary agents. She drips with expensive jewels and a Dior jacket is draped over her shoulders. Her Chanel purse fits comfortably in her hand, and she exudes wealth. Her red-painted fingernails are so long they resemble the talons of a bird of prey, an apt description of her demeanor, some would say.

Bess is intrigued by her, and after being introduced and hearing about all the famous writers Knopf publishes, says. "I wish I could t'ink ob somethin' I could write fo' yo ta publish."

Blanche touches her red nails to Bess's shoulder. "Honey, it really doesn't matter whether you are a good writer or not these days. Just put any old words on the page, and I can make you a star. Look what I did for Pound and T.S. Eliot." She laughs at her own witticism, which Bess doesn't quite understand. Sportin' Life walks over and puts his arm around Bess, and Knopf winks at him. "Where have you been hiding this gorgeous creature, Mr. Big?"

"Everyone keeps asking me that. I haven't hidden her. Just waiting to bring her around. Didn't want anyone to scare her off." Sportin' Life smiles.

Gesturing with her hands at the people in the room. "This is really wonderful, Mr. Big. I've had salons where George Gershwin and Noel Coward have attended, and this is up there with them. I think I'd like to publish that *Nigger Heaven* book, and steal Zora Neale Hurston away from Lippincott. I am also looking forward to publishing more of Langston Hughes, too. This may work out very well for my company."

Sportin' Life is happy his lavish event is turning out to be a success. It is important for him to be seen as more than just the "numbers guy," and it worked. Bess looks first at him, and then around the room, respecting Sportin' Life's ability for putting on this party, and perhaps inadvertently, opening her mind to a whole new world.

CHAPTER NINETEEN

At the end of the evening, Bess and Sportin' Life are standing together as they shake hands and share embraces with their departing guests. Romare walks over to Sportin' Life. "What a successful party! I made new friends and a terrific new contact in Gertrude Whitney. She wants some new work from Richmond and me. I think I have the perfect piece I want to present to her. Zora Neale is going to have her book published by Blanche Knopf, and she will publish another one by Langston." He turns his attention Bess. "Bess, it was so lovely meeting you. I would very much like to paint a portrait of you, if you would be willing to pose for me."

Bess is shocked Romare is asking to do a painting of her. She thinks about her stash of cocaine and wants to pull it out right now to calm her nerves, but resists doing that for the first time in a long time. No one has ever flattered her like that before, so she doesn't know how to answer. She takes Sportin' Life's hand and squeezes it, unsure of what to say.

She turns to Sportin' Life and asks. "I . . . I . . . would dat be okay?" He smiles. "Yes, of course. That's fine. When people see it, it will bring in more customers."

Romare isn't sure what Sportin' Life means, but he has a pretty good idea, and smiles awkwardly. "Yes, it will be beautiful. I promise. So, what do you say Bess? Could I come back and do a painting of you?"

Her eyes are wide with anticipation. "Yes. Yes, I would lub dat berry . . . very . . . much."

Romare is excited. "Wonderful. I'll talk to Mr. Big about a date and I will see you soon." He shakes Bess's hand and then Sportin' Life's. He is the last one to leave.

The maids and servers have cleaned up after the party and have left for the night. Bess is in the bedroom, getting ready for bed. Sportin' Life comes in and flashes her an appreciative smile. He walks up behind Bess and holds her tightly. "You did great. I told you it would be easy. You are a star, and you make me look better. You are even beginning to talk like a New Yorker." He gives her a quick kiss on the cheek. "Don't I always take care of you?"

"Yes . . . war . . . was . . . all dose people at da paa'ty customahs ob yo numbahs game?"

Sportin' Life answers, "Yes. Many of them are customers, and the rest are the cultural elite of New York. I've been lucky, and smart too. I'm doing what I have to do to make it to the top." Pointing a finger at his chest, he says, "That's why they call me 'Mr. Big.'"

Bess knows how to flatter Sportin' Life and says, "Yo be Mistah Big. Do yo t'ink I will do good . . . wid . . . wit' . . . da painting?"

Sportin Life responds, "As long as you don't make me look bad. Just be your pretty self for right now. Here, calm your nerves." He places a small line of cocaine on the table and leaves. Bess is tired of Sportin' Life always acting like she can't do anything right, doubting her ability. She tries her best, but it seems she can never earn his respect.

Looking behind her to make sure Sportin' Life is gone, she wipes the powder off the table into a cup with her hand and washes it down the bathroom sink. With a clear head, she peers at herself in the mirror and says in a low voice, "Hol' fast tuh yuh dreams. Dis be how I staa't muh new life wid'out de happy dus'."

Thinking again about Porgy, tears trace their way down her face. She dries them off and goes back into the bedroom to try to fall asleep.

Sleep does not come easily to Bess as she struggles to withdraw from the cocaine. She has vivid and unpleasant dreams about the cruel and indifferent treatment she receives from the johns Sportin' Life brings to her. Chills and muscle aches wake her on and off all night. When she gave the drug up after meeting Porgy, she never suffered through any of these symptoms; his love and constant attention gave her the strength to overcome the withdrawal.

CHAPTER TWENTY

Porgy is breathing hard, and it takes a while for him to calm down after his disastrous and soul-wrenching accosting of the woman he thought was Bess. He wanted so much for it to be her. His head and his heart are hurting with his longing for Bess. He never stops thinking about her being in the grip of that vicious drug dealer and pimp, and fears for her survival.

Jonathan reminds Porgy. "I undahstan' yo is frustrated about tryin' ta fin' yo woman, but yo need ta concentrate first on gettin' a place ta live. You're gonna fin' it hard ta get a regular apartment heah, 'specially since yo gots . . . yo know . . . a goat. White people aroun' heah don' like Negroes as tenants already, let alone a Negro wit' a goat."

Porgy pulls out the little money he has left including what he has won playing craps. "I goin' tuh hab tuh fin' somet'ing tuh do tuh git me money." He pats his goat on its back as they move along the street. "When us fin' a place, do yuh t'ink I kin borruh some money somewheah tuh pay de rent 'til I git a job?"

William shakes his head. "Banks not loanin' ta anyone." They keep walking alongside Porgy in his cart, watching men and women showing the distress of the Depression. Porgy sees people waiting in line at the soup kitchen, and sitting on the pavement holding out a cup for a donation of even a few pennies.

"I t'awt dis' goin' tuh be a li'l bettah den Charleston, wheah I hab tuh beg."

"I don' know about Charleston, Porgy, but we is still Negro men, no mattah wheah we go. Da white bankah man is still finna keep us down. We can change our scenery, but we can't change da color of our skin, so they ain't givin' us no money."

Jonathan looks at the goat and takes a moment to think. He remembers something one of the dockworkers told him about a place Porgy and his goat might be able to stay. "What about da Goat House?"

"Wuh de Goat House?" Porgy asks.

"It's a li'l shack-house in Morningside Heights at West 120th street an' Amsterdam Avenue, where people can rent a room an' keep goats."

"Oh yeah! Da Goat House!" William exclaims.

"I t'awt yuh jis' say dat de buckruh ain't goin' tuh leh me stay ennyweh cuz ob de goat."

"Da white people ain't," Jonathan says. "But I was tol' da Goat House is run by Negroes, an' they will. Der is a lot of goats in Harlem, Porgy. I din't make da connection about havin' a place ta live an' gots da goat der too, until jus' now. Da people in Harlem love them. Der is an annual goat beauty pageant sponsored by da Beer Brewahs Board of Trade to fin' da best lookin' billy goats. People gots der goats in Central Park runnin' aroun'. I don' know what it is about goats, but they is a special part of Harlem."

Continuing down Amsterdam, they see men looking hungrily at Porgy's goat. You bettah keep yours close," William tells Porgy, half-joking.

Porgy clutches the harness tighter as they roll along. "Well, leh's go tuh de Goat House, an' hope dey hab a place fuh me." Jonathan takes the lead as they get closer to 120th Street and the Goat House.

The three men finally reach the ramshackle house Jonathan was talking about. It's a run-down two-story home, with a small front yard with more dirt than grass. There are two sets of stairs leading up to the porch of the home. There are tall wooden fences, once painted blue but now faded, on both sides of the property which hide the back yard from public view.

The men stop in front of the house and stare at it long and hard. "This be da Goat House," Jonathan says.

Porgy laughs. "I hope dey 'goat' someplace fuh me an' Sam tuh lib at." Jonathan and William roll their eyes and snicker at Porgy's joke.

"It's one of da only places like it in Harlem." The Goat House got its name from some students at nearby Columbia University who used to keep their school's mascot, 'Mathilda the Goat,' there. They thought, jokingly, she was a more fitting representative of the school than the "lion" symbol from King George's coat of arms.

"Does it seem like a Charleston-style southern home ta yo, Porgy?" Jonathan asks.

"It be somet'ing like us hab back der. It sho' be bigger den enny home I ebbuh lib en. Do us jis' walk on en?"

The sound of creaking floorboards catches their attention, and they see an elderly Negro woman get up from her chair on the porch of the house next door. She walks over to the men looking at the house from the sidewalk, barely lifts her feet off the ground as she moves. The woman has a cigar in her mouth and is wearing a bright floral print dress that drapes over her body from her neck to her ankles. Her eyes focus on William. "Yo' Jonathan?"

William points toward Jonathan, who says, "No, ma'am, dat's me. I'm Jonathan." He reaches out to shake her hand, but the woman just stares at him.

"One of da dockworkahs told me yo wanted ta rent a room heah. They came by earliah t'day." She blows smoke at the men. "Why would yo' want a room in dis house, boy? Ain't y'all leavin' in a few days ta go back on yo' ship?" She puts the cigar back in her mouth and puffs out another great cloud.

Jonathan puts his hand on Porgy's shoulder. "Well, ma'am, it isn't fo' me. It's fo' dis lovah boy right heah!" The guys laugh.

The woman eyes them suspiciously. "Lovah boy, huh? Does 'lovah boy' mean yo' finna bring in some women? You boys ain't plannin' ta run no funny business out of dis house, is yo? Cuz I don' do no funny business!" The woman aggressively sends out another gust of smoke at them.

They all yell "No! no! Dat was jus' a joke. Our frien' heah is a good man, an' gets aroun' in his cart an' on crutches."

Porgy rolls his cart over to the woman and, in an effort to gain her sympathy, tells his story. "'Scuse me, ma'am. Muh name be Porgy. I lukkin' fuh muh . . . muh wife. Her git tek up heah f'om Charleston ag'ins she will. I need somewheah tuh stay fuh de time bein' 'til I kin figga somet'ing out 'bout how tuh fin' she. I won't be a problem, as yuh kin tell by lukkin at muh condition. Dis heah is muh goat Sam . . ." Porgy rubs the goat on the head. "We won't cause yuh no haa'm. I don' hab a lot ob money, but I kin gib yuh all I hab an' I will come back wid mo'." He waits for the woman to answer.

The woman takes another puff. "Dis heah house was owned by mah brotha, Edgar . . . Edgar Riley. Long gone now." She blows out some more smoke as she appraises the men. "I take care of da shack an' rent it out ta da dockworkahs every now an' then. Da bad economic times be hittin' us hard, but I still gots ta eat." Sizing up Porgy and Sam, she says, "Rent is five dollars a week plus a dollar fo' da goat ta stay in da backyard. An' not a penny less. Yo bein' a cripple, yo can gots a room on da first floor in da back wheah yo can keep an eye on yo goat." Now finished smoking, she throws the stub of the cigar on the ground, and holds out her hand, palm up. Porgy looks at her hand, thinking, at long last, she wants to shake. He moves forward and extends his hand, but she pulls her hand back.

"No, boy. Da money. Twelve dollars fo' da first two weeks. Ta move in." She lowers her head down toward Porgy and scowls, challenging him to come up with the money. He takes out the rest of the cash he has and hands her ten one dollar bills and eight quarters. He frowns as he is now really almost out of money.

The woman pockets the money and her sour disposition turns to smiles. "There is a bed in da room an' a table an' chairs, an' a couch. Some pans fo' cookin'. Yo gots ta use da well in da backyard fo' yo watah an' heat it up on da stove fo' yo' baths. No hot watah runs through da house. I don' fix anythin' dat might go trippin' in der. Yo take care of it yo'self. Lights work except durin' a storm. I come by aftuh church on Sundays fo' da rent." The woman begins to walk off, but then turns back around. "By da way, mah name is Miss Glenda." She looks at Porgy's goat, who is chewing on the little patch of grass growing in the yard. "Don' let that goat tear up da house."

"No, ma'am. Him def'nitely will not." With a sense of relief, Porgy watches Miss Glenda walk back to her own house next door.

Looking at the Goat House, Jonathan says, "Well, that went pretty much how in mah head I hoped it would go. I think yo got lucky, jus' like da way yo play craps."

Porgy is a little uneasy about the rent. "I almos' out ob money an' I need ta fin' muh woman as soon as possible. How I goin' tuh do dat?"

William responds saying, "I got into trouble once up heah an' mah lawyah used a detective who might be able ta help yo. Let's go see him t'morrow an' try ta fin' some work fo' yo in da meantime." Down the street, they can see men just lingering around, downtrodden and obviously out of work. "Da Depression I think hit us Negro folk da worst of all." Shaking his head, he steps up onto the porch.

110

Jonathan turns to Porgy. "Welcome home." Jonathan follows behind William into the house.

Porgy takes a long look at the house and then down the street. *I goin' tuh fin' yuh, Bess. I be heah now.* He gets out of the cart and onto his crutches, leads Sam up the steps and walks into the house to settle in.

Later that evening, Jonathan and William are sitting in the Goat House at an old table with ancient wooden chairs. The room is sparsely furnished, plain and dark, but clean. Porgy has prepared dinner and brings soup and bread to the table. Jonathan takes a taste and is impressed by the amount of flavor. "How in the worl' did yo happen ta git dis cooked up?" William is hungrily enjoying the soup as well.

"I bin a beggah an' I kin git enny't'ing. I got some day-ol' bread f'om down de street at de bak'ry dat bin gettin' ready tuh put'um out fuh de crows. Den I trade some apple I hab fuh de potato. I mek de soup up wid dat well watuh an' season it wid some herbs I fin' growin' in de backyaa'd." Porgy blows on his bowl and takes a spoonful. "Yeah, dis be purty good."

They all continue to eat, using the bread to soak up the soup in their bowls. William questions Porgy. "So, honestly, do yo really think yo' gonna fin' yo' woman?"

"I know I am. I hab tuh. I hab tuh git she home tuh Jonah."

"Who is Jonah?"

Porgy grins from ear to ear. "We son."

"Wow, yo din't tell us yo gots a son" He takes a bite of his bread. "Dat makes da fight ta fin' her so much more important."

Porgy stares down at his bowl, the agony of his search almost too much to bear. He puts his hands on his head and begins to sob. "I dunno wuh I will do ef I don' fin' she. I hab tuh."

William throws an arm around Porgy. "It's gonna be okay. We're gonna go see dis detective I know t'morrow. We are gonna figure it out." Jonathan joins William with an arm around Porgy. "What is yo' wife name?"

He realizes he never told his friends his wife's name. "Bess. She name be Bess."

"Well, Bess, we're comin' fo' yo'!" William gives a comforting smile to Porgy.

Porgy wipes the tears from his face and watches them dunk the bread in the remains of the soup. He isn't embarrassed that he was crying, and his spirits brighten at the prospect of his friends helping him tomorrow to hire a detective. He is happy he met them and feels comfortable with them, knowing without their help he could not have gotten this far in New York. After eating, Jonathan and William wave goodbye to Porgy and return to the ship where they are spending their nights before it leaves on its journey back to Charleston.

CHAPTER TWENTY-ONE

The next day, the three men venture back out onto the Harlem streets. Porgy decided it was wiser to appear more business-like when he meets the detective and hobbles along on his crutches, instead of taking Sam and the cart. The terrible poverty of the city everywhere causes a stabbing pain in his heart. His throat chokes up, making it difficult for him to talk. "I nebbuh see so many homeless people an' beggahs en muh life. Eb'rywheah I luk I see people who be hungry an' en need."

They come to a small office building, but there is no sign on it listing the tenants. It is dark and a bit run-down, and a depressing and discouraged feeling radiates from it. In its heyday, before the Depression, it might have housed lawyers, loan companies, and small business owners.

Porgy turns to William and asks, "Are yuh sho' dis be de buildin'?" He is worried about the safety of going into this building. It doesn't look promising. William compares the address on the piece of paper with the address on the building.

"Yep! Dis is da address, an' da office is on da first floor. Mah lawyah said he was da best one in Harlem. So, go on in der an' talk ta him. We'll wait heah." William gives Porgy a "thumbs up."

Jonathan helps him climb the short staircase up to the front door where he makes his way inside. In the middle of the hallway, Porgy finds an office with printing on the glass door that reads,

"Elijah P. Morrison, Private Investigator." Porgy pushes the door open and enters.

In the waiting room, a pretty, brown-skinned girl is sitting at a desk filling out some paperwork. Behind her is a closed door. There are two chairs and a couple of faded generic prints are on the walls. Porgy approaches the young lady. "Hi. Is . . . Detective Morrison heah?"

The girl looks up and appraises Porgy's appearance and meager attire. "Have a seat." The girl continues to fill out the papers she is working on.

Not knowing what he is supposed to do next, he takes a seat. After the girl puts her file into a cabinet, Porgy sees her press a button on the desk. It surprises him when he hears a buzzing sound in another room. He is becoming restless and impatient, and starts to get up from his chair. "'Scuse me . . . ma'am . . ."

His question to the secretary is interrupted by a short, portly Negro man who comes in from the back room of the office. The detective has a thick mustache, a balding head and brown eyes that match the color of his suit.

"Yes, can I help you, sir?"

Porgy straightens up. "Good aftuh'noon. Muh name be Porgy. One ob muh frien's bring me heah. I would like tuh hiya yuh tuh fin' muh wife. I bin tol' yuh be de bes' detective en New Yawk." His eyes never waver from the detective's face.

Morrison looks Porgy up and down. He observes, but does not comment on, Porgy's physical condition, knowing it would be rude. He indicates the back room doorway and invites Porgy to come into his office.

Porgy makes his way toward the office on his crutches. The detective scowls at his secretary, who is staring with a frown at the crutches and the way Porgy walks, and closes the door behind them.

Inside the room, there is a large mahogany desk with neat stacks of files and papers on it. The room smells of tobacco. A pipe with a wisp of smoke coming from its bowl is resting on an ornately hand-carved stand on the desk. Also, on the desk is a plaque reading, "Elijah P. Morrison, Detective." Morrison sits behind his desk. "Have a seat." He points to the chair in front of the desk.

The chair is a little high, but as always Porgy tries not to show any weakness. Morrison raises his eyebrows as Porgy struggles to get onto the chair. "Do you . . . need some help?"

Porgy doesn't look at him until he is seated. "I got it." After settling himself on the chair, he lays the crutches next to his feet on the floor.

Detective Morrison picks up the pipe and adds more tobacco. "So, Mr. . . . ."

Porgy interrupts, and answers him. "Porgy. Muh name be Porgy."

Morrison asks, "Is that your last name?"

"No, dat's muh only name . . . it de only one I ebbuh hab."

Morrison re-lights the pipe, and blows out a puff of smoke. "Porgy. Right. So, you're here to find your wife?"

"Yaas. Muh wife. Bess. Her bin kidnap f'om Savannah an' bring tuh New Yawk. I bin en Charleston an' din't fin' out 'til I bin release f'om jail . . ."

Morrison is surprised. "Jail? For what?" He puts his pipe down.

"Cuz I wouldn' 'dentify a dead man, so dey t'row me in jail fuh contemp' ob court."

Morrison squints and he is now suspicious." Why aren't you still there?"

Porgy is now fidgeting with his fingers. "Cuz a white lawya frien' paid muh bail an' git me out."

The detective starts laughing. "Charleston is a long way from New York City, but they could still come here to arrest you for skipping out on your contempt charge and forfeiting your bail."

Now irritated, Porgy raises his voice, "I din't come heah tuh talk 'bout muh troubles! I came tuh fin' muh wife. Kin yuh help me do dat?" He is getting upset and wondering if Morrison can genuinely help him to find Bess.

The room draws silent after Porgy's outburst. Morrison clasps his hands together and looks at Porgy. "I can try to help you find your wife. Do you have a picture?" Porgy shakes his head. Then, with a tired sigh, he asks, "Do you have any money?"

Porgy pulls out a small wad of money. "I hab ten dollas lef'. Dat's all."

Detective Morrison tries, unsuccessfully, not to laugh. He is familiar with sad stories like Porgy's before. "I have a business to run, not a charity, even if it's for one of my Negro brothers looking for help. For me to even start, it would be sixty dollars, and that's the bare minimum."

Shocked by the amount of money it will cost to find Bess, Porgy gasps as though someone has just punched him in the gut. Tears well up in his eyes. "Wheah I s'ppose tuh git dat kin' ob money? I don' hab a job yet. Dis be all I hab lef'! I jis' need yuh help! Please, brudder. . ."

Morrison stops him. "Please, Porgy, I understand your problem. I understand your need to find your wife, but I have to eat too. It takes a lot of resources to find someone. So, once you find the money, I will be able to help you. I don't know how you're going to do that, but if you really want to find her . . . you will find the money." Stunned, Porgy gets onto his crutches and, in a dark mood, contemplates how he's ever going to manage that.

Morrison opens the office door and escorts Porgy out. Porgy leaves the building with shoulders slumped and his head down in total defeat, disappointment written all over his face. He spots

Jonathan and William across the street talking to some men and drinking soda pop. Cautiously crossing the busy street, he makes his way over to them. As Porgy approaches, William begins to smile but quickly erases it when he sees Porgy's anguished face. "How did it go?" But, he already knows the answer.

Porgy shakes his head sadly, "Him serbises staa't at sixty bucks."

William and Jonathan are startled at hearing the price. "Sixty bucks?" Jonathan yells. "How is yo finna git dat?"

"I don' know!" Porgy exclaims, dejected. He recognizes that he sounds angry, and knows he must calm down. These men are his only friends in the city, and the last thing he wants to do is offend them. Putting his hand on Jonathan's arm, he says, "I be sorry, man. I jis' tryin' tuh figga t'ings out. Well, I t'ink us bettah git back tuh Sam. I nebbuh lef' he dis long befo'. I be sho' him not happy tie up on de pawch."

William laughs. "He'll be fine. Who wants a goat? Unless they want ta eat him." His laughter stops when he looks around at the hungry and homeless people the Great Depression has created. "Let's go." The three men make their way back toward the Goat House.

CHAPTER TWENTY-TWO

A rriving back at the Goat House, they are in a panic as they realize Sam is not tied up on the porch where they left him. They check inside the house and out in the back yard, but he is nowhere to be found.

Jonathan turns to William, "See, yo jinxed it! They've eaten Sam!" Porgy comes back out onto the porch. Just the cart is on the front lawn, but Sam isn't there. Jonathan and William run next door to Miss Glenda's house.

They hammer on the door until she yells, "I'm comin'. . . I'm comin'. . . hold yo' horses."

When she opens the door, all three men shout, "Porgy's goat is missing! Do yo know anythin' about de goat? Gots yo seen him?"

Miss Glenda, annoyed by their shouting, answers, "I don' know nothin' about dat. I gots been busy in mah house all day."

They are distraught, but suddenly their anxiety is broken by the sound of Sam bleating nearby. Searching around for the source of the sound, Jonathan spots Sam surrounded by some Negro men down the street. He points toward them and shouts, "Der he is!" He starts running towards Sam and the group of men. Porgy and William follow after him.

As they approach the men, they see they are playing craps, and throwing dice. Porgy grabs the rope holding Sam and begins to walk off with him. "Dis is muh goat! Yuh stol'um an' I tek'um back!"

Davidson, one of the men shooting craps, stands up and glowers at Porgy. "Hold on now! Dat der be mah goat now. I won him fair an' square."

"Wuh yuh mean yuh win 'um? Dis is muh goat! Yuh stol'um!" Porgy yells, furious.

"Now, wait a minute, one of da playahs dis mornin' said he foun' him, an' when he lost his money he bet da goat, an' I won him. What is yo finna do about it?" The man gets very close to Porgy's face. "I bet mah cash against da goat an' I won. He's mine now. I had nothin' ta do wit' wheah he came from."

Porgy keeps Sam close by and then sizes up Davidson, who is at least a foot taller than he is and whose muscles bulge through his thin cotton shirt. Realizing there is no sense in trying to convince Davidson to give Sam back or to fight him for him, he says, "I'll buy'um back f'om yuh."

There are three other men on the sidewalk shooting craps. William and Jonathan have worried looks on their faces, anticipating what is about to happen next. Everyone can feel the tension, especially Davidson's friends, who know how volatile he can be.

Davidson guesses where Porgy is from based on his Gullah dialect and lets a malicious smile appear on his face. "Oh, yo poor, crippled, Southern country boy. Comin' ta da big city an' think yo can get whatevah yo want. Dis is how we do things heah. You can gots him back fo' ten dollahs." Davidson and the other craps players begin to laugh. Porgy knows if he pays ten dollars it will almost completely wipe out his supply of cash.

Porgy smirks. "Well, wheah I f'om, us don' steal proputty. But 'nuff talk. I want'um back an' ef dat's wuh it tek, let we roll de dice, an' when I hab win ten dollahs I will pay yuh." Sitting himself down, Porgy gets ready to gamble.

119

Davidson hunches down across from Porgy, and one of his men says, "Heah's da dice Davidson, I warmed them up fo' yo."

Turning to Porgy, he says, "Alright. I'll put two dollars on da pass line. Match dat mistah. Or don' yo even gots dat much?" And with that Davidson throws two one-dollar bills into the 'Pass Line' circle drawn with chalk on the sidewalk.

Davidson's men start snickering but hold back on placing bets. Porgy is used to people thinking he doesn't know how to shoot craps. He pulls two dollars from his pocket and places it in the 'No Pass Line' circle. He figures if Davidson 'craps out' by shooting a seven or an eleven, he'll win two dollars on the first roll.

Scrawled on the sidewalk are the street craps rules and odds which Porgy now studies. He calculates he would only lose if Davidson' first roll comes up a two or a three, with a roll of twelve resulting in no winner or loser. He is confident he is as canny a craps player as Davidson. The men on Davidson's side start hooting and hollering as the game begins.

Davidson blows on the dice to "warm them up" even more, and tosses them against the building wall. They bounce off the bricks and land in the middle of the sidewalk. Staring up at them are a three and a two, adding up to five. He is upset as he now must throw again and roll another five before he rolls a seven. He throws again. A four and a three turn up, for a losing toss. Davidson and his friends have now become very quiet.

Porgy drops his original two dollars and the two dollars he just won on the 'Pass Line' circle. Davidson must now match the bet according to the rules, and he puts four dollars on the 'No Pass Line" circle. He is convinced he will win, and Porgy will be forced out.

It is Porgy's turn now to roll the dice. He shoots them against the wall, and they bounce back, landing with a one and a two for total of three, and Porgy wins. Doing a quick calculation, he knows only needs to win another two dollars to buy Sam back. Jonathan and William are elated while Davidson, across from Porgy, is fuming.

It is Davidson's turn to roll the dice again, and again, he decides to try to clean Porgy out, setting eight dollars down in the 'Pass Line' circle. The rules require him to bet the same amount as Davidson, so Porgy lays down his total of eight dollars in the 'No Pass Line' circle, wondering if his luck can continue.

Davidson sends the dice against the wall and lets out a roar as they roll to a stop showing a combination adding up to eleven, a losing bet. "Yo cheated! Yo gots to have cheated! I nevah lose dat many times in a row!" He is stomping around and yelling. Porgy now has sixteen dollars and hands ten over to him. "Well, yuh los' t'day." Porgy picks up Sam's rope again. Davidson approaches Porgy menacingly, as if he is going to punch him. Porgy, now back up on his crutches, stands his ground, and Jonathan and William step between them.

One of the guys with Davidson stands up and grabs him. "D-man let it go. We don' need anyone ta get hurt, an' what were we finna do wit' a goat anyway? Go take a walk or somethin'."

Davidson snatches his arm away and storms off. One of Davidson's friends extends his hand to Porgy. "Mah name is Timothy."

Porgy extends his hand to shake Timothy's. "Nice tuh meet yuh man. I be Porgy. An' dese be muh frien's Jonathan an' William." Relieved and now smiling, they all shake Timothy's hand.

Timothy points to the other men who are still sitting on the sidewalk. "This is Matt an' Colby." They smile and wave to Porgy and his friends.

Matt gets up and faces Porgy. "Man, I nevah seen anyone beat Davidson three rolls in a row. Dat was amazin'. Wheah did yo learn ta shoot craps like dat?"

Porgy, a little tired from the stress, lowers himself back down on the sidewalk and leans against the wall. "I use tuh shoot craps a lot back wheah I f'om, Catfish Row. En Charleston. I guess dat's de one t'ing I lucky at." Porgy laughs at himself.

Colby is sitting next to him and asks, "Were yo unlucky wit' yo legs? What's up wit' dat?"

He gives a sideways glance at Jonathan and William, indicating they should not say anything about his legs. Turning back to Colby, he hesitates for a moment. "I bin bawn dis way."

Timothy makes eye contact with Porgy. "Well, howevah yo got dat way, dat was great craps. Wit' yo luck I bet yo could make some real money bettin' in da numbahs game too. Gots yo evah played da numbahs?"

Over Porgy's shoulder, Matt can see someone walking up the street and waves to him. "Speakin' of numbahs, here he comes."

Timothy and Colby turn around and also wave as Joshua, Sportin' Life's numbers manager, greets them. Joshua has come into the neighborhood to collect the day's betting slips and cash from his runners. He stops and smiles. "Fellas. Fellas. Evenin'." Timothy and his friends don't smile back. Joshua turns his attention to Timothy. "What numbahs is yo playin' today, Tim?"

"Sorry, Joshua, not t'day. I ain't won anythin' in a month wit' Mistah Big. I'm out, an' so is most of da people aroun' heah."

Joshua is not happy with that answer. "What do yo mean yo' out? Yo gots to play yo' numbahs. Don' yo want ta make da big money?"

"I don' gots ta do anythin'," exclaims Timothy. "We learned through da grapevine Mistah Big has been rippin' us off anyways."

Joshua laughs at that statement. "Who tol' yo dat? Why would we gyp yo?"

Timothy scoffs. "Cuz we know it's not an honest system. Yo win. We don'. Yo take our money an' we slip deepah into da Depression hopin' we hit da jackpot. He's been cheatin' his brothas an' only cares about bein' hugged by da whitey police an' those fancy writahs an' artists. Someone tol' us he helped dat Sidney Cohen guy buy da Apollo an' now him an' Mistah Big is best of frien's, an' he don' give a damn about us."

Matt adds, "We heard about dat li'l party at his new house in Sugar Hill. I think he bought dat by cheatin' us. We don' want ta bet wit' yo anymore."

Joshua is irate but he tries to stay calm. He inherently knows they are telling the truth, but can see he is outnumbered, and can't win the argument. "If yo continue to bad-mouth Mistah Big yo will heah from him about dat soonah or latah!"

Timothy glares at Joshua and says with a sneer, "I can't wait." Joshua is unnerved and walks away.

Excited, Porgy taps Timothy on the shoulder, now really interested in their conversation with Joshua. "Wuh bin dat all 'bout? Numbahs? Wuh dat?"

"Yo *is* new heah." Jonathan laughs.

Timothy looks over at Porgy. "Here is how it goes. Ev'ryday, people, like yo an' me, bet on da numbahs."

A little exasperated, Porgy asks, "Wuh be de numbahs?" He is increasingly concerned about all the things he doesn't yet understand about living in the city, not the least of which is the question of how he will ever find Bess. As always, this is his most pressing problem.

"People can pick any three numbahs from 000 to 999. It can be 283, 840, 620 . . . whatevah three numbahs they choose. They write dat numbah wit' their name on a slip a papuh an' give it wit' der money to Mistah Big's runnah. Da runnah is da guy who collects all da bets. Mistah Big is da bankah who holds ontah all da money an' bettin' slips from his runnahs If yo numbah comes up, yo win 600 times da amount yo bet."

"An' da runnahs take all da risks," Jonathan says.

"An' how do yuh know ef yuh numbah come up?" Porgy is intrigued and even more curious now.

Timothy explains, "Dat's wheah da luck comes in. Ev'ryday Mistah Big spins a wheel in his office. It's like a roulette wheel dat gots numbahs on it. He spins it three times. Each spin lands on a numbah an' dat be wheah da day's numbah comes from."

Porgy knows all about the ways crooked gamblers can cheat. "So, do ennyone watch dis man spin de w'eel? Can him jis' . . . mek up de numba, or rig de w'eel so berry few people win?"

Matt joins the conversation, "Dat's what we all think, an' why we don' bet wit' him no more . . . he gots an office in da Apollo Theater wheah he does da spin, so people think dey can trust him."

"How do eb'ryone fin' out wuh numbah be da winnah eb'ry day?"

Timothy continues his explanation. "At da end of each day, Mistah Big tells da runnahs what da numbah was. Den, da runnahs tell it ta da winnin' customahs an' give them der payout."

Porgy is a quick learner and now understands the numbers game. "Seems like da runnahs be spendin' a lot ob time doin' all dis. How much do dey git fuh all ob dis?"

"They git about . . . a quartah of what is bet dat day. But, like Jonathan said, they is takin' all da risks. Since it is against da law, if they get caught wit' money an' bettin' slips, they can be arrested. Or, if da customah is mad, they can get into a fight. Da runnah is nevah happy an' always want to get a biggah cut. Da runnahs say Mr. Big get too much fo' just sittin' behind a safe desk an' bein' da bankah while they is out in da streets."

Porgy's gambler's mind is getting into high gear now. "An' how do de runnahs get people tuh play da numbahs?"

Timothy opens his arms wide and points around the neighborhood. "The numbahs man can be foun' in almost ev'ry factory, office building, on da street . . . tryin' ta collect dimes, quarters, an' dollars. Da runnah takes play from housewives in their kitchen, or anywheah. He mingles wit' ship crews on da waterfront. Yo can catch him hangin' out in a Harlem bar, da furnace room of an apartment buildin', or da back room of a grocery or candy store. He is ev'rywheah"

Jonathan nods toward Timothy in agreement and says, "Da runnahs get people ta buy into da dream. Numbahs is a way of life aroun' heah Porgy. We all hopin' to get rich fast. Bettin' wit' Mistah Big use ta give people hope."

William nods his head. "But now people gots been losin' der hope wit' Mistah Big."

"Many customahs do think dat he sometimes fixes da wheel so der is fewah winnahs an' payouts. It's kind a like a drug an' people keep comin," Timothy adds.

Colby had been quiet up to this point but now feels he needs to add to the complaints about Mr. Big. "An' if da numbah yo pick don' come up, yo get nothin'. When we first startin' placin' bets wit' him, a lot of us would win. Sometimes we would split da earnings among ourselves, an' it was bettah than nothin'. It was more than we were makin' anywheah else. But as da police started gettin' more payoffs, cuttin' into Mistah Big profits, fewah an' fewah of us hit winnin' numbahs. Too much of a coincidence? But we kept playin'. Nothin' fo' us, an' he kept gettin' richah. He's a cheatah an' a two-bit hus'lah."

Porgy ponders this for a minute. "Huccome no one hab staa't a numbahs game jis' fuh we? A fair an' honest one jis' fuh de po' Negroes an' get some runnahs like dis Mistah Big's game."

Timothy shakes his head. "No one wants ta go up against Mistah Big. An' no one is clevah 'nuff an' is willing ta take da risks ta pull it off, an' have nothin' ta lose if it fails."

Slowly raising himself up onto his crutches, and with a penetrating gaze, he points to himself. "Me! I be dat person. I hab nuttin' tuh lose."

The guys stare at him, wondering if he is serious. Timothy is the first to speak. "Yo actually could be da perfect person. Secrecy is needed in a numbahs game, an' it's good dat Mistah Big not knows who yo is. An' yo seem trustworthy. Dis might work, especially if we vouch fo' yo in da neighborhood."

Porgy realizes he has found a solution to his improbable situation. "Us all need money. I come heah tuh New Yawk tuh fin' muh wife, an' I hab tuh mek money tuh pay people tuh fin' she. I will tek on enny challenge an' risk tuh do dat. Leh's figga out how us kin set up us own numbahs game tuh compete wid Mistah Big."

Jonathan puts his arm around William's shoulder. "Well, it looks like we're stayin' in New York. Let's fo'get about workin' on dat ship evah again'." They all laugh, as Jonathan says, "Let da fun begin."

Porgy takes hold of the rope tied to Sam. "All ob yuh, come on back wid me tuh de Goat House an' us kin git tuh wuk."

CHAPTER TWENTY-THREE

Sitting on her living room couch, Bess is smoking a cigarette nervously, but at the same time thinking excitedly about what she is going to be doing today. She runs to the bathroom and looks in the mirror, tossing her hair around and fixing her lipstick. Hearing a knock at the front door, she takes one more look in the mirror, and opens the door herself, as she has given the maids the day off. Standing there with his bag of paints and brushes, his easel, and a blank canvas is Romare Bearden.

Romare enters the apartment and gives Bess a kiss on the cheek. "Good morning, Miss Bess."

She returns the kiss. "Mawnin'. How is yo?"

"I am well, and how are you, Beautiful?"

Bess is very nervous. "I be a li'l . . . ankshus. I jis' wan' tuh do well." Without realizing it, she slips back into her Gullah dialect.

Because Romare is from Charlotte, he is familiar with Gullah, having grown up listening to it. He smiles. "You're going to do fine. Where can I set up?"

Romare follows Bess into the living room where he starts setting up his easel, tubes of paint, and brushes while she sits on the couch. "Would yuh like some watah or ennyt'ing? Juice? Wine?"

"Sure, let's both have a glass of wine, please. It will help you to relax."

Bess goes to the kitchen to pour two glasses. Ever since refusing to use Sportin' Life's happy dust after the party, the anxiety and her racing heart have made her more tense than usual. She comes back and hands Romare a glass. "Heah yuh go Romare."

"Thank you! Let's make a toast! To having an amazing day of painting!"

Bess laughs and clinks her glass with Romare's. "Tuh hopin' I kin be a good model."

Romare puts his glass down and finishes setting up, as Bess sits again and drinks her wine. She is in a quiet mood, and he tries to get her to brighten up. "You can talk to me, I don't bite."

Bess giggles at Romare's comment and sets her glass down. "I sorry. I nebbuh done ennyt'ing like dis befo'. I hab nebbuh bin 'lone wid a man, 'cept wid Mistah Big, an' 'cept when I . . ." She stops herself and lowers her head.

Anticipating what she is about to say, he wants her to know he understands. "It's okay. Like I said, you can tell me whatever is on your mind. It will make it more real."

"T'ank yuh fuh dat."

"So, how did you meet Mr. Big? You said you were from the South . . . Charleston, right? What made you and him come here to New York?"

Romare gives Bess a comfortable feeling, and so she is willing to share her tale with him. She lifts her head and begins. "Well, wuh I say at de paa'ty 'bout me git in wid a bad crowd ain't bin de whole story. I bin wukin' as a maid . . . en da main house on a cotton plantation neah Charleston. . . I bin beat up ober an' ober . . . raped, 'most eb'ry day by de buckruh ownahs." Growing up in the South, Romare understands the unending campaign of terror against Negro women is as much a threat to them as lynching is to Negro men.

Bess starts to cry. "I bin jis' a young gal, not eben a full woman yet. Sportin' . . . I mean Mistah Big, hab come down f'om New

Yawk an' bin heng 'round Charleston sellin' happy dust. When him see me at de plantation him say him wan' tuh help me. Him rescue me. One day, him come intah muh room an' say him bought out muh peonage contrac'. Him git me ober tuh Charleston neahby an' dat's wheah him git me intah . . . cocaine an' . . . sleepin' wid mens fuh git him money. I guess I t'ink I hab tuh do it cuz him did sabe me, an' I owe 'um fuh dat." She pauses in her narrative to dry her eyes and lights another cigarette.

Seeing Romare's sympathetic gaze, she continues her story. "Den one day I meet Crown, a stevedore f'om de ha'bah. Him be berry good-lukkin' an' strong. Him says him lub me so much, an' us quick git marry. I din't hab tuh be a pros'tute ennymo'. But him bin a mean man, an' I wan' tuh leabe he.

"An' den Crown murdah someone when him got mad at a craps game, an' run'way tuh 'scape git 'rrested. I bin all 'lone ag'in, an' en a purty bad way. Mistah Big bin still heng 'round an' allus temp' me wid de happy dus'. I bin tryin' tuh keep a clean life, but, I be weak, an' Mistah Big git muhself back on de happy dus'. Den, a wondah'ful woman name Maria tek muh en. Her introduce muh tuh a man name Porgy who lib nex' door, an' us fall en lub.

"Libbin' wid Porgy bin some ub de bes' days ob muh life. He git muhself off de cocaine an' tek care ob muh w'ile I struggle comin' down. Us eben 'dopt a chile. Den, Crown sneak back en town lukkin' tuh git me tuh leabe Porgy an' go 'way wid'um. An' den one night Crown git kill, an' dey fin' his body ober at de ha'bah.

"De police come aroun' axin' me an' Porgy questions cuz I use tuh be marry tuh Crown. Dey need someone tuh 'dentify de body so dey tek Porgy down tuh wheah de corona kep' it. Porgy b'lieb en voodoo, so him' bin 'fraid ob bein' neah de angry spirits ob de murdah man's ancestahs, an' 'him wouldn 'dentify de body. So, de police 'rrested Porgy fuh contemp' ob caw't an' lock'um up en jail. I bin completely broke' up, an' Mistah Big fin' out 'bout Porgy bin gone, an' git muhself back on de happy dus'. Him tell me I prob'ly would nebbuh see Porgy ag'in."

Bess's tears are still flowing, and she suddenly realizes she has been telling her story in Gullah, and wonders if Romare understood any of it. Taking a deep breath, she continues. "One night I git berry . . . very . . . drunk an' gots kidnap' by dockworkers at da ha'bah an' dey take me down da rivah ta Savannah. An' then once again, Mistah Big save me. He ransom me from da kidnappahs an' now we are heah." Bess is sobbing as she finishes her story. Having now told this to someone who honestly cares, has given her an overwhelming sense of relief.

Romare moves next to her to comfort her, trying to understand the depth of her grief. He puts his arm around her shoulder. "You sure have had a terrible life, but I believe everything happens for a reason. You will be okay. Remember, you are strong and you can do whatever you put your mind to. You have to know that. Just believe you can make it, no matter what."

Bess wipes her tears away and hugs Romare. She hasn't felt this much kindness since Porgy was taken away to jail. "Thank yo so much. I needed ta heah dat."

"Of course. Hey, here is an idea!" He picks everything up and walks down the hallway toward the bedrooms. Bess follows him, and watches as he peers into each of them and then picks the one where the bed is draped by a white silk canopy. He sets his artist materials along side it. "I think this will be the perfect place for our painting."

When Bess told the maids she was going to pose for a painting, they giggled and told her stories about artists and their models. So, she is wondering if he is going to try to get her to sleep with him. Romare can sense her anxious energy. He senses her concern. "I can guess what you are thinking but I don't get into romantic affairs with my models. All I want to do is paint a picture of you. For the picture I have in mind I would like to paint you in the nude. Is that going to be alright?"

Bess is well accustomed taking off her clothes in front of men. She would like to trust Romare but her past experiences make her wary. Closing her eyes, she takes a moment to think. Romare seems sincere to her, unlike the johns who usually rip at her clothing. "Yes, dat is okay." Trying to reassure herself, she thinks, *Dis be diff'rent den wuh I do tuh mek money fo' Mistah Big.*

After she slips out of her dress and under-garments, he directs her into the pose he wants. "Please lie down on the bed." Slowly, Bess lies down, but doesn't know how to pose. "Lie on your back and put one knee up." Bess does as he says, while Romare prepares his paints on the palette. "Now put your arms up with your hands behind your head. Be seductive and tough, beautiful, and also vulnerable, like someone people can feel close to."

Observing Bess as she makes herself comfortable, Romare instinctively knows this will be one of his best paintings ever. He has never had a model that was so beautiful and natural, and he wants to capture her on the canvas quickly. "Breathtaking. Let's begin." Bess holds her pose as he begins to sketch with a charcoal stick.

As Bess watches him paint, she is intrigued and tries to understand how great painters take elements of the real world and copy them onto a canvas. Observing Romare work, she wonders how she can become a part of the world of writers and artists whom she has met in the last few days. Hours later, Romare is finally finished with the painting. "Okay, gorgeous we are all done! Come see!"

Bess lowers her knee and lets out a sigh of relief. She hops off of the bed, puts on a silk dressing gown, and walks around the bed to see the painting. Excited, she studies it intently and exclaims, "Yo have somehow capture mah mood, dreamy, relax' but troubl'd." She gives Romare a hug.

131

"You were a great model. This was easy. And there is one more thing to do. I would like you to come up with the title for it,"

Bess is surprised. "I get ta name'um?"

"Yes, you do. What would you like to call it?"

Bess stares at the painting. It is painted in a classic figurative style. She is in the foreground, stretched out on the patterned bedspread, her knee up, with her arms above her head. The image of her body is painted in dark shades of grey, with beautiful colors all around her. In her mind, it strikes Bess as the vision of tormented Negro women, like herself, who are trying to overcome the hard life they face. .

In the painting, she has a sleepy and melancholy expression on her face, and remembers Langston Hughes' poem. "Name it 'Fevah'd Dream '."

"Yes, I think 'Fevered Dream' captures what I was trying to paint. You really looked like you were having a bad dream, but it's over now, isn't it?"

Bess is so exhilarated by her life-affirming experience with Romare that she is more able to slip into the New York way of speaking. "Yes, Romare. Dis was such a wondah'ful day fo' me, an' from today on mah dreams is finna only be pleasant ones."

CHAPTER TWENTY-FOUR

With his friends sitting around the kitchen table in the Goat House, Porgy begins discussing how to start their numbers business. "Ef der be a mo' honest way tuh pick t'ree numbahs, 'stead ob spin a crooked roulette w'eel like Mistah Big do, customahs would know us wouldn' cheat dem. Den mo' people would place bet wid us. Do ennybody hab ideas?" They all look to Timothy, whose face shows he is thinking it over, and they watch as he gets up and walks out the front door. "Mebbe I scare 'um off," Porgy jokes.

A moment later, he comes back in with a newspaper. "There is otha' ways dat it's done. Der is parts of da city, like in Brooklyn, wheah they git da three numbahs from da winnin' payouts fo' bets on da horse races at Aqueduct race track." He opens the newspaper to the race results. "Everyday, da newspapah print da win, place, an' show payouts fo' all da races at Aqueduct, an' ev'ryone can fin' da results, so da numbah can't be fixed."

Timothy shows them the horse racing results page in the paper. "Let's say we picked our three numbahs from da fourth race yesterday. Heah, a horse named "Gee Wiz" won . . . Da newspapah says da payout fo' "Gee Wiz" was $74.25 fo' win, place was $13.56, and show, $7.61." Timothy points to the payouts. "We could use da last three numbahs of da payouts fo' da winnin' horse . . . dose numbahs is 5, 6, an' 1. Dat would be da winnin' numbah fo' da day.

Anyone who picked 561 the day befo' would be paid 600 times what they bet. Dis is a really honest way ta do it. Ev'ryone can check da numbah fo' themselves"

Porgy and his friends nod their heads in agreement. "Leh we git some runnahs den, an' git goin' on de bid'ness."

Only a few weeks have passed, and Porgy and his friends have gotten his numbers operation set up. Jonathan, William, and Timothy have spent hours each day spreading the word that a new game is starting up and runners were needed. It wasn't very difficult for Porgy's friends to recruit the runners, many of whom came from the ranks of the unemployed.

On a bright Harlem morning Porgy finds himself standing with his crutches on the porch of the Goat House. In front of him is a large group of men, and some women too, who have congregated on the lawn. Next to Porgy are Jonathan, William, and Timothy. Down on the lawn are Colby and Matthew, paper and pencil at the ready to sign up Porgy's new numbers runners.

Porgy looks out at the crowd, confident in his ability to take on his new mission. Since arriving in Harlem he has been trying to adjust his Gullah dialect and learn to speak like the Negroes who live in New York. "Good mornin', fellas an' ladies. I t'ink mah frien's gots tol' yo, it has come ta mah attention dat dis 'Mistah Big' t'inks he gots da numbahs game in da palm of his hands. However, his runnahs is takin' da mos' risk an' gettin' paid li'l.

"I gots a proposal fo' ev'ryone. I am startin' our own numbahs operation. A mo' truthful, honest system. One dat will not cheat da bettahs an' will get them ta trust us, an' they will bet mo'. I will be da bankah an' Timothy, Jonathan, an' William will collect da bettin' slips an' da cash ev'ryday. Yo will bring da slips an' cash ta them each night by 11 p.m.

"As Jonathan, William, an' Timothy explained ta yo, customahs can check da winnin' t'ree numbahs by lookin' in da newspapah fo' win, place an' show in da fourth race at Aqueduct.

No cheatin'. No stealin'. No dishonesty. An' I will pay yo thirty pa'cent commission 'stead of da twenty five dat Mistah Big pays his runnahs . . . an' I will make shuh da police don' hassle yo. Dis operation will work wit' no trouble at all. Let's build somethin' really big heah. Is y'all in?"

While Porgy watches the expressions across his prospects' faces, trying to gauge whether he has convinced them to join their operation, one of the men standing on the lawn, Earl, raises his hand. "I use ta be a runnah fo' Mistah Big. He is not finna take too kindly ta someone else steppin' into this game, especially if he starts losin' money. What is we finna do then?"

The men look at Porgy as he responds, "We will handle dat when we get ta dat point. I ain't worry about Mistah Big. Well, since yo quit bein' one of his ol' runnahs an' yo is heah, he was not handlin' da bid'ness fair. We will be tough an' protec' ourselves. Let's jus' get it goin'. Yes?" Colby and Matthew begin walking among the men and women, signing them up and giving them instructions about their neighborhood assignments.

Once the last of the new runners have been sent off, Timothy walks up to Porgy and asks, "Yo' think dis will work?"

"I know it will. It's gots ta. It is da only way I know ta make 'nuff money ta fin' Bess." Looking past Timothy, he watches the new runners disperse down the street, ready to make some much needed cash.

Porgy's new numbers operation has gotten off to a booming start, and bets and money are rolling in. Porgy and his friends are able to keep more than ten percent of the cash bet. Using the Aqueduct fourth race payouts as the way to pick the winning number is making bettors feel they can trust the system, and the runners are also happy with the higher commission.

At the Goat House, Porgy sits at the kitchen table, which is also now his office desk where he keeps track of the bets. Jonathan walks in and drops a stack of cash and betting slips onto the table. "Anothah five hundred bets t'day."

Thrilled, Porgy exclaims, "Anothah five hundred? It's not even two o'clock yet."

Jonathan laughs. "Everyone loves da new system. An' even though we gots some large payouts they were not 'nuff fo' us ta go broke. We is not quite swimmin' in cash, but things are workin' out."

"We're finna need ta get mo' organized if we keep it up like dis," Timothy says as he enters the house with his own bag of slips and cash. "Colby jus' brought these in." Timothy places them on the table, and he is troubled by what he sees in the kitchen. There are money and betting slips on the floor, the kitchen counter, the table, everywhere. "We're finna need somewhere else ta run dis. 'Specially if people catch on dat we work out of dis house, we could be robbed, or some cops we're not payin' off could come bargin' in. Plus, you've made 'nuff money now ta become a mo' visible numbahs bankah, an' a target fo' competition ta try to take us down."

Jonathan adds, "Porgy, I don' think anyone knew dat it would be dis big dis fast."

"I agree. I don' want us ta be robbed. Is der anywheah else we can run dis out of?"

Timothy thinks for a moment. "Mistah Big uses da Apollo fo' his office an' he doesn't care if anyone knows dat. But we need someplace secret wheah people can't fin' out it's our office, so we stay safe from Mistah Big. I know a place called Smalls Paradise Club in da basement of an office buildin' on Seventh Avenue. Da ownah is Ed . . . Ed Smalls. Not too many people know where it is, an' we can gots good security. Maybe he will give us a space ta operate. We're gonna need a regular office soon."

Porgy surveys the disorder in the kitchen. "Yes, we will. Can we go der t'day?"

"Let's go tonight aftuh da deadline fo' t'day's bettin' cut-off time at 11." They begin to organize the previous day's betting slips and wait for the newspaper and the results from the fourth race at Aqueduct.

CHAPTER TWENTY-FIVE

After the Goat House numbers business closes down at 11 p.m., they leave and walk down Seventh Avenue toward Smalls Paradise Club. They reach the office building and find the front door is locked.

"Is dis it?" Porgy asks, puzzled.

Remembering where the club's entrance is, Timothy leads them around the corner of the building to a concealed basement doorway and helps Porgy down the stairs. At the bottom, a bodyguard checks them out and then opens the door when he recognizes Timothy. As he lets them enter, the silence from the outside is immediately shattered by loud music from the club. The jazz is upbeat, with Fats Waller and his band performing tonight.

Smalls Paradise is unique, catering to both Negro and white customers. Unlike other Harlem clubs which close around three or four in the morning, Smalls stays open all night. A specialty of the club is a breakfast-time floor show beginning at 6 a.m. with waiters dancing the Charleston and skating around on roller-skates while serving food and drinks.

As he enters, Porgy scans the surroundings. *Wow, dis be sho' a lot fancier den de dinin' room on de ship.* Smalls has a large dining room with a stage at one end and a dimly lit taproom with a shiny, black, metal trimmed bar. They approach the bar where Timothy introduces them to the bartender, a pretty young lady who knows him.

She smiles and flirts with him. "Hey there, sexy man. I haven't seen you here in awhile. You didn't miss me?"

Taking her hand, and with a wide grin and a wink, he answers, "Otelia, why do yo think I'm heah?" They both giggle and hug each other across the bar. "Let's get some shots of bourbon fo' me an' mah boys. An' I need ta talk ta Sugar."

Otelia's smile disappears. "You want to talk to him, now?"

"Yep. Now. We have a business proposition fo' him."

"Yo gots it." Indifferent to the rest of Timothy's friends, she shrugs, pours them all shots and passes the glasses across to them. "Wait here. I'll be right back."

Timothy leans over to Porgy, and in a low voice, whispers. "Ed Smalls is da only Negro man ta own a club in Harlem. He used ta own anothah place, called da Sugar Cane Club, an' so ev'ryone jus' calls him Sugar."

The Sugar Cane Club was also a place where Negroes and whites could mingle. During Prohibition, it had been a speakeasy as well as a cabaret, but Ed Smalls had to close it. It could not turn a profit, even though it attracted many patrons who came to hear jazz performers like Bessie Smith, Ethel Waters, Duke Ellington and Louis Armstrong. The high cost of illegal liquor and mob protection payoffs took their toll.

"Otelia knows me because I used ta work fo' Smalls years ago when I set up craps games fo' his customahs. He loves anythin' dat makes money, so I think we gots a good shot at sellin' dis idea to him."

Porgy is nervous, but hopeful. Otelia comes back after a couple of minutes, and sidles up to Timothy. "He's waiting on you in the back. Only two of you, though."

Timothy puts an arm around her and gives her a kiss on the cheek. "Dat's all I need, baby. Thank yo."

Playfully, she rolls her eyes at him and goes back to her spot behind the bar. Timothy turns to Jonathan and William. "We'll be back." He helps Porgy off the stool, hands him his crutches, and they walk to the back of the club. Timothy carries their drinks, and they walk past the restrooms and on down a dark hallway. At the end they come to a door to an office where there is a burly bodyguard on either side.

One of the bodyguards knocks on the door. A deep, sonorous voice from inside yells, "You can let them come in." The guard slowly opens the door and Porgy follows Timothy in. The bodyguards close the door behind them. Inside the office, a short, stout, nattily-dressed man sits behind a desk looking over receipts and an accounting ledger, but doesn't look up at first.

Walking up to the desk, Timothy exclaims, "Sugar! How are yo doin', man?"

Timothy reaches out to shake his hand. Sugar lifts his head from what he was doing, and guardedly asks," I'm fine. How about you?" They clasp hands and Timothy leans over to give him a hug and a light pat on the back. "What are you doing coming here to bother me during my work hours, man? You know I don't like that! Are you here to talk to me about setting up craps games again?"

In an apologetic tone, Timothy says, "No, no. Somethin' diffuhrent. I'm sorry, man, but I really needed ta talk ta yo right away."

Smalls turns and focuses his attention on Porgy. "Who the hell is this?"

Patting Porgy on the back, Timothy says, "He's who I want ta tell yo about."

Sugar apprises both of them suspiciously, and now notices Porgy is on crutches. He leans back in his chair. "You have five minutes," and motions for Timothy and Porgy to sit.

Timothy begins the conversation. "So, a lot of us is short on money durin' dis damn Depression."

Laughing, Smalls says, "We're Black men. We're always going to be short of money during hard times . . . good times too."

"Dat's true too, Sugar. Because Davidson took ovah da sidewalk craps games, yo and me can't make money dat way anymo'. Now, what if we can make us all some extra cash by settin' up a numbahs bid'ness wit' an office heah?"

Sugar is quick to respond. "That would be crazy. No! There is no way we can run a numbers operation here! Mr. Big controls this part of Harlem and I don't want to get tangled up in all that mess, and have him get me shut down. I'm losing money during this Depression as we speak, and a numbers game would be too risky. I don't want no police and Mr. Big sniffing around in here!"

Timothy is about to speak but Porgy interrupts. "Sugar is it?"

Sugar stares at him. "It is."

Porgy takes a sip of his drink and begins to speak. "Mah name is Porgy, an' no one knows me. An' no one will figga out who I am or dat der is a bank runnin' a numbahs game heah. We will take Mistah Big down so yo won't gots ta worry 'bout him. We gots hired a lot of his runnahs an' we gots da mens ta puhtek . . . protec' . . . us too. I can brin' money in heah an' us . . . we . . . is already runnin' a successful operation."

"How can I trust you? I don't know who you are, either. If you're just another poor crippled World War veteran, I'd like to help. I'm picking up a bit of Gullah patois, so I can tell you are from South Carolina, like me. But going into business with you is another matter."

Timothy steps in. "This is already workin' really well. Like he says, no one has any idea who he is. Customahs an' runnahs have faith in our operation, 'specially since we bin vouchin' fo' him in da neighborhoods. Porgy is real sharp at gambling, an' dealin' wit' tough guys. I saw him stand up against powahful people. He beat dat bully Davidson at craps an' stared him down. We jus' can't keep runnin' our numbahs game out of da house wheah he lives."

141

Sugar is painfully familiar with how Davidson's took control of the sidewalk craps games. He is surprised by Timothy's account of Porgy's daring, and his demeanor changes. "You beat out Davidson at craps and were able to come out whole?"

"Yes, I did stand up ta Davidson. It is a long story, but I only played craps long 'nuff ta win muh goat back, which dey stole from me." Hoping he won't be caught in a little lie, he continues. "An', yes I am cripple' from da War. Got mah legs shot out from undah me in da battle of da Somme in Belgium, but it made me toughah. I gots people who have become runnahs fo' me. I gots da money fo' da numbahs bank an' I gots a new honest system fo' pullin' da daily numbah. People is tired of Mistah Big an' his cheatin' ways. Yo club is da perfec' secret place fo' our office, an' ya'll get five pa'cent of da money bet. I am sho' yuh kin use da extra money, so let's do dis."

Porgy and Timothy patiently wait as Sugar thinks about it. "Okay. Let's see how it works. A couple of weeks to start. There is a storage room upstairs. It should be big enough for you to turn into an office. You will report to me every day, and we'll see how this goes." He shakes hands with Porgy and Timothy who are excited about starting up a real office and getting to work. Looking at Porgy, he says, "Also, you need another name. Never use your real name in this type of business. What can we call you?"

Porgy thinks about it for a second, and then responds, "Mistah Goat Man"

He laughs. "I'll bet there's a story behind that name." He presses a buzzer and one of the bodyguards opens the door to let them back out into the corridor. From his desk, Sugar waves his hand toward them and calls out in Gullah, "Alright, Mistah Goat Man, an' git tuh it." Timothy and Porgy walk out of the office, chuckling, and head upstairs to find the storage room.

142

CHAPTER TWENTY-SIX

Romare is packing up his tubes of paint and brushes in the bedroom, when Bess hears a knock at the front door. She is puzzled because no one comes to the apartment without Sportin' Life being home. The only person who was expected to come over today was Romare. Bess adjusts her silk dressing gown and slowly walks to the door as Romare prepares to leave.

Cautiously she opens the door and is relieved to find familiar faces in the hallway. Crossing into the large foyer are Richmond Barthé, Zora Neale Hurston, Benny Carter and Langston Hughes, the friends she met at the party. Along with them is another woman, someone Bess has not previously met.

Langston Hughes hugs her. "We have exciting news to tell you and Mr. Big!"

Zora Neale gives her an affectionate hug too and notices Bess's dressing gown. "Hello, Miss Bess! You look beautiful, but what are you all dressed up like that for in the middle of the day?" Before she can answer, Romare comes out of the bedroom. They all greet him, a little suspiciously, as Bearden is known as a lady's man.

Langston asks, "What are you doing here Romare?"

Romare smiles at Bess and turns his painting around. "We had some business to take care of today. Bess modeled for me, and I am going to leave the painting here with her for a while before I show it at a gallery."

Everyone knew how talented he is, but they gasp in astonishment at the painting. Barthé carefully takes the painting over to the window to view it in natural light. "This is beautiful! I think this is your best work ever. Of course, with Bess as your model, how could it be anything but great."

Zora Neale turns to the other woman who came in with them, and whispers, "I told you she was gorgeous, but we don't see too much of her because Mr. Big likes to keep her close by, in the apartment."

The woman smiles. "You're right, she is," as she turns toward Bess.

Langston takes Bess's hand. "I'm so sorry. We are so rude. This is Josephine Baker. Josephine, this is Mr. Big's lady, Bess. "

Bess takes a long look at Josephine Baker. She is not beautiful but is quite stunning in a certain exotic kind of way. She is adorned with flashy costume jewelry and is wearing a long red dress. Her short haircut frames her face perfectly, with a lovely smile that lights up the room, and Bess is in awe. Josephine shakes Bess's hand and kisses her on both cheeks. "My, my, my . . . I can see why Mr. Big keeps you hidden away. He doesn't want anyone to get their hands on you."

Flattered by all the attention, she throws her head back with a carefree laugh, something she has not done since she left Catfish Row and Porgy. She is now more confident in her ability to switch from Gullah to the dialect she learned from the maids. "Yo so nice. Thank yo."

"He shouldn't be allowed to keep you hidden away. He needs to let you out of this cage, even though it's a very comfortable cage." To make her point, Josephine swirls her scarf flamboyantly through the air, and they all laugh. Josephine, knowing Mr. Big's history of providing good-looking women to his customers, is fairly sure he is using Bess as a courtesan, as well.

"Speaking of Mr. Big, where is he?" Benny Carter asks.

"We need to talk to you both about something very important," Richmond Barthé says.

"He's not heah yet, but y'all can come in an' gots a seat. He bes' be back soon." They all walk in and take seats in the living room. "I'm finna get some champagne an' some snacks. I'll be right back." Returning to the kitchen, she starts to cut up cheese, and puts some fruit and cold-cuts onto a tray. Josephine twirls around in a little dance as she follows Bess into the kitchen. Bess watches her and is charmed by her quirky appearance and dazzling mannerisms.

Josephine pops a grape into her mouth. "Do you need some help?"

Gaily, Bess says, "Shuh, if yo want ta."

Josephine opens the bottle and begins pouring the champagne into the exquisite crystal flutes Bess put on the tray. She pours herself a glass. "So, why doesn't Mr. Big ever bring you out of the apartment?"

Not sure what to say. she hesitates. "I did . . . I . . . uh . . . he thinks it's safah in heah fo' me. He takes care of me, so I kin' of do what he says because I feel like he knows what's bes' fo' me."

Taking a sip of champagne, Josephine says, "I had a guy once who thought it was 'safe' for me to stay inside too. I was homeless on the streets in St. Louis and I came under his control, and I married him when I was just thirteen. I'm still under someone's thumb, even now where I work, being one of the Negro girls in the chorus line at the Plantation Club." When she mentions where she works, she grimaces and takes another sip.

"Listen to that name, 'Plantation Club.' Only white patrons can come there. For us Negro performers, it is pretty horrible, with paintings of slave cabins and picket fences on the walls, and lots of mirrors. There are scenes painted on the walls of dutiful, chuckling mammies, like Aunt Jemima tossing waffles and flapjacks for the plantation owner and his family. The ceiling over the dance floor is painted like a nighttime sky, filled with stars and moons which glitter at night above the dancers' heads." Josephine adds, sarcastically, "The only thing missing is a picture of Eliza running across the ice in *Uncle Tom's Cabin.* At one end of the dance floor there is a poster from that racist movie, *Birth of a Nation,* and there are tiny models of plantation cabins set on shelves on the walls." She snickers at her own sad dilemma.

Bess takes a break from preparing the food and faces her with a sympathetic gaze. "I am sorry dat yo gots had such a bad life."

"I think I can see the pain on your face, Bess, because you have been there too."

She stares at her and her cheerful mood instantly changes to sadness "Yo can see dat?"

"A beautiful girl like you? From the South? Being cooped up in this apartment? I can guess what Mr. Big is using you for, and I wouldn't like that myself. Why are you living here like that?"

Bess doesn't want to cry and have to tell her story all over again, but she does. "I tol' Romare about my life earliah so fo'give me fo' cryin'. I was . . . rape by da ownahs of da plantation I was at. I work der as an indenshuh servant. Sportin', I mean Mistah Big, had come down from New Yawk, an' bought out mah work contrac' from da ownahs. He introduce me ta da happy dus' ta ease da pain. In retu'n, I did whatevah he ax me ta do. I did . . . I do . . . favahs fo' all his frien's, an' anyone else, so we could make money. I was young an' din't know any bettah at dat time. I was hypnotize by him, an' by da happy dus', but I nevah wanted dat feelin'. It numb me. Still do."

Bess wipes the tears from her face. Josephine brushes her own tears away as well. She is exhausted from telling her story once again, and her anger spills over. "I hated da white men. Our bodies

. . . our Black bodies . . . were a playgroun' fo' them. An' it was alright fo' them ta come in an' take what they wanted. We were fair game fo' da plantation ownahs, da Ku Klux Klan . . . ev'ryone!" She pauses for a moment and then tells Josephine about meeting Porgy, how he was the only man she has ever loved, and how she ended up in New York with Mr. Big.

Because Josephine shared with Bess the details of her life, Bess feels she can bare her soul as well. "Livin' in Charleston was so hard, an' up heah in Harlem is not much bettah. I gots gone from one cage ta anothah. I wish I could get away from it all somehow, an' be mah own woman . . . live life as a free person. At a party da othah night I saw how Mistah. Big's white frien's got wit' Zora Neale an' Langston an' Romare an' even wit' me. It open mah eyes dat I could be treated like dat. Like a star. A human bein'. It change da way I t'awt about mah life. I want more. I need more."

Josephine moves next to her and dries her eyes. "Only you can decide what's best for you. I understand what it's like to be a doormat for men, white men especially. It is hard to shake that off. Why do you think I'm here looking for him? It gets so bad and sometimes I need a little something to keep me going. I'm not stuck in a cage anymore. I'm on my way to greatness. I know I am . . . and you can be too." Josephine hugs Bess. "I heard you had a great singing voice. am I right? And can you dance too?"

She nods her head, excited. "I really love ta sing. I do. I gots since I was a li'l girl. An' I use ta dance at our plantation parties too."

"Then why don't you?" Bess shrugs her shoulders. "Live out your dreams. Or you're going to regret it. Don't let these men dictate what you do with your body and your life. If you want to sing and dance, then . . . sing and dance."

Bess fills her hands with cool water and splashes her face. "I jus' don' know how ta do dat."

Handing her a towel, she says, "It must have been meant for me to come and see you today. I was like you once upon a time, but I got to be a performer, a singer and dancer. With your good looks, you could be a singer and a dancer too. There aren't any jobs where I work, but there's another place called the Apollo Theater and now they have an Amateur Night where they audition new talent"

The words "Amateur Night" remind her of the party. "I met da ownah of da Apollo Theater at dat party dat I tol' yo about, Sidney Cohen. Dat's wheah Mistah Big's office is."

Josephine pours more champagne. "Great, that's your way in. It's the least he can do for you. You won't have to be a courtesan anymore under Mr. Big's thumb."

"I don' think Mistah Big will let me audition."

"Don't worry. Somehow we will find a way to convince him." Josephine pats Bess on the arm, as they hear the front door open and see Sportin' Life enter the apartment. "Come. Your man is here."

CHAPTER TWENTY-SEVEN

Josephine picks up her champagne glass and walks out of the kitchen to meet Sportin' Life. Bess fills the rest of the glasses and takes them into the living room. *What kin I say tuh convince Sportin' Life dat I need tuh audition on Amateur Night?* She puts the drinks on a cocktail table and watches their visitors say hello to Sportin' Life. He walks over to Bess and puts his arm around her in a possessive manner. Visibly perturbed at seeing her serving the drinks to their friends, he asks, "Where are the maids?"

"I give dem a break, so I could pose fo' Romare's paintin'." She goes into the kitchen and gets the tray of snacks which she also places on the cocktail table.

Sportin' Life turns to his friends. He doesn't remember inviting any of them over today. "What are you all doing here?"

Langston Hughes looks at the group and takes a sip of champagne. "Things keep getting worse for us here, man. You have been such a great help and support for all of us, and we really appreciate it. But we have come here to tell you that it is time for us to leave America."

Sportin' Life takes a swallow of champagne, shocked. "Leave? And go where?"

Zora Neale was expecting his surprised reaction. "Paris. We have been considering it for a long time."

He wrinkles his brow. "Paris? What do you mean, Paris?"

"Paris, France, Mr. Big," Zora Neale says in a serious tone of voice, "We are sick of the discrimination and dangers here in Harlem . . . in New York . . . in this whole country."

Carter chimes in. "We want to live our lives with dignity. Not just as artists, but as people, Negro people, trying to thrive and make it in this world. Paris is where we will be treated as equals and with respect."

Langston takes a sip of champagne. "Paris will be a place to escape racism and take our dreams to the next level! Whatever it is that we want to do! Music, writing, painting, anything. Imagine a world where you can produce your art in peace and not be looked upon as second-class citizens. My friend, Paulette Nardal, is one of the founders of the 'Negritude Movement' in Paris that promotes Negro culture and history. She has already translated some of my poems into French, and she will help make us feel welcome there."

Zora Neale Hurston exclaims. "Negroes going from America to France is not a new thing. Our people have been doing that on and off for about the last hundred years. This time, it's artists, writers, and musicians like us who are tired of the vicious bigotry in America."

Because he is wealthy, Sportin' Life is not personally affected very much by racism in America and asks, "How do you know things will be better in Paris?"

She digs in her purse and takes out a copy of the *Chicago Defender*, the largest circulation Negro newspaper in America. "Mr. Big, we know it from reading columns like 'The Street Wolf of Paris' by Edgar Wiggins in the *Defender*. Look here in his latest column. The article is all about the Pan-Africanism movement based there. It includes people from America, Africa and the French West Indies, who are interested in literature, culture, and political awareness. Moving to Paris will give us a chance to be a part of that."

Sportin' Life is trying to take it all in. Their connection is important to his view of himself as a member of their cultural community. "I don't want you all to leave. Are you sure this is a good idea? How will you make a living there and where are you all going to live?"

Langston says, "We all have jobs lined up, so that is taken care of. Look at this Paris city map. We are going to live in the Montmartre section, where Negroes can feel free to be human. The area has a fancy name, 'Arrondissement Dix-Huit,' on a hilltop where you can see the entire city of Paris. The Moulin Rouge cabaret is nearby, and we heard Picasso and many other famous artists used to live there, too."

Benny says. "Over there I am going to write music for Willie Lewis' band and not have to be subservient to 'the white man' anymore."

Langston adds, "I've got a job writing for Aimé Césaire's magazine, *L'Etudiant Noire,* 'The Black Student.'"

Pointing his finger at Bearden, Sportin' Life asks. "And you? Going to paint more pictures of my girl?"

Romare knows Mr. Big is being a little sharp because they are springing this on him so suddenly, so he ignores the sarcasm. "I'm going to work in the studio of Lois Mailou Jones, a really fine abstract painter of African-themes. Her artwork is really original and beautiful. Barthé here will be close by working at Nancy Elizabeth Prophet's sculpture atelier. So, you can see we are well-prepared for this move."

Bess listens and is in awe of how amazing these artists are, and how they are all using their gifts from God to live out their dreams. She wants very much to be part of this circle, and thinks about what Josephine told her about not hiding in the shadows any longer.

Zora Neale tells Sportin' Life, "I have a writing assignment from *Opportunity Magazine,* the National Urban League's publication. They want me to write a series of articles about what Negroes are doing in Paris, like the ones in the *Defender*. Everyone there will be a valuable source of information for me. It will be so much more exciting, and safer too, than staying here."

Josephine smiles. "I'll give you all the material you need, Zora Neale. I am going to audition for a dancing job at the Folies-Bergère. I'm already designing my costume with ostrich feathers."

Benny adds, "We all got great opportunities from your party, and we really appreciated it. But, as Negro people, we're getting killed everyday in this country, and, the effects of the Depression are out of control. So, why wouldn't we want to go to Paris? Our people are making moves over there! Negro artists like us are thriving!"

Romare jumps in. "Paris is a new world that we can make our own."

Sportin' Life's friends continue to extol the virtues of Paris for a few more hours before they leave the apartment. They promise to return to say goodbye before departing America to start their new lives.

Josephine approaches the door last and Sportin' Life hands her a small paper packet of cocaine. "Something extra for you, beautiful."

She kisses him on the cheek and puts it in her purse. Glancing at Bess, she says, "Remember, Bess, go out and do your own thing. Don't let Mr. Big keep you caged up here . . . like we talked."

His face turns red at Josephine's accusation, but he is defiant. "What will she do out in the world without me, besides get hurt?"

Irked by the comment, she flashes her eyes. "So you're saying since she's a woman, she can't be out on her own without the presence of a man?"

"You know how it is out there, Jo."

"Yes, I do. That's why you're going to let her audition for Amateur Night at the Apollo."

Bess looks at Sportin' Life's surprised expression, fearing his reaction. He turns toward Josephine. "You mean where stars like Ella Fitzgerald and Thelma Carpenter got their start? I don't think they will let her go up on the stage, even if I did allow her to try."

"That's the whole point of Amateur Night. It's a way for new performers to try out for a job there. You're going to convince Sidney Cohen to let her audition, so she can have her own shot at stardom. We will be at the Apollo to support her dreams. I expect to see her there. I don't want to hear anything more about it."

Josephine gives Sportin' Life a hug. Turning to Bess, she assures her, "I will be your champion. Let me know when you will be performing and I'll pick out a costume and help you dress." She walks out of the apartment, feeling she was able to save another sister from a lifetime of despair.

Sportin' Life closes the door and shouts angrily at Bess. "What was that all about?"

"I really do want ta do it. I want ta sing an' dance. I know I can do it."

He is still negative, "You can't go up on that stage, Bess. They will eat you alive if you mess up. You're not ready for something like that. No."

Bess is insistent. She grabs Sportin' Life by the arm. "I can't jus' sit heah an' rot away. If they boo me away, den dat was mah destiny. But I gots ta do somethin'. I'm done wit' cocaine. I don' want ta do it anymo', an' I don' want ta do favahs fo' yo' frien's anymo'! I want ta do somethin' fo' me! Dis is mah dream."

Sportin' Life looks at Bess and sighs. He realizes her whole outlook on life has undergone a dramatic change, and he reluctantly gives in. *Why did that crazy Josephine put these ideas into her head? I'll just let her do this and when she fails, I will be there to rescue her again, and then this will be over for good.*

CHAPTER TWENTY-EIGHT

The Apollo Theater is getting ready for another Amateur Night as Sportin' Life and Bess walk into the opulent lobby, a gaudy mix of various architectural styles. There are pillars topped by Ionic and Tuscan capitals, and walls decorated with neoclassical reliefs of Greek urns. Garlands and portrait medallions of Roman Gods, all highlighted with gold-leaf paint, add to the spectacle. Bess is overwhelmed, never before having been in any kind of theatre.

A comedian is on the stage, and the audience is laughing. There is an easel on the right side with a sign reading, "Amateur Night." The comedy act finishes and the master of ceremonies introduces the next performer, a female singer who launches into a fast-paced jazz number. The audience likes her performance and some patrons start dancing and clapping in the aisles. Bess watches the performances nervously, praying she won't let Josephine down.

Sportin' Life leads Bess to the back of the theater, where Sidney Cohen is in his office. "Sidney, Just the man I was looking for."

"What is it this time, some problem with the numbers racket?" Cohen chuckles and turns to give Bess a kiss on the cheek, "Nice to see you, gorgeous girl. I'm glad to see you out of the apartment."

She giggles nervously. "Yes, I am too."

Sidney stands back and looks at the couple. "So, what's going on?"

Sportin' Life clears his throat. "No, no problems. I want you to let . . . Bess here . . . . perform tonight."

"No, Mr. Big. Now you know I can't do that. I can't just let anyone get up there at the last minute. Tonight's entertainers have been booked for weeks."

He leans over the desk getting into Sidney's face. "Wait a minute! She's not just anyone. She's my woman, and you owe me for all the money I bring in here."

"That doesn't make her exempt from the way Amateur Night works. I can't make exceptions."

Interrupting, Bess implores, "Please, let me do one song. If they boo, yo can both blame me."

"Oh, don't worry about blame. There's a guy behind the curtain called 'The Executioner.' He uses a real broom and will sweep you off the stage if the audience howls for your removal."

"Like you, I am not happy about this, but Josephine Baker put the idea into her head. She will be here with all the rest of our friends. Do me this favor, Sidney . . . come on."

Cohen takes some time to think about it. "Fine. Do it. Go tell Cooper, the master of ceremonies to add her name to the list."

They walk out of the office and, as they re-enter the lobby, Sportin' Life takes hold of Bess' arm. "Don't mess this up and make me look bad," and goes off to find Cooper. Bess waits there for a few minutes, gripping her little case which holds her costume and makeup. She is jittery and nervous, looking around for Josephine Baker during the intermission.

The intermission is over and the people are returning to their seats. The flash of newspaper photographers' cameras at the front of the lobby attracts Bess's attention. Her dismay turns to relief as she gets a glimpse of Josephine's flamboyant entrance. Now that the lobby has emptied, they find one another and walk arm-in-arm to the performers' dressing rooms.

She fixes Bess's makeup and helps her with her hair. Bess puts on a shiny blue dress Josephine picked out for her. It shimmers and sparkles with every move of her body. She turns Bess's head toward the mirror. "That woman is exquisite."

"I am so scared, an' I am havin' a hard time breathin'." Josephine goes over and rubs her back as Bess slumps in the chair. "I can't do dis, I can't. I don' know why I said I could. I don' wan' ta go out der." She fights the urge to ask Josephine for some happy dust.

Taking Bess's hand, she says, "You can, Bess! You can do this! I can't tell you how many people tried to hold me back. But I proved them all wrong, and so will you. You will do great!"

Bess's heart is racing and her palms are damp with perspiration. They look in the mirror together. She tries to keep calm and remembers something she heard on the radio, and recites it out loud. "Day by day, in ev'ry way, I am gettin' bettah an' bettah."

She hugs Bess and they walk out into the theater. In the orchestra section there are tables set up where patrons can order food and drinks. They sit down with Sportin' Life, Langston, Romare, Richmond, and Zora Neale. Their friends are all drinking champagne or bourbon, except Bess, who is drinking water.

Ralph Cooper returns to the stage in time to see a tap dancer being swept off by 'The Executioner'. Watching that puts Bess more on edge. She leans over to Josephine. "He is finna sweep me off too."

Josephine playfully taps her on the knee. "The dancer they booed was terrible, but you are going to be great."

Cooper speaks into the microphone, "Alright! Alright! Settle down!" The crowd quiets down, waiting for his announcement. He picks up his paper with the names on it. "We have one more act for the show . . . Miss Bess! Where are you? Miss Bess come on up." She doesn't move from the table, and Josephine gives her a nudge. Cooper continues to call out Bess's name until she finally gets up and slowly walks to the front of the theater. The applause from the audience starts hesitantly and then builds as they see Bess start up the steps, and marvel at how lovely she is.

Earlier in the evening Josephine told Bess about an Apollo tradition that is supposed to bring luck to people who are auditioning, so Bess touches the special piece of "lucky" wood near the railing before going onstage. The chunk of wood was taken from the 'Tree of Hope', a legendary shade tree behind the old Lafayette Theater. This was where Cooper originated the idea for an Amateur Night. Once on stage, Ralph Cooper escorts her to the microphone. The room falls silent. Bess stands there frozen, paralyzed with stage fright.

Sportin' Life glares at Josephine. "I knew I shouldn't have let her go. If people connect her to me, it will make me look bad and hurt my business."

Josephine glares at him and shushes him, "Don't be ridiculous. The only person who will be embarrassed if she doesn't do well will be her, not you."

Standing up, Josephine claps and shouts out, "Come on Bess." Moving closer to the microphone, she speaks almost in a whisper, "Hi, I'm Bess . . . an' . . . I'm . . . goin' ta sing . . . I'm finna sing a song by Irvin' Berlin."

This is the tune Benny Carter worked on with her. The band waits for her to start. The spotlights have blinded her, and she can't see her friends sitting at their table.

Momentarily, the words to the song escape her. Bess thinks about walking off but her legs won't move. She stares at the orchestra and begins singing. "Blue . . . skies . . . smilin' . . . at . . . me . . ." The band picks up on the song, and they begin to play. With the band accompanying her, she calms down, and sways and snaps her fingers. Quite a few patrons from the audience leave their seats and move into aisles to dance as she sings.

> *Blue skies smilin' at me,*
> *Nothin' but blue skies do I see.*
> *Blue birds singin' a song,*
> *Nothin' but blue birds all day long.*
> *Nevah saw da sun shinin' so bright.*
> *Nevah saw things go oh so right.*
> *Noticin' da days hurryin' by.*
> *When you're in love, my how dey fly.*
> *Blue days, all of dem gone.*
> *Nothin' but blue skies from now on.*

Bess's performance is hitting every note, high and low. More patrons are now up dancing in rhythm with her singing, feeling every beat of the music. Even Sportin' Life is entranced, seeing Bess on the stage, confidently singing and swaying to the music. As Bess finishes, the place erupts into cheers. Ralph Cooper rushes back and embraces her with an affectionate hug. Waving his arms and facing the audience, he yells, "Wasn't she amazing!"

Bess is excited and happily speaks into the microphone. Her face is glowing and she is radiant. A dozen or more new fans rush up to Bess and reach up to shake her hand. She shakes hands with each one, repeating over and over, "Thank you, thank you, thank you. Dis night was so wondah'ful fo' me."

The last person to come up to Bess is Josephine, holding a huge bouquet of red roses. "I told you you would be a star!" Bess realizes she accomplished something on her very own for the first time in her life, and she is jubilant. Josephine hurries her back to her friends at the table, where they are standing and applauding. She runs around the table and gives each of them a big embrace. Still bustling with energy, she sits down next to Sportin' Life who doesn't share in her excitement and has remained seated.

Later in the evening, Sportin' Life and Bess return to their apartment. "Well, you did surprise me. I can't believe it was you up there, especially without any happy dust."

"I know. I don' know what came ovah me, but it felt wondahful."

Sportin' Life laughs. "Well, I'm glad you got that all out of your system. It was only an Amateur Night, baby. You can't just wake up and be a famous singer and dancer. You aren't Josephine."

"Wow, dat's really encouragin'." Bess says in a sarcastic and defiant tone.

He has never heard her speak to him like that, "You are beautiful, and you have some talent, but you have no training. I don't have the time right now to manage your career. Someone called Mr. Goat Man is taking away all my numbers business, and I have to take care of that. I'm sorry Bess."

She bristles, irritated, at his statement. "Back at da dressin' room aftuh da show, Ralph an' Sidney came in an' offah me a job in da chorus line, an' I am finna take it. Josephine will help me, so yo don' gots ta get involve." Bess turns and walks into the bedroom on the kind of high that comes only from the discovery of newly-acquired self-worth.

CHAPTER TWENTY-NINE

Porgy is now dressed in a well-tailored grey pin-stripe suit, and he has on an imported Italian Borsalino hat. Long gone are the shabby clothes worn when he was a beggar. Only a few weeks have passed since he started his numbers business and it is already much bigger than he and his friends ever imagined. Additional runners have been hired, and he expanded his territory to more neighborhoods across Harlem.

He now moves around in a shiny new wheelchair instead of on his crutches. Sam is being cared for by another resident of the Goat House, and he is enjoying his retirement on the back lawn. There is no longer a need for him to pull Porgy in the cart.

Now having made enough money to start Detective Morrison's search for Bess, his bodyguards take him over to Morrison's building. One of the bodyguards wheels Porgy into the office where he greets the secretary. In his new clothes, wheelchair and refined appearance, she does not recognize him.

She politely asks, "Who should I tell Mr. Morrison is here to see him?" There is a surprised look on her face when Porgy reminds her who he is. Hesitantly, she calls her boss on the intercom to tell him who the visitor is.

Recognizing Porgy, Morrison comes out and waves his secretary off. "It's okay Candace. You remember Porgy, don't you?

He was here before." The secretary rolls her eyes as Porgy joins the detective in his office.

Porgy wheels up to Morrison's desk and puts down sixty dollars. "If I 'membah correc'ly, dis is how much yo need ta start lookin' fo' mah wife. I gots ta fin' her soon as possible, so we can get back ta our son in Charleston. I jus' receive an urgen' lettah from da lady who is takin' care of him. She write how relieve she was ta heah from me. She is worried about me findin' mah wife Bess cuz she have a visit from chile protection services. They tol' her dat me an' Bess gots ta be in caw't ta sign 'doption papahs a month from now. Otha'wise, da baby will be made a ward of da caw't an' be put intah an orphanage."

The detective takes the money and starts counting it. It adds up to what he told Porgy the first time. "I realize you are in a hurry, but these things take time."

Porgy is frantic. "Like I tol' yo da fust time, she was kidnap. Dis guy, Sportin' Life, foun' her down in Savannah an' brought her ta New Yawk. He prob'ly gots her on drugs an' pimpin' her, an' I gots ta fin' her befo' things get even worse."

Morrison nods his head. "All right. So, tell me all about your wife. Start from the beginning." They spend the next hour talking about Bess, and Porgy also tells him everything he can remember about Sportin' Life.

The detective says he will do his best to find her. "Without a photograph it will be difficult, but I will contact my friends in the police department who are familiar with all the local drug dealers and pimps. Maybe someone has heard of this Sportin' Life. How will I get in touch with you if I hear something?"

Porgy recalls Sugar's advice about secrecy, and hands Morrison a slip of paper. "Here is da address of mah frien' Jonathan. He will know how ta get ahold of me."

After he leaves, Morrison picks up his phone and calls two of his friends in the police department to see if they have come across a pimp and drug dealer named Sportin' Life. His first call is to Samuel Battle who was the first Negro officer hired by the New York Police Department. Battle was Morrison's superior officer when he was on the police force, and he feels if anyone knows the Harlem underworld, it would be Battle.

Morrison's other friend is Johnny Broderick, an Irish-American cop. Years ago he and Broderick patrolled the Broadway theater district and became close friends. If Sportin' Life is providing Negro prostitutes or dealing cocaine to the white community, Broderick would be aware of it. For an additional source of information, Morrison tells Candace, "Tonight, walk around the streets and ask if any of the prostitutes or their pimps know someone in the business named Bess." Reluctantly she agrees. She finds the prospect of doing that distasteful, but she does not want to displease her boss and lose her job.

CHAPTER THIRTY

A few days later, Porgy is sitting in his storage room office in Smalls Paradise. He picks up the afternoon newspaper and writes down the winning number for the day, based on the fourth race at Aqueduct. Jonathan comes in and Porgy shows him, "The winnin' numbah t'day is 730."

Jonathan says, "We made a killin' yesterday since der were only ten winnahs. Let's see how da rest of dis day goes." Porgy opens a safe they have installed in the office, and they remove the betting slips to determine if anyone hit the number "730" for the day.

"How many runnahs do we gots now?"

Jonathan checks his "runners book," and does a quick count. "Forty-two."

Porgy looks at a Harlem map on the wall with push pins showing all his runners' neighborhoods. "I think we need ta add more."

Jonathan is troubled by Porgy's plan. "We just added twelve runnahs last week, an' I'm concerned we is movin' too fast an' atttractin' too much attention."

Ignoring Jonathan's concern, Porgy says, "Let's hire eight mo' ta make fifty. Even dough we is busiah than evah, I want ta make shuh we gots 'nuff runnahs ta covah dat rich Hamilton Heights neighborhood." The neighborhood Porgy wants to send runners into is at the northern end of St. Nicholas Park. It didn't take Porgy long to familiarize himself with all the neighborhoods in Harlem, and to figure out which would be the most lucrative. After he and Jonathan finish looking through the betting slips, Jonathan takes the winning slips and cash and leaves to distribute them to the runners.

Porgy rolls toward the door, reaches up and grabs his hat. He picks up his new briefcase and, with a sense of pride, surveys his office. While he is very anxious about finding Bess, he is pleased he now has the cash coming in for Morrison to find her.

Two bodyguards now accompany Porgy. The bigger of the two, Mitch, turns to Porgy and asks, "Are you ready to go, sir?" With a nod of his head, Mitch pushes him in his wheelchair out through Smalls Paradise, where waiters and kitchen staff are getting ready for the evening show.

The bright, sunny day puts him into a happy mood as they make it to the street. The other bodyguard, Tony, joins them. "Ok. Let's go. Da winnin' numbah be circulatin' an' I want ta get some rest befo' we start receivin' t'day's bettin' slips." They roll Porgy toward his new home.

Porgy's new residence is in a stately apartment building at 409 Edgecombe Avenue. It is a thirteen-story building, the tallest in Sugar Hill, Harlem's ritziest area, and he lives in an elegant apartment on the 10th floor. Sugar Hill extends north from 145th Street to 155th and is bounded by Amsterdam to the west and Edgecombe to the east. 409 Edgecombe is the best address in Harlem. It is very near to where Sportin' Life and Bess live, but of course, Porgy isn't aware of that.

Porgy goes into his bedroom and lies down on his new bed. He falls into a deep sleep filled with dreams of now being able to afford the search for Bess. After being awakened by the voices of Jonathan and William entering the apartment, Porgy transfers himself into his wheelchair and rolls into the living room to meet them.

Jonathan gives Porgy a report on the day's results. "I can't believe how far we all gots come so fast.

William adds, "An' Jonathan an' me aren't missin' workin' fo' slave wages on dat ship. Like yo, we all gots nice places ta live now. Pretty soon we be sendin' fo' our fam'lies."

Porgy is pleased is friends are doing well. "An' wit' da money I made, I met Detective Morrison again an' hire him ta fin' mah woman. . . . What can I say? Bein' a fair an' honest bankah in da illegal numbahs game is profit'ble." They all start laughing.

A few minutes later, Timothy rushes in. "Hey guys, we gots a serious problem an' we need ta deal wit'!" They turn toward the front door and are startled to see Timothy's face, which is bloody and badly bruised.

Porgy yells, "Mah gawd, Timothy, What da hell happen ta yo? William, Jonathan, go get some peroxide, bandages an' ice. Hurry!"

"Mistah Big's numbahs manager, Joshua, an' two of his men attack me an' they stole all da money fo' t'morrow's numbahs pull!"

Timothy winces as his face is cleaned and bandaged, and he holds an ice-pack to his rapidly swelling eye. His friends sit down on the couch and urgently wait to hear what happened. Jonathan, with a worried look on his face, says, "Dis means we is turnin' intah powahful competition fo' Mistah Big."

Standing up, William says angrily, "Of course we're a problem fo' him! We're lucky they didn't kill Timothy!"

Porgy had been told about other bankers getting into territory fights, especially with the important names like "Bumpy" Johnson. He was aware that Johnson, like himself, was from South Carolina, and was careful to avoid encroaching on his territory. However, he didn't think he was cutting into Mr. Big's business enough for him to retaliate. Porgy is visibly shaken and turns to Timothy. "Is dat all they did was take da money?"

Now that Timothy's cuts and bruises are taken are of, he finishes telling about what happened. "Yes, jus' da money. Befo' they let me go, Joshua said Mistah Big wan' ta gots a meetin' t'night wit' da head of our operation at his office at da Apollo Theater." Porgy is surprised. "How did he learn yo' workin' fo' an independent banker an' not some organization like Stephanie St. Clair or Dutch Schultz? He would gots ta be crazy ta attack one of der people."

Timothy turns to Porgy. "This is New York. Da numbahs game is only so big. An' I am shuh Mistah Big planted informahs among our runnahs. Once he started losin' money, he want' ta kill off his rivals."

Jonathan says, "Dat's what I was always afraid of, dat they wouldn' wan' anyone else runnin' numbahs in der neighborhoods. We is movin' on up an' they wan' ta beat us down!"

Timothy is defiant." No one gonna beat us down. What do yo wan' ta do? They asked fo' Mr. Goat Man specifically ta meet them at da Apollo. "

"Okay, we will go. I will try ta end dis peaceful an', if necessary, divide up da terr'tory, if dat's what we gots ta do. If not, we'll deal wit' it anothah way. Let's get ready fo' t'night. Yo guys know what ta do. Tell mah bodyguards Mitch an' Tony what is goin' on an' make shuh they gots der guns wit' them. They gots a way ta conceal them in case they pat them down at da door." After Porgy moves back into his bedroom, Jonathan, William and Timothy begin talking among themselves about how to handle the confrontation with Mr. Big if things get rough.

It is a short taxicab ride from Porgy's apartment to the Apollo, and they enter the theater to meet Mr. Big. The doorman and security guards had been alerted to watch for them, and they are patted down roughly.

One of the guards, satisfied they are not carrying any guns, orders them, "Wait at the bar."

William says to Porgy, "They know who we is, obviously, an' were waitin' fo' us."

"I think they is stallin' us ta keep da uppah hand, but it won' work. I'm not finna be sway' by enny of his strong-arm games." Porgy is in a confident and relaxed mood. "Jis' take a look at dis place. Der is as much glass in it as all da windahs in mah apartment. I nevah knew der were so many diffuhrent kin' of likkuh."

A few minutes later, Mitch and Tony, Porgy's bodyguards, arrive with their girlfriends, who are wearing long cocktail dresses. They have concealed their boyfriends' guns in ankle holsters, just in case the guards found a reason to search the men. They cross the lobby and sit at the bar, so they can keep an eye on Porgy and his friends.

Porgy looks around and recognizes Mr. Dooley, the same tour guide who was working on the ship he came to New York on. Porgy's mood turns dark as he remembers his experience in the ship's dining room. Dooley is there with another group of passengers from Charleston, and has taken them on an excursion to visit Harlem's night spots. "We are now in the Apollo Theater, famous for elaborate Negro shows. In a little while, you're going to see for yourselves how entertaining they are."

Sitting at the bar, Porgy hears one of the white passengers say, "I hope these niggah performahs will be better than the ones on the rivah showboats back home." He hasn't heard Negroes referred to like that since coming to Harlem, and thinks for a moment about going over to their table and calling them out.

Within earshot he hears another passenger complain, "Why did Mr. Dooley bring us to a nightclub where we have to sit next to Negroes? He should have taken us to the Cotton Club where they don't allow them in." Porgy is frustrated but realizes people from the south will probably never change.

The bartender has also heard the passengers, and whispers, "Those white tourists are here just to gawk at us . . . makes me feel like we are animals in the zoo. Their conversations show they have no real interest in the great music, the beauty of our race, or the talent of our Negro artists." Now that the bartender has kept Porgy and his friends waiting at the bar for the time he was told to, he goes to the back of the theater to Sportin' Life's office. "They're here. I saw the guy with bruises, the one Joshua gave the 'message' to, and there are three guys with him."

There are four bodyguards in Sportin' Life's office. He motions for one of them to go get Mr. Goat Man and his associates, and the bodyguard follows the bartender out of the office. "This is going to be an easy meeting. I'm sure I can destroy these upstarts. This is my territory and I don't want anybody think they can step in and steal a part of it. That is not going to happen." Sportin' Life opens his desk drawer and checks to make sure his gun is loaded. "Just in case, I am ready for war."

Sportin' Life's bodyguard steps up to Timothy at the bar. "Let's go fellas." Porgy and his friends leave their barstools and follow him. They enter the large area behind the stage filled with props, costumes, lights and scenery. Crossing this area they can see doors to storage closets and dressing rooms. As they pass one of the doors, they can actually hear the chatter of women's voices. Porgy passes right by the door to the dressing room where Bess and the chorus girls are getting ready for their show. Unaware of her presence, he takes no notice.

When they arrive at Sportin' Life's office, the bodyguard walks in first, followed by Porgy in his wheel chair and his friends, Jonathan, William, and Timothy. "The visitors are here, sir," and then moves next to the other bodyguards to wait for instructions.

Sportin' Life is seated in a swivel chair at his desk, and has his back turned to the door.

CHAPTER THIRTY-ONE

Across from Sportin' Life's office, behind the curtain, the performers are getting ready for the show. Bess now has a regular singing and dancing job at the Apollo in the Ralph Cooper and Benny Carter production, "16 Gorgeous Hotsteppers." The chorus line girls are in their dressing room, putting on elaborately sequined costumes that are made like two-piece bathing suits, leaving little to the imagination.

As Bess puts on her costume, she gushes to the other girls, "I love dese outfits. I nevah get tired of lookin' at da rhinestones, fringes an' sparklin' buttons dat glittah like diamonds in da stage lights. An' dese harlequin stockin's an' high heels make us look . . . well, like Benny say, 'gorgeous'."

Bess has combed her hair into a finger wave style and put on her red lipstick. She and the girls in the show are practicing their routines for the night, which include a variety of dances they choreographed themselves. One of the dancers is rehearsing a Spanish flamenco dance, a popular number in the show. The program also includes a traditional dance from Corsica, a cowboy number, a Hawaiian dance, and a tap routine. For some routines, they dance on large serving trays.

The chorus line is the opening act, and they do three dance productions for each show. At the Apollo, there are at least four shows a day and sometimes eight when the big name bands and stars perform. On those days, the girls might be dancing as many as twenty-four numbers. The chorus line consisted of six short girls, nicknamed, "ponies," and six tall girls, called "show girls." Bess was a "show girl," and was in the group that also did the tap dance routines.

With a few minutes before the show is set to start, Mabel Lee, one of the "show girls," is working on her steps. Bess takes a drink of water and then joins her chorus line sister in rehearsing. "Mabel, slow down a bit," and tries to catch up.

The chorus line was hard work for only twenty dollars a week, with little recognition. But the chorus girls prided themselves on their versatility. During her rehearsal, Bess savors her new found freedom from being Sportin' Life's courtesan money-machine and cocaine addict. This is the happiest she has been since her life with Porgy, which now seems like a very long time ago. As they hear the music start, the girls grab their serving trays, walk onto the stage and take their positions behind the curtain. Bess passes by Sportin' Life's door, unaware that Porgy is right on the other side.

CHAPTER THIRTY-TWO

Inside the office, Porgy stops his wheelchair in front of Sportin' Life's desk. "Hello, is yo Mistah Big?"

With his back still turned he returns the greeting, "Hello, Mr. Goat Man." Sportin' Life swivels around to face him.

Porgy's shoulders stiffen in shock and his hands grip the wheelchair arms painfully. His heart begins to race and his head feels like it is going to explode. They face each other with mouths agape. After months of looking for Bess, the link to the love of his life is sitting right in front of him. Porgy yells at him, "Sportin' Life?! Yo' Mistah Big?! What da hell is goin' on?"

Sportin' Life screams back, "Porgy? You're Mr. Goat Man? In New York?! What are you even doing here? Oh, this is great! This is too funny for words!!" He can't control his laughter. "Everybody out, now!"

The bodyguards check with their boss. "But Mistah Big . . ."

Sportin' Life points toward the door. "Out! Everyone!"

William leans down and whispers into Porgy's ear, "Yo gonna be okay?"

He nods his head, determined he will not leave this office until Sportin' Life tells him where Bess is. Sportin' Life shouts, "Go have a drink on me fellas. Everyone out!"

The room is now empty except for Porgy and Sportin' Life. The atmosphere is electric between the two men. Porgy rolls his wheelchair closer to the desk and glares at him. "Where is Bess?"

Sportin' Life takes his gun from the drawer, waves it in front of Porgy, and then slams it down on the desk. He moves forward in his chair, puts both hands on the desk, and growls, "You're not going to get Bess, Porgy. Ever! Even if you pay me the all money you stole from me, I will still never let you get your hands on her.

Thinking only about Bess, Porgy is confused. "What money?"

"What money? What money? The money you've been stealing from me with your bootleg numbers operation. I have eyes and ears all around Harlem and that's how I found out about your amateur operation. I was ready to make a deal about splitting up the territories, but that's out of the question now that I know who Mr. Goat Man is."

Porgy taunts him." Well, yo din't gots 'nuff eyes if yo din't figga out it was me."

Sportin' Life starts laughing. "That's true. They didn't tell me a poor, crippled beggar was running a numbers operation." Leaning back in his chair, his laughter becomes hysterical.

Porgy focuses intently on Sportin' Life with a penetrating stare. "An' yo is right, der ain't finna be enny deal. I is finna put yo out of bid'ness completely," which stops Sportin' Life's laughter short.

As Porgy starts to move around the desk, Sportin' Life reaches for his gun. "Don't come any closer!"

Porgy's eyes follow his hand as he picks up the gun, and he stops advancing. "Where is Bess?! Tell me Sportin' Life! Tell me! Where is yo keepin' her?" His voice is threatening and his anger builds.

Sportin' Life grips the gun tightly and jumps up out of his chair. Fiercely, he snarls, "You think you can love her like a real man? A weak cripple like you? Huh? I take care of her! She's my woman. She won't go back to you."

Porgy sits up straight, furious. "Yes she will. Bess an' me gots a son, an' she loves me an' dat chile! Yo could nevah look out fo' her in da right way. Evah! All yo evah did is drug her. Yo sold her ta othah men. Yo nevah care about her or gots any good' feelings fo' her."

"It's not really your son, just adopted! You think you can play house but all it is is a broken down cripple's excuse for a home! I can give her more than you ever could! Forever!" He rushes around the desk and leans over Porgy with a wild look in his eyes.

Porgy looks at the gun and then at Sportin' Life's eyes. Guessing he won't have the nerve to use it, he demands, "Fo' da last time, where is she?" Porgy's mind is in turmoil trying to figure out how to make Sportin' Life reveal where Bess is, and then he hits on the solution. "Now dat I know who yo is, mah detective and his police frien's will beat it out of yo!"

Realizing now there is only one way to prevent Porgy from getting Bess back, and taking over what remains of his numbers business, he points the gun at Porgy's head. "She's out there, dancing in the chorus line. Doing what I tell her to do. And, you'll never see her again. I kill those who stand in my way. She will never even know you were here!"

Porgy can now see the danger he is in and, using all of his strength, he propels the wheel chair forward into Sportin' Life's legs. Sportin' Life loses his balance and falls hard onto the floor, sending the gun flying. Porgy launches himself off the wheelchair, landing on top of Sportin' Life, and they begin to grapple, rolling back and forth. Porgy's arms and shoulders are very strong, and he lands some solid blows, but Sportin' Life is much more agile and gets the upper hand. He punches Porgy repeatedly in the face and Porgy's nose starts to bleed. "I'm going to kill you, cripple.

Nobody is going to take my numbers business or my woman away from me!"

Porgy tries to go for the gun, but Sportin' Life jumps on him before he can reach it, knocking the breath out of him. Even though winded, he still has the strength to ram his fist into Sportin' Life's face, knocking him backward. Porgy sees his chance and lunges onto Sportin' Life. He puts his neck into a headlock and squeezes hard. "Now yo is finna die! Dis be fo' Bess!"

Sportin' Life gasps for air, his hands clutching Porgy's arm, trying to free himself. His powerful grip can't be broken and Sportin' Life's arms and legs are flailing, no longer able to defend him. His body finally goes limp, his eyes bulge, and he loses consciousness. Porgy loosens his hold and pushes himself off Sportin' Life. Believing he has killed him, alarms go off in his head. He quickly scrambles back onto his wheelchair hoping he can find Bess before Sportin' Life's bodyguards realize what has happened. He bends down, picks up the gun, and rolls the wheelchair out of the office.

As Porgy reaches the area behind the stage to look for Bess, Jonathan spots him and runs over. "What happened? Yo gots blood on yo face!"

Porgy is frantic and yells, "Bess! Bess!" waving his arms at the performers who are getting ready to go on. "Jonathan, mah wife is heah! Mistah Big is da one who kidnap mah wife."

Sportin' Life's bodyguards have finished their drinks and come back from the bar to check on the meeting. They see Porgy rushing out of the office, covered in blood, which puts them on high alert. Fearing the worst, one of the guards goes back into the office and finds Sportin' Life motionless on the floor. "What da hell?" He darts out of the room, and shouts, "He killed Mistah Big. Get him!"

William and Timothy catch up to Porgy and Jonathan and move as fast as they can through the doorway into the packed theater, keeping an eye out for Mistah Big's bodyguards. Porgy yells over the music. "Bess! Bess!" Not seeing Bess on the stage, they leave the orchestra section, and rush again to the backstage area of the theater to find her.

Porgy locates the door of the chorus line dressing room and pushes it open. A dozen dancers in various states of undress call out to him, "Hey, no men are allowed in here. Get out!" Ignoring the women, he moves farther into the room.

The shows Bess was dancing in are now over, and she is back in street clothes. She is leaning into the mirror, brushing her hair. He glances at each of the beautiful faces in the room, searching for Bess. Suddenly, she is there. Her face is reflected in a mirror across the room. His heart skips a beat, and he whispers to himself, "Bess." Then he screams, "Bess!"

Bess turns around and looks at the man who just yelled her name. She sees a well-dressed man in a wheelchair, but has no idea who he is, and continues to brush her hair. Again from the far end of the room comes the voice, "Bess!"

"Who is dat callin' mah name? Do any of yo girls know who dat is?" As she speaks these words, the voice calling her name triggers her memory. Realizing who it is, she screams, "Porgy! I must be dreamin'. Porgy! Oh mah gawd!! Porgy!" Dropping the hairbrush, she runs into his arms. She kneels in front of the wheelchair and kisses him wildly as tears stream down her cheeks. Bess wraps her arms around Porgy, and they stare into each others eyes. The words come rushing out, "Is yo real? Be dis real? What be yuh doin' heah. Why be yuh bleedin'?"

Porgy is crying tears of joy. "It be real! I came tuh fin' yuh! Tuh rescue yuh f'om Sportin' Life." They hug and kiss again.

Jonathan spots Mr. Big's bodyguards with their guns drawn looking for them inside the theater, and hears them shouting that Mr. Goat Man killed Mr. Big. He rushes into to the dressing room to warn Porgy. "We gots ta git out of heah!! Now! Da bodyguards say yo kill Mistah Big." Porgy turns and sees them rapidly approaching.

Bess grabs his hand. "Dis way! Leh's go out one ob de side exit!" They all follow her to the end of the dressing room where there is a door leading outside.

The bodyguards race after Porgy and Bess as they run through the exit door leading to the street. "Hey! Stop!" one of the bodyguards screams. He fires his gun toward them, but they are already out on the street. Mitch and Tony have been covering Porgy's escape and return the gunfire.

The patrons in the Apollo until now had been watching a delightful musical revue. They managed at first to overlook a man in a wheelchair yelling at the performers. Then, when they saw two men with guns running through the orchestra section and heard the gunshots, it was too much to ignore. The theater-goers are now screaming, stumbling over the seats and running up the aisles to get to the doors to the outside, adding to the overall chaos. With the help of their friends, Porgy and Bess are able to disappear into the crowd that is overflowing onto the street.

Giving up the chase, Sportin' Life's bodyguards go back to his office. One of them bends down close to Sportin' Life and can see he is still breathing, and they help revive him. Looking around, they realize he must have been in a fight with Porgy but had only been rendered unconscious. "Mr. Goat Man tried to choke me to death! What happened? Did you catch him?"

"No. We saw all the blood and thought you were dead, so we went after him. Some woman helped him and his friends get out of the building. We lost them in the crowd on the street."

"Bess! Bess is the one who helped them escape. I hate him! I have to destroy him! I won't let him ruin my numbers business."

Sidney Cohen, the owner of the Apollo, dashes over to Mr. Big's office, screaming, "You've created chaos in my theatre! My terrified customers got stampeded out of the building, damaging everything while they ran. I'm going to have to close to fix this place up. I heard gunfire and now the police are here. That's it, I've had enough! Go find a new place to run your business, at once!"

Sportin' Life can't believe the turn of events and tells his bodyguards, "We will get revenge."

CHAPTER THIRTY-THREE

Porgy and Bess work their way through the milling crowd to the front of the theater. They spy the police cars that have responded to the gunfire and look around for a place to hide. They hear one of the theatre-goers say to a policeman, "A man in a wheelchair came into the theatre screaming a woman's name during the show. Then two men with guns came rushing in and ran after him. After we heard gunshots, we all rushed out of the building."

Panicking patrons are pushing and shoving at the taxi stand, trying to get away from the Apollo as fast as possible. Bess rolls Porgy into the line in an effort to blend in alongside the people waiting. When they reach the front of the taxi line, the doorman hails a cab and helps them into it. Once they are in the taxi and the wheelchair is stowed safely in the trunk, she questions Porgy, "Wuh happen en der? Why be Sportin' Life's bodyguards shootin' at we?"

"I kill Sportin' Life. Him t'reaten' me wid a gun. I knock he ober an' git on top ob he an' choke he tuh deat'. Dey mus' hab foun' he an' figga I done it."

"Why war him t'reatenin' yo wid a gun? War yuh fightin' ober me?"

"It be a long story." He puts his finger to his lips and points to the driver. "I will tell y'all 'bout it when us git tuh muh apartment.

An', I wan' tuh heah how come yuh be en de Apollo chorus line. Right now I be jis' so happy tuh be wid yuh ag'in".

"Me too."

As Bess enters Porgy's apartment at 409 Edgecombe, she realizes it is just a few doors down from the building she lived in with Sportin' Life. "Tuh t'ink him war keepin' me right up de street f'om yuh all dis time an' I din't know it. Porgy, dis place be boot'ful. De furniture an' carpetin' be so fancy. How war yuh ebbuh able tuh afford all ob dis? I caint b'lieb I not be dreamin'."

"Leh's sit down on de couch an' I will tell yuh all 'about it."

She settles down onto the couch and Porgy shifts himself from the wheelchair next to her. Both of them are exhausted from the evening's traumatic events.

Porgy smiles and puts his arms around her. "No. Yuh be not dreamin'. I allus war sho' I would fin' yuh an' tek yuh back tuh Catfish Row. I lub yuh so much, an' nebbuh realize how much, ontel I foun' out yuh war gone."

Bess begins to cry. "I lub yuh too. Yuh hab no idea wuh I bin t'rough. It bin so tough. I finally hab a chance tuh git free f'om muh ol' life when I gots de job at de Apollo en de chorus line. I sang an' dance en front ob an audience, an' war no 'fraid! 'Membah when us would sing en our room en Catfish Row? Yuh allus encourage' me, an' I be so happy dat I done it."

With a sense of sadness, Bess continues, "I war desp'rate cuz I couldn' figga out wuh I war goin' tuh do when yuh went tuh jail." Bess's voice lowers almost to a whisper, and she continues remorsefully, "I be so sorry, but I got back on de white dus' an' leh Sportin' Life brin' me up heah tuh New Yawk. I be sorry. I war . . . I din't t'ink I would ebbuh see yuh ag'in. An' dey all took 'vantage ob me. An' now yuh . . . yuh foun' me. Yuh hab sabe me."

Porgy kisses Bess. "Us be allus goin' tuh be tuggedah. I lub dat yuh sing an' dance now. I ain't surprise' cuz I knew yuh hab dat kin' ob talent de fust time I saw yuh."

"But Porgy, how did yuh fin' me, an' how did yuh git heah tuh New Yawk? How did yuh eben git heah?" Bess asks in amazement.

"Mistah Archdale, de lawyah, git me out ob jail an' I wen' back tuh Catfish Row. Maria tol' me dat Sportin' Life tek yuh up heah. I snuck ontah a cruise ship an' pose as a kitchen wukah. Some frien's help me an' Sam fin' a place tuh stay en Harlem."

"But Porgy how did yuh git intah de numbahs bid'ness?"

"When I bin playin' craps I foun' out 'bout de numbahs racket. I war allus good at gamblin', so when I learn 'bout how someone name Mistah Big war runnin' a crooked numbahs system, I staa't' muh own honest game tuh git de cash I needed. Tuh keep f'om bein' foun' out, an' cuz Sam be heah too, I call muhself Mistah Goat Man."

"Oh, I 'membah Sportin' Life tol' me someone name Mistah Goat Man war hurtin his bid'ness."

"De police say de numbahs be agains' de law, an' mebbe it is, but it gib po' Negro people a way tuh git a li'l money, an' dat's good. I din't want tuh do somethin' agains' de law, but it war de only way fuh me tuh mek money. Aftuh I gots 'nuff, I hiya a detective tuh fin' yuh, but nuttin' happen. Sportin' life hab yuh too well hidden away."

'Yeah. Sportin' Life nebbuh leh me leabe de apa'tment."

"I b'came berry successful an' cut intah his bid'ness, like him tol' yuh. Him ax me tuh come tuh de Apollo t'night tuh mek a deal 'bout splittin' up de territory. Befo' I got der, I hab no idea who him be. At de meeting him realize I be Mistah Goat Man, an' couldn' b'lieb it be me who bin messin' wid his profits."

Porgy stops talking for a moment and his mind jumps back to Sportin' Life's office. "I demanded dat him tell me wheah yuh war. Him tol' me yuh war his fuh'ebbuh, an' would nebbuh gib yuh up, an' him t'reaten me wid a gun. Us end up fightin' on de floor, an' I choke him tuh deat'."

"It mus' hab bin fate fo' yuh ta walk intah da Apollo an' fin' me en muh dressin' room." She closes her eyes, snuggles next to Porgy, overjoyed her time with Sportin' Life is finished. "It be hah'd heah at fust. I bin on de white dus' heaby, an' him force me tuh entuhtain his frien's. An' den I met a dansah, Josephine Bakah, an' many ob de Negro artists and writahs heah en Harlem, an' some ob der famous white frien's too. Josephine convince' me I hab tuh git out f'om undah Sportin' Life, an' so de fust t'ing I did war gib up cocaine."

Tears fall from Bess's eyes. "I caint imagine wuh would hab happen' ef I habn' met Josephine. Her gib me de idea tuh try out fo' Amateur Night at de Apollo, an' dat be how I got de chorus-line job der." She turns to Porgy. "Muh life war already gettin' bettah an' den yuh walk intah de Apollo."

Porgy wipes away her tears as Bess says, "I t'awt 'bout yuh an' Jonah all de time but I could nebbuh figga out a way tuh 'escape. Eb'ry time I wen' tuh sleep I dream 'bout yuh an' our son. Eben when I war awake too, yuh an' de baby came intah muh t'awts." A picture of Jonah floats into Bess's mind. "I caint wait tuh see our son an' hold he. Him hab prob'ly grown so much. I hope Clara an' Jake be lookin' down on we f'om hebbin an' guide we tuh bring he up like dey would hab demselves."

Bess stops abruptly in her reverie and guiltily remembers that she had abandoned Jonah. "Oh mah gawd! Who hab been tekin' care ob he all dis time?"

"Maria, ob course."

She gives a sigh of relief, "I be goin' tuh owe she eb'ryt'ing. Maria be a godsend."

Porgy's revelation that he is Mr. Goat Man, and that Sportin' Life is dead, has put an idea into her head. *I know how much it tuk fuh he tuh rescue me, so how kin I tell he wuh I wan' tuh say wid'out hurtin' his feelin's. I lub he so much.*

She takes Porgy's hand. "Do yuh like libin' en Harlem? It luks like yo' numbahs bid'ness be mekin' yuh a lot ob money, an' dis place be berry nice. Now dat I be use tuh it, I jis' lub it heah, an' muh new careah at de Apollo. An' I hab also met lots ob new frien's . . . could us stay heah?"

Porgy's mouth drops open and his eyes become wider. "Wuh! Wuh be yuh t'inkin', Bess? Yuh don' wan' tuh goin' back tuh Charleston? Wuh 'bout Jonah?"

"Us hab a bettah life heah. A bettah chance at survivin' an' a bettah future fuh he. Sho', eb'ryone der lub we, but us hab money now. Yuh hab a bid'ness, sort ob. I hab a careah. I don' t'ink it be de bes' t'ing, us goin' back. Us could git Maria tuh brin' de baby heah. Wuh ef her would like it heah an' wan' tuh stay?" Bess looks at Porgy but he doesn't reply. "Don' dis mek sense? Wuh do yuh t'ink?"

I wonda ef she be right. Do I really wan' tuh be goin' back tuh muh life as a beggah? I wuk so haa'd tuh mek a bid'ness, do I wan' tuh gib dat up? Do I wan' tuh raise Jonah en de Jim Crow Sout'? An' her seems so happy heah dancin' an' singin'.

Squeezing her hand, he says, "Yes, I t'ink us could try dat. Fust, I hab tuh figga out wuh be happen now wid Sportin' Life's terr'tory, an' den I will write Maria a lettah. When I heah back f'om she, I will send someone tuh git she an' de baby tuh come heah." Bess kisses Porgy on the cheek and claps in excitement. He caresses her and says, "I miss yuh boot'ful face so much." They embrace and renew their vows of love until they fall asleep in each other's arms.

CHAPTER THIRTY-FOUR

A few weeks later, on a beautiful Saturday morning, Porgy and Bess awaken in their sun-filled bedroom. They are watching a pair of blue jays on the window-sill. "Bess, luk. I t'ink dat bird be de same blue jay dat war outside muh jail cell windah en Charleston."

"The smallah one mebbe be de lady blue jay dat war on muh windah sill when I fust came tuh Harlem." She turns to Porgy with a sweet smile, her face radiant with love. "Dey mus' be heah tuh remind we dat blue jays mate fuh life." Their Saturday morning blue jay moment stretches into the early afternoon, until it is interrupted by the telephone.

Bess picks it up to answer, and after listening for a few minutes, she puts the phone back down. In an agitated voice she tells Porgy, "Dat war Mabel Lee f'om de chorus line. Dey wan' me ta come en now fuh a dance rehearsal. Her said Sidney Cohen prommus de theatre be goin' open ag'in soon. Her tol' me dat him war intendin' tuh fire me when him foun' out I war de reason fuh de disruption an' gun-fight. But her an' de othah dancahs convince he dat I be popular wid de audiences."

She puts her hand on Porgy's arm. "An'. . . heah's de bad news. Someone tol' she dat Mistah Big be still alive an' dat Sidney hab kick he an' his numbahs bid'ness out ob de Apollo."

"Oh muh gawd. Sportin' life be alive!? Dey say I hab kill he! I really t'awt I hab kill he an' I war happy 'bout dat. I war not worry 'bout gettin' caught cuz no one knows who Mistah. Goat Man be, an' us mek a clean 'scape. Now, I hab tuh worry 'bout he tryin' tuh git revenge."

After Bess leaves for the Apollo, Jonathan, William, and Timothy arrive at the apartment to check the day's winning number listed in the afternoon newspaper. Porgy tells them, "I jus' heah dat Mistah Big is not dead, so he must be lyin' low."

"So, what is we finna do about him now?" asks William, "Most of his runnahs gots signed up wit' us, so his business must of really dropped off. He probably is hurtin' bad."

Porgy agrees. "He is done fo' now. If it looks like he is tryin' ta get even, we gots ta be ready, so let's hire some mo' muscle ta protec' our runnahs. Also, I want bodyguards wit' Bess all da time when she is out of da apartment now dat she gone back ta performin' at da Apollo.

"One othah change. I am finna send fo' our son ta be brought ta New Yawk, an' I goin' ta spend mo' time at home when he get heah. Timothy, yo can run da office an' da bettin' slips an' cash at Smalls when I is not der. An' Jonathan an' William keep managin' da runnahs like always."

Timothy looks at Jonathan and William for their silent approval. "No problem Porgy fo' us gettin' mo' involved handlin' da game as long as yo is nearby in case trouble brews. It's Mistah Goat Man who da runnahs an' customahs trust."

"Don' worry, I am always finna be heah ta take care of things." With a broad grin, he adds. "Jus' ask Sam about dat. I hope he is gettin' his daily outin's in Central Paa'k." As Porgy's friends leave the apartment, he reminds them, "Don' fo'get t'night's party heah. Bess is lookin' forward ta seein' y'all."

CHAPTER THIRTY-FIVE

The sun is going down as the time for their party approaches. Bess is helping the maids to fill the ice buckets for champagne, and set the dinner table. The party is for their artist and writer friends who will soon be leaving for Paris.

Once the Paris-bound artists and writers learned how Mr. Big tried to keep Porgy from finding Bess, and attempted to kill him, they broke off their association with him. They were also moved by what Romare and Josephine told them about Bess's struggles and how she had gained a new sense of independence. It was also unbelievable to them how Porgy found Bess, and wonderful they had all become friends of the couple. Sadly, though, they told them it was now time for them to leave America and relocate to Paris.

Before their guests arrive, Porgy is in the office in his apartment with Jonathan and William, who have arrived early for the party. "Where is Timothy?" enquires Porgy.

William looks up from his paperwork, "He is ovah at Smalls finishin' up some details."

Bess hears voices in the hallway outside their apartment and a knock at the door. She leaves the maids to finish setting up and opens the door to invite in Langston, Josephine, Romare, Benny, Richmond, and Zora Neale. Porgy rolls his wheelchair into the living room, and he and Bess greet their guests, and introduce them to Jonathan and William.

"We is so sorry ta see y'all go, but we prepared a real Charleston-style dinnah so yo won' fo'get us. First yo' finna gots she-crab soup made wit' crabmeat, crab roe, sherry, an' plenty of heavy cream." Porgy motions for them to take seats at the dining room table and Bess continues, "Then fo' an appetizah der's Beaufort Boil."

They all nod their heads in knowing anticipation, except for Benny Carter. "Well, you all were from the South, but I was born and raised here in Harlem, so what is Beaufort Boil?"

She puts on a happy smile and mimes adding the ingredients into a gumbo pot. "Beaufort, South Carolina is wheah I is from. Dis dish is a combination of shrimp, sausage, corn, potatoes, an' Old Bay seasonin' served on grits."

Porgy proudly points to Bess. "An' then fo' da main course, Bess is goin' ta cook fo' y'all a dish our baby Jonah's Godmothah use ta prepare. It gots fried catfish, fried cabbage on good ol' Carolina rice, lima beans, an' pieces of sweet caw'nbread."

"Don' fo'get, fo' dessert, pralines," Bess adds.

Dinner conversation revolves around their friends' description of the Montmartre section in Paris where they are going to live. "Our house agent already thinks he has found apartments for us on a street called Rue de Clichy, near the famous Moulin Rouge," Zora Neale says.

On a somber note, Romare adds, "It looks like we are getting out of here just in time. You heard about that Negro kid, Lino Rivera, who was beaten up by those supposedly upstanding white citizens . . . at Kress' Five and Ten, right across the street from the Apollo Theater. "

"Yes, I heah about it as I was gettin' der fo' da first show."

Romare continues, "Well, the police did nothing, and that's what started the riot."

Richmond Barthé holds up the newspaper. "It says here ten thousand of our brothers and sisters took to the streets to protest.

Three of them were killed, one hundred twenty-five were arrested and more than a hundred were injured."

Zora Neale bows her head, and in a sorrowful voice says, "That's why we're going to get the hell out of here. Life in America won't be any better until white people change."

Langston Hughes closes his eyes momentarily to jog his memory. "That reminds me of the poem by my friend Claude McKay:

If we must die let it not be like hogs
Hunted and penned in an inglorious spot,
While around us bark the mad and hungry dogs,
Making their mock at our accursed lot."

"Lets jus' relax an' enjoy da wondah'ful meal Bess prepare fo' us. Mebbe someday it goin' ta change, an' we will see yo heah again, but fo' t'night, we finna celebrate our frien'ship wit' each othah. So, no more talk about depressin' things. "

Dinner is over, and they are enjoying their coffee and pralines. Bess, laughingly says, "I bet yo won' fin' dis kin' a cookin' in Paris." They all smile, and agree.

Suddenly, the front door flies open and Timothy rushes into the apartment. Jonathan and William jump up from the table, fearing that something is wrong. Porgy straightens up in his wheelchair and shouts, "What da hell is goin' on, Timothy?"

Running over to Porgy, Timothy yells. "We gots ta get yo out of heah, right away!"

"Fo' what?" asks Porgy. Everyone at the table is alarmed by Timothy's urgency, their faces frozen in fright.

He catches his breath and blurts out, "The cops is on der way heah ta arrest yo! Dey came lookin' fo' me at Smalls, but I gots away. I think they must gots somehow figured out yo is Mistah Goat Man, Porgy."

"I don' undahstan'. I pay dem a lot of money fo' protecshun an' secrecy. Da local beat cops git one thousand dollars a month ta ignore mah numbahs bid'ness. Dey is suppose ta tip me off if someone at headquartahs is plannin' a raid." Porgy's disposition remains calm. "Pastor Adam Clayton Powell, at da Abyssinian Baptist church tol' me he warn da chief of police not ta put us Negro numbahs bankahs out of bid'ness an' let da Italian Mafia take ovah. An' mah operation is too small ta be a serious problem fo' Dutch Schultz, da big numbahs bankah."

Bess is frightened and yells out, "Porgy! What if dey really come in an' . . ."

As she moves over to be next to Porgy, two uniformed policemen and a plain-clothes detective barge into the apartment. The guests are no strangers to police harassment and cautiously stand and move away from the table. Porgy holds Bess's hand to help calm her down.

The detective walks straight over to Porgy. "I have hyah a warrant for your arrest for the murder of a man named Crown, in Charleston, South Carolina. We have a signed statement from a witness who says he saw you do it."

The guests look at the detective, shocked expressions on their faces, finding it hard to believe Porgy could have killed someone. He recognizes the man walking toward him as Raymond Foster, the detective who arrested him back in Charleston for not identifying Crown's body. Porgy looks at him and whispers, "What?! I din't!" For a moment he thinks about reaching into the dining room sideboard drawer for the gun he took from Sportin' Life, but realizes that would be hopeless.

The policemen shoo all the guests in the apartment toward the doorway, "Everyone out! Move! Out!"

After their friends are gone, Bess and Porgy are the only ones left in the apartment. Bess shouts, "Detective! He din't do it!"

One of the officers hand-cuffs Porgy and Foster, ignoring Bess, says, "We will be takin' you back on the train to Charleston to stand trial."

"I din't murdah Crown. I din't murdah anyone!"

The police roll Porgy in his wheelchair out of the apartment as he screams. "Bess! Bess! I will be back. Wait fo' me! Ev'rythin' will be okay. I promise"

Bess tries to stop them from taking Porgy toward the elevator, "Porgy! Porgy! Please don' go!" She attempts to push her way into the elevator, but they shove her roughly away as the door closes. She falls to her knees wailing. "Oh mah gawd, Porgy. How could dey take yo away from me all da way back ta Charleston? How is I goin' ta survive wit'out yo?"

CHAPTER THIRTY-SIX

At the 30th precinct on West 151st Street, Porgy is booked, and then transported to the jail on Rikers Island to await the train ride to Charleston. The prison is in the middle of the East River and holds around 10,000 defendants awaiting trial. Porgy's cellmates have told him no one has ever escaped from there, so he doesn't think he can break out and get back to Bess.

It has been a week since Porgy's arrest and Jonathan has finally been able to track down the jail where Porgy was taken. On a grey and dismal day he and Bess have now made the trip to Rikers Island. They sign in at the visitor's desk and wait their turn to see Porgy. Only one visitor is allowed in at a time, and Jonathan goes first. Porgy is in prison garb and sits in his wheelchair behind the glass partition.

Porgy and Jonathan pick up the telephone receivers. "Sorry it took so long fo' us ta fin' out wheah yo was. I gots Bess some cash from da safe at Smalls, but she is very worried about yo. I tol' her ta stay out in da waitin' room until I talked ta yo first."

"Thanks fo' dat. T'day, dey let me talk ta a lawyah dat private investigator, Elijah Morrison, foun' fo' me. But, he say once a judge heah signs off, der is no way ta prevent dem from takin' me back ta Charleston."

"We all know yo' innocent an' dat yo will be back soon. Howevah, soon as our runnahs foun' out yo was arrested, a lot of them started ta join back wit' Mistah Big's operation. Da runnahs an' customahs stood by us cuz of yo."

We is hurtin', an' Mistah Smalls say we need ta fin' anotha place ta run da bid'ness. He's worry da cops will shut his club down. While yo is gone, we will try ta keep it going, but it will be tough."

Porgy isn't concerned about the prospect of starting all over again when he returns to Harlem. "Jonathan, don' worry, jus' do da best yo can. An', please keep an eye on Bess." Jonathan gets up and signals the guard to let him out so that Bess can come into the room.

Porgy is pained, because he can tell she has been crying from the redness in her eyes. "Bess, dis too will pass. I goin' come back heah."

She holds the receiver with a shaking hand, and speaks into it with a trembling voice. "I lub yuh so much an' I be 'fraid ob wuh dey goin' tuh do tuh yuh back en Charleston. Dat Charleston detective hate eb'ryone en Catfish Row."

Porgy puts on the best face he can. "Now dat I foun' yuh nuttin' goin' tuh stop me f'om bein' wid yuh. I will write tuh tell yuh when I be back." With that the guard comes in and tells them their visiting time is up. They blow kisses and then they are separated.

The guard wheels Porgy out of the visitor's room and the steel door closes behind him. *I hope her kin stay strong ontel dis be ober. Her luks an' sounds depress'. I be worry 'bout she.* In the waiting room Jonathan tries his best to console Bess, and they depart for the ride back to Harlem. When they arrive at her apartment, she looks around, defeated. *How kin I go on wid'out Porgy?*

With the extradition papers approved by the judge, Porgy is now released into the custody of Detective Foster. The New York police bring a car around to the jail to transport them to Penn Station for the fifteen-hour trip to Charleston. They have given him back only his old crutches because the detective didn't want to deal with putting the heavy wheelchair onto the train. As the people around them move along the platform, they stare at Porgy as he struggles to board.

The train moves off after all the passengers have boarded and their luggage has been loaded by the porters. Porgy sits across from Foster, staring out the window, thoughts of Bess occupying his mind. The detective notices the sad look in Porgy's eyes and says menacingly, "You're gonna have a long time to think on the trip 'bout what we do to murderers in Charleston." He doesn't respond to Foster's taunts as he watches Penn Station fade into the distance. *Is dey goin' heng me? Be der ennyone en Charleston who kin help me?*

Four hours later, they reach Washington, D.C. The detective grabs Porgy by the arm and pulls him roughly out of his seat. They must switch train cars because the remainder of the trip is through the South, in cars set up with segregated sections. Once they are on the new train, Foster pushes him onto a hard seat behind a screen that separates the Negro section of the car. Satisfied his prisoner is secure, he moves forward to sit in the white section.

Porgy tries to figure out how he could somehow sneak off the train at one of the stops and escape, but he has been chained to the seat, and he gives up that idea. He watches the train's doors close and his hopes of freedom vanish. Foster smiles at Porgy's defeated appearance.

The next day they arrive at Union Station in Charleston. Porgy is taken off the train and hobbles on his crutches out to the street with Raymond Foster by his side. The Charleston police are there waiting for them, and he is driven through the town in a horse-drawn jail cart, which resembles a circus cage on wheels. There was an article about the upcoming murder trial in *The Post and Courier*, so many citizens of Catfish Row have come out to watch the arrival of the train.

Maria spots Porgy, and she cries out, "Oh no Porgy. Wuh now?!" He makes eye contact with her through the bars of the cart, but doesn't know what to shout out to her. In his mind he is fearful and thinks this is the beginning of the end.

Porgy is transported to the Old Charleston jail where he is removed from the cart. It is the same jail that he was in before. Even though Porgy is crippled, as an added injustice to Negro prisoners, his hands and feet have been manacled. The jailers part carry and part drag him up to the third floor, and he winces in pain as his knees and shins bang against the edge of each step.

The white inmates in the surrounding cells taunt Porgy. "Hey cripple! What didja do? Try to steal someone's legs? Hey boy! We gonna tear you up!"

Dese buckruh trash nebbuh change. Dey scream da same t'ings at me de las' time I bin en heah. As Porgy is shoved into a cell, he questions the guard, "Wheah be Bookah? Caint I be en a cell wid Bookah like befo'?"

Removing the manacles and locking the door, the guard laughs, "That nigger was hanged right after you left." The bile rising in his throat, Porgy is frightened practically out of his skin, and thinks, *Gawd, jis' fuh stealin' chickens! Wuh be dey goin' tuh do tuh me? How will I ebbuh git out ob dis mess?* He lies on his cot and prays, "Gawd please mek de trial verdic' go muh way."

"I need tuh call muh lawyah, Mistah Archdale! I need tuh contact muh lawyah!" Laughing cruelly, the jailers ignore him and continue to walk away. Porgy tries again, "I hab tuh call muh lawyah!" Porgy's voice is drowned out by the noise and yelling of the other prisoners. He looks around in despair at the cage he is now in. His cry echoes down the hall. "Bess!"

CHAPTER THIRTY-SEVEN

In the new office Sportin' Life has set up, he is meeting with Joshua. "My friends in the police department told me Mr. Goat Man was arrested and sent to Charleston to stand trial for the murder of some guy back there. Now with him out of the picture, and thanks to you and our old runners, we have won back almost all the business we lost." Timothy had been right, that without Porgy their numbers business would not last, especially after Ed Smalls heard about what happened at the Apollo Theater, and kicked them out.

With his numbers business now recovered, Sportin' Life has devised a plan to get Bess back, and is now ready to put it into action. She was his prized possession and it bruised his ego when Porgy took her away. Now that Bess's bodyguards are gone, he is able to take the elevator up to Porgy and Bess's apartment and ring the bell. Through the speaker he tells one of the maids he is an old friend of Bess's and sweet-talks her into opening the door to let him in.

Sportin' Life enters the apartment and there, curled up in a chair in the corner, is a totally despondent Bess. She is wearing a drab grey dress. Her usually beautiful hair is in disarray and with no make-up on, she appears very fragile. Alarmed, she looks up, startled. Sportin' Life is standing in the doorway, smiling at her.

"What is yo doin' heah?" He doesn't move, and stands there as Bess moans, "Why is yo heeeeah?"

He slowly approaches her and says in a deceptively sympathetic tone, "I heard on the street the police arrested Porgy, and he was taken back to Charleston. I came to check on you and see if you were okay."

Hoping he will have an answer, Bess's blood-shot eyes gaze up at him. "Do yo know who tol' da police dat he kill Crown, an' how dey could fin' him?"

Inching closer to Bess, he says, "No, I don't. Maybe it was someone in Catfish Row who lost to Porgy at craps and wanted to get even. The police were probably happy to pin it on Porgy and close the case."

Bess jerks her head away, angry that he had the nerve to come to her apartment. "Okay, yo check on me. I is fine now. Jus' get out! I don' wan' tuh be aroun' yo anymo', not aftuh yo try ta kill Porgy."

Sportin' Life kneels down next to her. "It was just a big misunderstanding between me and Porgy, and it's all in the past. I came to console you, that's all. He can't take care of you anymore, Bess. Look at him. He's always in jail. Come on. Come back to my apartment, to your real home."

Curling tighter in the chair, Bess whispers, "Jus' go away."

In a sing-songy voice Sportin' Life cajoles, "I have something to make you feel better." Bess covers her face with her hands in total despair, wondering if she will ever see Porgy again. Reluctantly, she takes the cocaine, puts three lines on the table next to her chair and sniffs them all in. She instantly goes into a powerful high, her brain completely fogged.

This is a sensation she hasn't had since she quit months ago, and it hits her hard. Sportin' Life has a "Cheshire Cat" smile on his face and helps her out of her chair. He gently leads her out of the apartment where she had been living so happily with Porgy.

Since returning to Sportin' Life's apartment, Bess has hardly noticed the luxurious surroundings. Most of her days are spent high on cocaine which puts her mind into a pain-free muddle. She only picks at her food and doesn't give her hair or makeup the attention it needs. The maids keep their distance, and she meanders from window to window gazing listlessly at nothing. She dwells dispiritedly on how wonderful the short time she had with Porgy was and how happy they were before he was taken away.

On a typical dismal morning, Bess is sitting her bedroom, staring at the windowsill, hoping the blue jay will find her and bring good news. To add to her depression, she is no longer dancing at the Apollo Theater. Mabel Lee had called her and said, "Brace your self for a shock, Honey. Sidney Cohen is dead. He had a sudden heart attack. The Apollo has new owners, and they are going to do a variety show and no chorus line. We are out of a job."

After the call, Bess's mental state declined even further. *Wid'out muh careah an' muh frien's I will jis' sink back tuh muh ol' life wid Sportin' Life an' nebbuh 'scape.*

While looking out the window, she becomes aware of voices in the living room. Turning toward the bedroom doorway, she sees Josephine Baker talking to Sportin' Life, suitcases sitting next to her. Bess walks in, and Josephine smiles and hugs her.

"What's goin' on, I t'awt y'all hab already left fo' Paris?" All of Sportin' Life's artist and writer friends had distanced themselves from him once they learned how he had tried to kill Porgy. They came to realize he was no better than the cops who were killing people in Harlem. His old friends were even angrier with him now that he had coerced Bess back into her former life. Josephine was angry too, but she depended on Sportin' Life for happy dust.

She grasps Bess's hands. "We are leaving for Paris today. I came here to try to convince your man to let us take you there with us. I can help you find a job singing and dancing just like me."

"Are yo really shuh things will be bettah der?" *Could I get away an' do dat too?*

"Yes, after the latest riots, it's not safe here in Harlem either. We have to get out."

Bess is in an almost continual cocaine haze, and Sportin' Life has gotten her back into doing sexual favors for his friends and customers. She now believes Sportin' Life is right, that she will never see Porgy again. She pleads with him. "Please, I wan' ta get out of heah. Please." Bess really wants to leave behind the life she has been forced into, but she doesn't have the will to break free.

Sportin' Life shakes his head, "No."

Bess's shoulders droop; she is looking at the floor and can't bring herself to look into Josephine's eyes. She thinks this is her last chance to escape. Josephine picks up her suitcases and heads to the front door. Taking hold of Bess's arms, she gives them a little shake. "If you ever make it out of here, come find me in Paris." With another shake, "Find me. Promise me."

Tears rolling down her cheeks, Bess says, "I promise."

Josephine hugs her one last time and, kisses her on the cheek. "Remember what I told you. Don't let your life here keep you stuck in this cage. Do something." Bess takes a step toward Josephine but Sportin' Life quickly moves between the two women, snarling, "Goodbye, Josephine," and closes the door.

CHAPTER THIRTY-EIGHT

Bess's artist and writer friends have moved to Paris, and she has also lost contact with her fellow dancers from the Apollo Theater. Completely alone again, and without dancing and Josephine's support, she wanders listlessly around the apartment all day. The only change to her sad days is the anguish that overtakes her by the occasional "servicing" of one of Sportin' Life's customers or friends. She has never understood why Sportin' Life continues to pimp her out since she is sure he no longer needs the money.

With the passing weeks, her renewed cocaine addiction keeps Bess's mind in a muddle, and she is not able to figure out what to do. On one ordinary afternoon, Bess is sitting on her bed in a confused daze, and begins talking out loud to herself. "Porgy. I miss yuh . . . why habn' I heah f'om yuh? . . . Wuh should I do? . . . Oh, I know . . . I will write an' tell yuh I be comin' tuh git yuh an' Jonah, an' us will go back tuh our room en Catfish Row. I prommus."

The day's happy dust is starting to wear off and Bess's whole body is chilled. She slides off the bed, puts a robe on over her dress, and walks into Sportin' Life's office. She rummages through the drawers of his desk looking for paper, pen and ink, and an envelope.

On the desk she notices the unopened mail placed there by the maid. The letter on top is addressed to Sportin' Life with Detective Raymond Foster at the Charleston police station as the return address. Bess is curious as to why Sportin'Life would be receiving a letter from Foster, and thinks it might contain some news about Porgy. She picks up a letter opener and slits open the envelope. She reads, "Thank you for your help," and sees the detective's signature at the bottom.

As Bess is reading the detective's letter, she hears the door to the apartment open. Sportin' Life shouts, puzzled, "Who left the door to my office open?" He walks through the doorway and sees her standing next to his desk.

Bess holds up the letter and shouts, "Yo gots Porgy arrested, din't yo!"

He lets out a surprised laugh. "Yeah, I did. Why not? Porgy tried to ruin my numbers business, and somebody killed Crown, so I figured the police would be happy to arrest anyone if they had a witness. With Porgy out of the way, I got my numbers business back."

Glaring at him, her fury explodes. "Yo' a liar! I'm finna go ta Charleston ta tell da police yo is lyin' about seein' Porgy kill Crown. Yo not even in Catfish Row when he was kill cuz eb'ryone knows Maria chase yo out long befo' dat."

His face contorted in anger, Sportin' Life kicks the office door shut, strides over to the desk and grabs Bess by the arms. She tries to twist out of his grip, but he is too strong for her. "You think you can go to Charleston all by yourself? You have no money. You have nothing but me!"

"Yeah, cuz yo set it up dat way! Dat's da way yo want' it! Not anymo', I'm leavin'!" She tries to pull away from him, but he continues to hold on tightly, shaking her hard. Bess, frightened, begins to cry, thinking he could seriously hurt her.

"You aren't going anywhere! I am not going to go to jail for perjury! You're not leaving me!" He keeps on shaking her violently, determined to scare her out of going to the police.

She struggles against Sportin' Life's grip, stamping her feet and kicking him. "Yo' evil! I hate yo! If yo don' let me go, I will scream an' da maid will heah. I'm leavin'! I hope dey arrest yo fo' lyin'. I hope yo rot in hell!" Sportin' Life, his heart now pounding, tightens his hold and won't let her go. He pushes her back hard onto the desk, sending the day's mail flying. She grimaces in agony as her head hits the desk lamp, making her dizzy.

It suddenly dawns on Sportin' Life that he must prevent Bess from leaving, at all costs, and puts his hands around her neck and begins to squeeze. Bess's arms, now free, begin to flail at him, scratching his arms and his face. Grunting in pain, he continues the pressure on her neck. In a savage whisper he says, "You have left me no choice, I have to kill you."

Bess is fighting to breathe and is slowly losing consciousness. She frantically gropes around the desk for something with which to defend herself, and finds the letter opener. He sees her reach for it, and takes one hand off her neck to keep her from grasping it. But, in the few seconds his hand is off her neck she is able to take a deep breath and secure her grip on the letter opener. As Sportin' Life tries to regain his strangle-hold on her, Bess swings her arm up with all her strength and plunges the letter opener into his neck. His hands stop squeezing her throat, and he backs away and falls to the floor. Blood is spurting out of his neck, and he gasps for air but cannot take in a breath. He finally stops moving, lying there, silently, in a pool of blood.

Sprawled on her back on the desk, Bess is almost as lifeless as Sportin' Life. Lifting herself up, she stares at the scene before her. She can't believe what she has done. She nudges Sportin' Life's leg. Nothing. She kicks him to see if he moves. Nothing, again. "Sportin' Life? Sportin' Life get up!" His hands jerk wildly and he takes one final gasp. His eyes are frozen in their gaze at Bess, and she jumps back in horror.

Bess kneels down on the floor and crawls over to him crying. "Oh mah gawd! Oh mah gawd! What hab I done?" The sight of the blood covering the front of her robe and arms sends her into a deeper panic as the severity of the moment fully registers. "I din't mean tuh, him mek me do it," she tells herself over and over as Sportin' Life's dead body continues to bleed on the floor.

Bess realizes she must think fast. Removing her bloody robe, she uses it to wipe off her arms as best she can, and drops it on the floor next to the body. She opens the office door leading to the living room and, as calmly as possible, walks out, closing the door after her. *I hab tuh keep muh voice calm so de maid won' t'ink somet'ing be wrong.* She calls to the maid who is in the kitchen, "Viola, Mistah Big is busy in his office an' does not wan' ta be disturb'. He'll come out an' gots dinnah latah."

Trying not to make any noise, Bess enters the bathroom adjacent to her bedroom, takes off her clothes, and steps into the shower to wash all the blood off. Still shaken from her ordeal, she can't believe how it all really happened, and tries to concentrate on scrubbing herself clean. Once she has washed all the blood away, she steps out of the shower, towels herself dry and goes back into the bedroom.

In a very few hours, Bess is sure Viola will discover Sportin' Life's body and call the police. She knows she must get away quickly because it won't take the police very long to figure out who killed Sportin'Life, and arrest her, and she will never get to Charleston. She must tell the police in Charleston Maria can prove Sportin' Life wasn't in Catfish Row when Crown was killed, and he lied about seeing Porgy kill him.

Bess chooses a non-descript cotton house dress and low-heeled Oxfords from the closet. She hopes this outfit will be comfortable to wear for the long trip to Charleston, and not draw any attention to her. Quickly packing additional clothing into two suitcases, her escape plan becomes clear.

She takes a picture off the wall revealing the bedroom safe. She used to watch Sportin' Life open this safe, and without him knowing it, had copied the combination onto a piece of paper, which she now retrieves from her vanity. Bess opens the safe and is astonished to discover how large a quantity of cash is inside. She fills her purse and one of the suitcases with as much of the money as they will hold. With great willpower, she leaves the cocaine in the safe. In her closet she finds the rolled-up painting Romare did of her and places it in the other suitcase. The picture represented to her the awakening of her new life.

It is one of the maid's days off, so she only needs to leave the apartment without Viola seeing the suitcases. Checking to make sure the maid is still in the kitchen, she softly opens the front door and puts them into the hall. She returns to the apartment and peers into the office one more time. Sportin' Life lies there alone, dead and cold. *I be glad him deat'. Him caint rule muh life ennymo'. I goin' tuh Charleston tuh sabe muh Porgy.*

At the doorway to the kitchen, she tells Viola, "I is goin' out fo' a li'l while. Remember, don' disturb Mistah Big." Her nerves are now steady, and she closes the apartment door behind her, never looking back.

Bess is firm in her conviction she must go to Charleston to help free Porgy from jail, even if they find out she killed Sportin' Life and arrest her. She remembers Jonathan told her the detective took Porgy on a train from Penn Station to Charleston. Once in the lobby of the apartment building, she tells the doorman to take her suitcases to the curb and hail a taxi. She tells the driver to take her to Penn station.

At Penn Station, she buys a ticket and finds her way to the departure track, hoping no one will remember seeing a lone Negro woman board a train to Charleston. Once on the train she now realizes that a chapter in her life has ended for good. Calmed down from her ordeal, she watches the New York City skyline fade into the distance as the train makes its way south.

CHAPTER THIRTY-NINE

Alan Archdale received word about Porgy's arrest from the servants at the Rutledge estate and decided to go see Porgy in jail. His arrival at the jailhouse surprises Henry Jeanes, the head of the South Carolina Law Enforcement Division. Jeanes is a man in his forties who had risen quickly in South Carolina's legal system. He was one of the few white officials friendly to the Negro community and had helped prosecute many civil rights violations by the Ku Klux Klan.

"Well, hello Alan, not used to seeing fancy corporate lawyers like you here."

Archdale shakes his hand. "Yes, you're right. I'm here to defend the beggar Porgy who was accused of murdering another Negro in Catfish Row. Perhaps you remember seeing Porgy in his goat cart over the years."

"Yes, I remember him. Hard to believe he could kill someone. Good luck, I hope you get a sympathetic judge and jury. At least he didn't kill a white citizen or you'd have no chance."

Archdale asks, "And what brings you over to our neck of the woods from Columbia?"

Henry Jeanes has an exasperated expression on his face. "Do you remember that Greene boy who got lynched over in Walhalla in Oconee County? Well, we arrested the perpetrators, but I am trying to move the case to Charleston. No way could we obtain a conviction in Oconee County where the Klan is so powerful. Hope it goes well for Porgy."

Archdale goes up to the third floor to meet with Porgy. He reminds Porgy the prosecutor claims to have a signed statement from a witness who says he saw Porgy kill Crown. "Unless we can debunk that witness's testimony, or come up with evidence showing he died some other way, you are going to be convicted of murder."

Porgy tells Archdale, "Well, it was a dark night, so I wondah, could da witness only think it was me killin' him. If yo go talk ta Maria an' da othah people who live in Catfish Row, maybe they can think of some otha way Crown might gots died." The lawyer thinks it will be hard to debunk the witness, but he agrees to set up a meeting with the citizens of Catfish Row to come up with alternative ideas about Crown's death.

A few days later, Alan Archdale is sitting on a bench in Washington Square Park across the street from the courthouse. He is wearing glasses and is writing some notes in his legal pad. Freshly mowed grass surrounds the benches and a flower-lined pathway leads to a fountain. The park is serene and beautiful with blooming pink azaleas and Spanish moss hanging off ancient live oak trees. People stroll through just for their enjoyment, or to take a break from the business they are conducting at City Hall or in the courthouse across the way.

Maria, along with Peter and Mingo, residents of Catfish Row, walk together down the pathway to meet Alan Archdale, as Porgy had suggested. Peter is an elderly, grizzled Negro denizen of Catfish Row, much respected for his wisdom and common sense. He drives a horse-drawn wagon and, years ago, his friends at the Snee Farm prevailed upon him to relocate Porgy from there to Charleston. Before Porgy built his cart and found Sam the goat, Peter would also drive him around the city.

Peter was the one who originally told the police he saw Crown kill Robbins during the craps game, and he was initially held as a material witness in the case. He was indebted to Alan Archdale, who got him released from custody, and would do anything to help get his friend Porgy acquitted.

The other resident whom Maria asked to come along is Mingo, a deck-hand on the ferry that plies the waters between Charleston and Ediwander Island. Ediwander, one of a hundred Sea Islands is sparsely inhabited. Its terrain is mainly salt marshes and live oak forests. It has two light houses and islanders say there are gold-laden Spanish galleons sunk off its beaches.

Mingo owes Porgy a favor from the time when Bess was in a coma with a high fever. Porgy had paid him to buy a "spell" to break the fever from Lody, the voodoo conjurer on Ediwander. Lody lived in the former plantation slave quarters in a shack painted 'haint blue,' a color she believed evil ghosts mistake for the sky, and move on by. Instead of going to see Lody, Mingo spent the money on corn liquor, got drunk, and never bought the spell. Bess did recover, and although Porgy never found out it wasn't the "spell" that cured her, Mingo felt guilty.

Alan Archdale has also brought along Simon Frasier, a local Negro attorney, who can help him better understand the conversation with the Gullah-speaking townspeople. Frasier is actually not licensed by the State of South Carolina, but the court lets him handle cases for the people who live in Catfish Row. Frasier looks upon the white lawyer as his savior since he once kept him from being jailed for granting divorces, which are not legal in South Carolina.

The three denizens reach the lawyers' park bench and Maria says, "Mistah Archdale?"

The lawyer sets aside his notes and stands to greet them. "Hello. Yes, I'm Archdale. How did you know?"

Maria laughs. "Yo de only white man sittin' next tuh a Negro man in de paa'k."

Archdale and Simon Frasier smile and shake the hands of Maria and her friends. They all walk over to a bench where there is a table and take seats. Frasier sits across from them and takes out a file from a well-weathered briefcase. "Okay, leh we b'gin. De trial be t'morrah an' 'less us come up wid somethin' tuh show Porgy din't kill Crown, he will heng."

With tears streaming down her face, Maria says, "Us caint leh dat happ'n, him hab a son an' wife."

Archdale nods his head in agreement. "Yes. That's why we're all here. All right, you all are possible witnesses in this trial, and we need to come up with a compelling story about why Porgy is not guilty of murdering Crown."

Maria begins. "I could tell de jury dat mebbe someone bin chasin' aftuh he, tryin' tuh capcha he fuh de murdah ob Robbins, Serena husbin'. Us could say dat w'ile him bin runnin', him fell on de stevedore hook at de ha'bah."

Archdale asks, "Okay. Anyone else?"

Peter speaks up next. "I could say dat Crown try tuh steal one ob muh hawses dat pull muh waggin, but him bin so drunk him fell off ontah muh blacksmith axe an' die."

Mingo, the boat deck-hand, breaks in. "No, no, no. Leh's say dat him git a bad potion f'om Lody, de voodoo conjura woman on Ediwander Island, an' him go crazy an' stab heself ta deat'!"

Alan Archdale understands that tradition and history in Charleston lean heavily toward voodoo, and superstitious beliefs to justify the way bad people should be punished. Therefore, he realizes why Maria, Peter, and Mingo have come up with these fanciful scenarios about how Crown could have died.

With a kindly smile, he shakes his head at the stories they came up with. "No, what I meant by a 'compelling story' was something backed up by new evidence, or witnesses who may have known something about how Crown might have died. Your ideas are too unbelievable. They sound like something out of a storybook, and won't stand up in court."

Maria is dejected but takes heart when she hears the bells at the church across the street ring through the park. "Kin us goin' intah dat chu'ch an' pray fuh Porgy? Fuh a miracle?"

Archdale looks toward the church and smiles. "Of course we can," and they all walk over to St. Michael's Episcopal Church. It is on the other side of Washington Park, directly across from the jail and courthouse.

St. Michael's is one of the few white churches in Charleston that allow Negro parishioners inside. Since its establishment in America the Church of England had always been a place embracing all people, without respect to race. In 1919, it was the first church to adopt an anti-lynching resolution. Alan Archdale is a member of the church's Standing Committee, and helped draft the resolution.

Entering the church, Maria and her friends are struck by how beautiful it is. The brown wood-paneled interior is warm and welcoming. Archdale turns to Porgy's friends and points to St. Michael's north wall. "Look up there at that beautiful stained glass window. It was installed there in 1898, and the design in the window is called 'Easter Morning.' Maybe there's a message of hope there for our friend Porgy."

The Catfish Row residents and Archdale walk toward the altar, and Maria and her friends kneel in the pews. They each begin their own prayers for Porgy's release, hoping for a miracle at the trial in the morning. Archdale watches them, and while a believer in the power of prayer, he doesn't think it alone will help Porgy.

As Maria is getting ready to leave the church, she says to Archdale. "I jis' 'membuh somet'ing 'bout de night Crown git dead." After listening to her, Archdale and Frasier exchange knowing looks, and realize they might now have a plan for the trial that could free Porgy.

CHAPTER FORTY

Porgy has been transferred to a cell in the basement of the Charleston County Courthouse the evening before the trial. The Courthouse is on Broad Street at the southwest corner of Washington Park. It is a cream-colored three story brick structure with four columns rising from above the entrance to the roof. Negroes who see the building are intimidated because it represents the oppressive Jim Crow laws.

The walls in the cell are painted grey, and it is very cold and damp. Porgy sits in the corner on a cot, oblivious to his surroundings, worrying more about Bess and Jonah than himself. *Ef dey heng me, how will her fin' out an' git back heah tuh Jonah? Oh gawd, wuh ef Sportin' Life fin' she an' gits she back?*

His jailers would not give him any writing materials, so he had Alan Archdale write her at the address of their apartment in Harlem. But, he did not get any letter back because Bess had already moved out, and was back living with Sportin' Life. She had not left a forwarding address. Of course, Porgy was not aware of that.

A police officer escorts Simon Frasier to Porgy's cell, and turns to him. "You have fifteen minutes," and walks away. Porgy sees Frasier approach and makes his way to the bars on his knees. Frasier bends down to be at eye level with him.

"Hi, Porgy, Mistah Archdale ax muh tuh help wid yo defense. How yuh doin' en heah? Yo eatin'?"

"I caint eat. Too nerbus 'bout t'morrah. So, wuh de verdict goin' tuh be? Will I goin' tuh heng t'morrah?"

Simon Frasier smiles. "I goin' tuh mek sho' dat don' happ'n. Dat wuh Mistah Archdale an' me be wuk'n on fuh yuh." Frasier lowers his voice and says, "Now, listen careful tuh wuh Mistah Archdale an' me wan' yuh tuh do at de trial."

Porgy listens quietly and without comment until Simon Frasier is finished. He considers what he has heard, and asks, "I onduhstan', but wuh 'bout de jury?"

"Us won' know 'til t'morrah. Us Black, 'membuh? Us git wuh us git."

Porgy stands with the aid of his crutches and hobbles back to his cot. "It figga's."

Simon raises himself up. "Don' gib up hope an' 'membuh wuh I tol' yuh tuh do. Yuh hab a son tuh git home tuh"

The officer walks over to Simon and taps him on the shoulder, "Time's up."

"I see yuh up der," and walks off with the police officer and out of the basement.

Now left alone, Porgy sets aside his crutches and kneels next to the cot and prays. "Gawd, please mek dis jury fin' me inn'cent. It be de only way fuh me tuh git back tuh Bess an' Jonah."

CHAPTER FORTY-ONE

On the morning of the trial, Porgy is brought upstairs from the holding cell in the basement. People who want to attend are gathering at the entrance to the courthouse. Maria catches up to Simon Frasier as he arrives, and says, "Jis' tuh leh yuh know, I hiya'd Doctah Buzzard fuh de trial. Him be well-known en dis courthouse, an' him goin' sit en durin' de trial. Yuh will know he cuz him be chewin' a root an' keep him purple sunglass on. Us collec' money tuh pay'um tuh sway de jury usin' Gullah voodoo."

"Jis' mek shuh him don' disrup' de proceedin's, okay?"

Porgy is taken into the defendants' waiting room outside the courtroom and ordered to stand and wait. He is nervous and rocks back and forth on his crutches. His breathing is short and shallow, but, at the same time, his confidence is sustained by the trust he has in his lawyers.

The courtroom is filling up quickly. There hasn't been a murder trial like this in a long time. The room has a brown railing with white spindles dividing the spectators from the lawyers, witnesses and defendants. An elegant brass chandelier hangs from the ceiling, and there is a fireplace built into one wall from the days before central heating. The judge's bench sits on a higher level and is flanked by two large draped windows.

White spectators have the seats downstairs, and Negroes must sit in the balcony. Simon Frasier and Alan Archdale have taken their seats at a table in front of the railing, at one side, and are going over their notes. On the other side, the prosecutor, Frank A. Mcleod, and his partner sit at a similar table discussing their opening statement. Simon turns around to view the crowd and sees Maria is upstairs with Porgy and Bess's baby. She nervously smiles at him, and under his breath says to her, "It goin' tuh be okay."

The courtroom is noisy, but the chatter dies down immediately when two officers escort Porgy on his crutches into the courtroom and seat him next to Simon. Everyone's eyes are on Porgy, who looks up and spots his son with Maria. He blows a kiss to Jonah and Maria, and then listens to Frasier who leans over. "Okay. 'Membuh eb'ryt'ing us talk 'bout." Porgy nods his head.

The gallery is hushed as the jury members enter and take their seats. Every person on the jury is white. Frasier is upset about this, but not surprised. The Negroes in the balcony sound a collective and anguished sigh. Porgy notices one member of the jury staring at him intently. He recognizes him as Osgood Hamlin, the owner of the Snee Plantation, the farm where his legs had been broken. Porgy wonders if Hamlin thinks he had something to do with his son losing his legs in the cotton gin "accident." Porgy thinks he's doomed.

The bailiff walks in to announce the entrance of the judge, and yells out, "All rise! Court is now in session. Presidin' is the honorable Judge J.C. Klugh. The Court of General Sessions will now hyah the case of Charleston County versus the beggah known as Porgy, charged with the murder of the stevedore known as Crown."

J.C. Klugh enters the courtroom and receives knowing murmurs from the public in attendance. Archdale turns to Frasier and whispers. "We are up against a very tough judge, and are in for a fight."

Every Negro defendant was terrified of getting Klugh for their trial because of the Franklin murder case. Pink Franklin, a Negro, shot and killed a sheriff who had come to arrest him for violating the Peonage Laws. Franklin's lawyers claimed it was self-defense and that, in addition, impaneling an all-white jury was unconstitutional. Judge Klugh ruled against Franklin and sentenced him to be hanged. Franklin appealed to the U.S. Supreme court but it was denied. A semblance of justice did prevail when his sentence was ultimately commuted to life, and he was paroled a few years later.

Judge Klugh steps up to the bench and takes his seat. He surveys the filled courtroom, hoping the trial will be over quickly, as he feels it is a waste of his time. "You may all be seated." While everyone is taking their seats, the bailiff hands Judge Klugh the Grand Jury's indictment, which he skims through quickly and repeats the bailiff's announcement. "This court is presiding over the case of Charleston County versus Porgy for the murder of Crown. The trial will begin with any concerns, motions or statements from the prosecutor or the defense attorney."

Frasier immediately stands up to address the judge. "Yuh honnuh, muh client an' me be concern' wid de all buckruh, I means all white, composition ob de jury. Us b'lieb Negroes bin 'scluded an' de jury bin chose delib'rately tuh be bias' agains' muh client."

Klugh looks at the jury and then back at Frasier. "Are you saying that because these twelve jurors are all of the white race they can't render an honest judgment?"

"No, but . . ." Frasier tries to speak but the judge interrupts.

"If the defendant did not commit the murder he is charged with, then why should he be worried about the composition of the jury?"

Frasier is trying not to show his frustration with the judge. At this point Alan Archdale gets up from his seat. "Your Honor, we just want a fair trial. The defense moves to have this jury disqualified based on the Code of Civil Procedure, Title 8, Chapter 3, Article 1, Section 599. As you know, this section asserts the jury pool must be representative of the community and should not exclude anyone because of their race or gender. We believe this jury, being all white, is not representative. It may therefore have some prejudice or bias against my client, just because he is a Negro. Therefore, we request a new jury, including Negroes, should be impaneled."

Judge Klugh exclaims, "A fair trial is what you want and a fair trial is what you're going to get. In this court room, only registered voters can be part of the jury pool. It's my understanding there aren't any Negroes here in this county on the voter rolls. Am I correct?"

Archdale bites his lip. He thinks for a moment about reminding the court that Negroes are kept from voting because of onerous literacy tests and restrictive property ownership requirements. But, he holds back because he doesn't want to find himself on the wrong side of Klugh. Instead, he nods his head. "Yes, your honor. But, as you well know, they are not on the voter rolls through no fault of their own."

Judge Klugh laughs and, with a malicious smirk, points to the voodoo root "doctor" in the balcony. Looking out at the galley, he says sarcastically, "Your client shouldn't worry about the jury anyway, because Dr. Buzzard will spook them and get him acquitted!" The whites in the courtroom and the jurors burst out laughing.

"Motion to have a reselection of the jury is denied." Klugh bangs his gavel as Frasier and Archdale take their seats. "Alright, let's start these proceedings. Prosecution, please call your first witness to the stand."

Frank A. Mcleod, the prosecutor, stands up. "Your honor, we have only one witness. We call Detective Raymond Foster to the stand." Foster leaves his seat in the gallery and walks toward the witness box.

Porgy leans over to Archdale. "Dat be de detective who 'rrest me when I wouldn' 'dentify Crown body, an' de same one who 'rrested me en New Yawk an' brin' me back tuh Charleston."

Mcleod starts questioning Foster and the trial officially begins. "Detective, you were involved with Porgy's detainment on contempt of court charges after he refused to identify the body after Crown was killed, correct?"

"Yessuh. That's correct."

"And you arrested Porgy as well when he escaped from Charleston to New York?"

"Objekshun yo' honnuh!" Frasier yells. "Muh client did not 'scape tuh New Yawk. He bin out on bail an' jis' temporarily lef' de jurisdiction."

"Okay, a minor difference, but I will sustain the objection," Judge Klugh says. Porgy looks at the Judge, surprised at this unexpected little victory.

The prosecutor clears his throat. "I'll rephrase, your honor. Were you the one who arrested Porgy in New York, and brought him to Charleston?"

"That's correct," Detective Foster states as he stares at Porgy.

"Would you please tell the jury what happened at the time you investigated the murder of Crown and Porgy refused to identify his body here in Charleston?"

Foster begins to go over the events that took place when he interrogated Porgy the first time. "At the harbah where they foun' Crown's body, the coroner showed me his death had been caused by a chest wound. After furthah examination, we discovered the victim was stabbed in the heart with a knife by a person or persons unknown." He points to his chest.

Mcleod opens a folder and removes a photograph of Crown's body and shows it to him. "Is this the murder victim, Crown? With a stab wound to the chest?"

Foster nods his head, "Yessuh, that's Crown."

The prosecutor turns to show the photograph to the jury. "Please enter this picture as Exhibit A showing the wound in the victim's heart. Let's continue. Who found the body?"

"A sailor down at the docks discovered Crown."

"And did you question the sailor?"

"Yes, we questioned him, but he said he didn't see anythin'."

"And then how did your investigation proceed?"

"Since we knew Crown had killed a man named Robbins, we went to see Robbins' widah, Serena. I thought perhaps she might have tried to git revenge. She was our first suspect."

"And what did this woman have to say?" McLeod asks.

"Serena had an alibi with witnesses provin' she was in her house at the time Crown was killed."

"So, she was ruled out as a suspect?"

"Yessuh."

"And then what happened? Who was the next person you questioned?" The prosecutor paces the floor and stops back in front of the witness stand.

"I then went to question Porgy." He points to Porgy. "That man at the defendant's table ovuh there. Porgy was livin' with Bess, Crown's formah wife . . . not actually sure if any of them was legally married . . ."

Alan Archdale stands and raises his hand. "Objection, your honor. The witness is trying to impugn the character of the defendant without any evidence."

"Overruled. Mr. Archdale, when it is your turn, if you want, you can present evidence on that issue. The witness may continue." Archdale is reasonably certain Porgy and Bess were not legally married, but he felt he needed to plant some doubt in the minds of the jurors.

"Thank you. We believe Porgy was worried if Crown came back to Catfish Row, he would sweet-talk Bess into goin' away with him. It was common knowledge the defendant hated him an' wanted him out the way, an' that's why he killed him."

Archdale raises his hand again. "Objection, your honor! Speculation on the part of the witness and not based on evidence!"

"Sustained. Stick to what you know for certain detective," Judge Klugh rules.

"I *do* know that for certain, your honah. The locals tol' us Crown was hidin' on Kittiwah Island an' Bess went off to meet him when she was at the Catfish Row annual picnic. This took place while she was livin' with Porgy, an' we was fairly sure Porgy knew about it."

At this painful disclosure, Porgy's memory went back to Bess's confession about meeting Crown and still being under his sway. He could still visualize Crown, a tall man, with strong legs and muscular thighs, everything physically he was not. But Porgy also knew Bess loved him for transforming her life and for his decency. When they first met, he helped Bess quit the happy dust. They moved in together and created a loving home for themselves. Then, after they adopted Jonah, life was wonderful, and she had promised to stay with him even if Crown showed up again.

The white citizens in the courtroom find Foster's testimony about Bess and Crown meeting in the wild-hog wilderness of Kittiwar Island very amusing and start laughing. Klugh bangs his gavel on the bench, "Order! Order! Detective . . . Please stick to the facts."

The courtroom quiets down again as Foster continues. "I went to Porgy and Bess's room in Catfish Row to question him. Porgy admitted to me he knew Crown. While we was interviewin' him, I noticed a broken windah in their room and thought it might be evidence of the crime. I immediately accused him of killin' Crown, but Bess said the windah shattered when Porgy, being crippled, had a fall. She tol' me neighbors witnessed him fallin' an' breakin' the windah.

"With that explanation, I initially had to rule out Porgy as the killah. Also, we foun' Crown's body at the docks, quite a distance from Porgy's room. Since Porgy is crippled, we did not think he could have dragged him down to the docks. Latah, I thought someone could've helped Porgy, or he could've hauled him down there in his goat cart. When Porgy refused to identify Crown's body at the inquest, my suspicions only grew.

"We did lock him up awaitin' his trial for contempt of court for refusin' to identify Crown's body an' attend the inquest. Counsel for the defense, Mr. Archdale, put up his bail, so we had no choice but to let him go. Without any concrete evidence, we had to eliminate Porgy as a suspect in the murder. The next thing we learned was Porgy had left Charleston and no one would tell us where he had gone."

The crowd begins to whisper amongst themselves. Judge Klugh pounds his gavel, "Order! Order!" The gallery becomes silent.

McLeod summarizes, "So, there was a broken window in his home. And at that time Porgy was living with Crown's ex-wife and wouldn't identify the body . . . and then later on he ran from the court's jurisdiction. Does that pretty much sum it up?"

"Yessuh, that's correct."

The prosecutor sneers at Porgy and then turns back to the detective with a warm smile. "So, why did you now decide to arrest him for the murder? Could you also tell us how you tracked Porgy down after he jumped bail, pardon your Honor . . . was released from jail here in Charleston awaiting trial on the contempt charge?"

"I received a sworn written statement from a Catfish Row resident named Sportin' Life that he saw Porgy kill Crown and that various residents of Catfish Row dragged Crown's body to the harbah and covered it up with a tarp. Sportin' Life is the one who tol' us where to find Porgy in New York. Upon receivin' that information, I went to New York, and with the assistance of the New York City police, took Porgy into custody and brought him back hyah."

Porgy exclaims "Sportin' Life! Him be a liar!"

The prosecutor tells the judge he is putting Sportin' Life's sworn written statement into the court records as Exhibit B and asks the detective, "And when you found Porgy in New York, was he living with anyone?"

"Yes, he was with Crown's ex-wife, Bess."

He smiles and walks back to his seat. "No more questions, your honor."

Judge Klugh turns to Archdale and Simon Frasier. "Defense, please proceed with your cross examination."

CHAPTER FORTY-TWO

Archdale takes a few minutes to consult with Porgy and rises. He walks up to Detective Foster and begins his cross examination. "Detective Foster, isn't Sportin' Life a known drug dealer and a pimp?"

Foster looks to the judge and then back to Archdale, not wanting to undercut his testimony by having to admit Sportin' Life was involved in criminal activities. The prosecutor, Frank McLeod, raises his hand to object to Archdale's question but Klugh rules, "The witness will answer the question since it relates to the veracity of Sportin' Life's sworn statement."

"Detective, remember you're under oath. I'll ask you again. Isn't Sportin' Life a known drug dealer and a pimp?"

Foster nods his head, and stutters before answering. "Yyy . . . Yes, he is . . . was."

"And where is Sportin' Life now? Why isn't he here to give his statement in person?"

"I jus' learned he was . . . murdered . . . in New York. They are still lookin' for his killah now, or for . . . ah, someone who maybe hired someone to kill him." Foster abruptly turns to look at Porgy.

Porgy is shocked, gasping in disbelief, "Sportin' Life dead?" After a moment, he sighs with relief, realizing even if he hangs, Bess won't have to worry about Sportin' Life anymore. The audience again starts to whisper loudly among themselves.

Judge Klugh bangs the bench again with his gavel. "We will have order in my courtroom!"

Porgy leans into Simon and says, "Sportin' Life be dead? Fuh sho' muh frien's would hab tol' Bess dat, an' her would hab write tuh tell me." Porgy moans audibly, "Why din't I heah f'om she?"

"I dunno. De pros'cution din't eben tell we Sportin' Life bin dead. Dis may wuk en yuh fabuh."

Archdale moves closer to the witness box and asks, "You're not suggesting my client killed Sportin' Life too, are you? There was no way he could have killed him, because he was on a train with you coming to Charleston, right?"

"Yes, that's right."

Sensing a ray of legal light for Porgy, Archdale addresses the bench, "Your honor, under Section 803 of the South Carolina Rules of Evidence, I move the written statement from Sportin' Life be stricken from the record since he is not here to testify in person and to be cross-examined."

Judge Klugh takes a moment to consider the motion. "No, Mr. Archdale. Section 803 of the South Carolina Rules of Evidence allows for the admission of such sworn written statements if the decedent had nothing to gain by proffering it before passing away."

Archdale goes back to sit next to Porgy. Somewhat defeated, "No more questions your honor."

"You may step down, Detective Foster."

He glares menacingly at Porgy and returns to his seat in the gallery.

Judge Klugh turns to the defense's table. "Mr. Archdale, please call up your first witness."

Archdale rises. "I would like to bring Porgy to the stand, your honor." Simon Frasier helps Porgy to get situated in the witness box. They are trying to show the judge and jury Porgy is crippled in the hope of gaining some sympathy. Simon pats Porgy on the back and gives him a knowing nod of his head, and Porgy nods back signaling he is ready to tell the judge and jury what they agreed upon the day before.

Archdale approaches the witness box and asks, "So, Porgy, why would this man named Sportin' Life lie and say he saw you kill Crown?"

Porgy decides the jury will understand him better if he doesn't give his testimony in the Gullah dialect. "Crown's formah wife Bess an' me bin livin' tagethah an' we adopted a chile. Befo' I met her, Sportin' Life gots her on drugs and war her pimp. Mistah Archdale, aftuh yo paid mah bail, I foun' out Sportin' Life' take her ta New Yawk while I bin in jail. So, I lef' Charleston an' went ta look fo' Bess in New Yawk an' bring her back."

"Did he have something hanging over Bess so that he could talk her into going with him?"

Porgy, embarrassed for Bess, his face pained, lowers his head before he answers. "My frien's tol' me Bess war very depress an' Sportin' Life talk' her intah goin' back ta her ol' life. I knew I hab ta fin' her an' save her. So, in ordah ta get money an' hire a private detective . . ." Porgy pauses and looks at Archdale, not sure if he should tell about his illegal numbers operation in New York.

Archdale knows what he is thinking. "Go on, Porgy. You can tell about how you made a living in New York. It will show what Sportin' Life had against you and why he wrote Detective Foster and lied he saw you kill Crown."

Porgy takes in a deep breath. "There be a gamblin' business I started up in New Yawk, workin' out of an office in a dance club, ta make money . . . Da gamblin' game people bet on is called . . . da numbahs. Befo' I arrived der, Sportin' Life, he go by da name Mistah Big, war da 'main man' in da numbahs game in Harlem. . . . dat be a place in New Yawk. But, aftuh a short period of time I took away almost all his bid'ness.

"And den I foun' out dat Mistah Big war really Sportin' Life, an' I war able ta rescue Bess from him. Bess war back livin' wit' me when I got 'rrested an' brought back ta Charleston. He had mo' den 'nuff reasons ta lie an' tell da detective I kill Crown. Sportin' Life want' me an' mah numbahs bid'ness out of da way, an' he wan' ta git revenge fo' me takin' Bess back."

At this point, Attorney Archdale addresses Judge Klugh. "Your honor, going back to Section 803 of the Rules of Evidence, as you can see Sportin' Life did have an incentive to lie in his statement. I respectfully request his statement be stricken from the record and the jury instructed to ignore it."

McLeod jumps up. "Objection, your honor! I thought we were sticking to the facts! What we just heard about Sportin' Life is some dime-novel back alley gambling war story from up North in that fancy New York City. The defense has no way to prove any of this."

"Sustained." Klugh points a finger at Archdale. "I will only tell everyone this one more time. Stick to the facts you can prove. Counselor, continue with your witness."

Archdale nods. "Yes, your honor. Porgy, could you please tell us what happened here in Catfish Row the night Crown was killed?"

Porgy, tentative, begins to tell the judge and jury the story Simon Frasier told him to relate. He glances up at Maria holding Jonah, and then back to Simon. "On da night Crown die, he came ta da room Bess an' me were livin' in." Porgy's breath quickens as he thinks about the events that took place. "Crown broke da windah in our room an' was finna, I mean fixin' ta fo'cebly abduct Bess. He was still on da run ta keep from bein' 'rrested fo' killin' Robbins, but din't wan' ta leave wit'out her. Crown was tryin' ta kill me first an' den take her away an' I . . ."

Porgy looks up to the balcony again. He sees his adopted son, and his thoughts focus lovingly on him and Bess, and then he visualizes the scene he is about to describe. What happened that night in Catfish Row comes tumbling into his mind. He hopes this is the right thing to do.

He pauses. "An' when he crawl through da broke windah holdin' a knife, I fought wit' him an' grab' his knife away from him, an' den I stab' him wit' it." Porgy turns toward the jury and, in tears, shouts. "I did it ta defen' Bess an' me!"

When he admits to killing Crown, astonished gasps come from every corner of the room, and soon the people in the gallery are all talking loudly among themselves. Even the jurors gasp. Judge Klugh hammers his gavel furiously, yelling for quiet in his courtroom. In the upstairs gallery, Maria starts crying and clutches the baby tighter.

The courtroom gallery quiets down as Porgy continues. "I love Bess. I love mah son who we took in aftuh his mama die in da hurricane. I now had a family wit' Bess. Crown was a murderah, a monstah, an' a drunk. He tried ta kill me an' Gawd knows what he would hab done if he hab got ahold of Bess. I done it ta protec' mah family!"

The atmosphere in the courtroom has changed since the start of Porgy's testimony. The gallery watches his tear-stained face, hears the plaintive tone of his voice, and the nods of their heads show they believe he is telling the truth.

Archdale approaches the bench. "Your honor, in the upstairs galley is a resident of Catfish Row, named Maria. To corroborate what you just heard from Porgy, she is prepared to testify Crown visited her the night he was killed. He told her he had come to take Bess back from Porgy, whether she wanted to go with him, or not. He also said he would kill Porgy if he got in the way. Therefore, as counsel for the defendant I am asking you to bypass the jury and render a verdict of self defense and acquit Porgy of murder."

In the balcony, the Negro residents of Catfish Row start clapping when Archdale makes his statement. Klugh bangs his gavel once again, and motions Archdale, Frasier and Mcleod to the bench. He converses in a low voice with Mcleod who has no objection to Archdale's motion. Klugh then turns to the jury. "It is the judgment of this court that the defendant, Porgy, be acquitted of the charge of murder. We rule he killed Crown in self-defense and was also preventing his wife from being kidnapped. Porgy is free to go. Court is adjourned." Judge Klugh thumps his gavel for the last time.

Before leaving the bench, Klugh leans down and, in a snickering voice, says to the lawyers, "To be honest, no one really cares if one Negro kills another Negro as long as they don't disrupt the lives of the rest of the citizens."

Porgy is helped out of the witness box and hugs Archdale and Frasier. "Y'all save mah life. I din't think I hab a chance. I thought fo' shuh I war goin' ta heng. Thank yo so much fo' comin' up wit' da idea fo' me ta tell dat story."

Maria, holding Jonah, comes down from the balcony, runs over to hug Porgy and kisses him on the cheek. She hands him baby Jonah whom Porgy hasn't seen since he left Charleston.

"T'ank gawd de judge b'lieb muh story 'bout killin' Crown. Ef him habn', fo' sho' I would hab heng. Maria, 'membuh de lettah I sent yuh f'om New Yawk befo' I bin 'rrested? I ax ef yuh would come tuh New Yawk wid Jonah? Hab yuh t'awt 'bout it? Will yuh come?"

CHAPTER FORTY-THREE

Porgy and his friends from Catfish Row walk across Washington Square Park and enter St. Michael's Church to celebrate Porgy's release. It is near sunset and while the light in the vestibule is dimmed, colorful rays shine into the sanctuary through the impressive stained glass windows. The choir begins singing to signal the start of the Evensong Service.

He has never been inside a white church before. The only church music he is familiar with is called "shouting," a rhythmic pattern beaten out by feet and hands as an accompaniment to Spirituals. The choir's serene voices enhance his renewed sense of freedom.

He is seated in a pew and thanks everyone for all they have done to keep his spirits up during the trial. Simon Frasier puts his arm around Porgy and points to the church's "Easter Morning" stained glass window. "Befo' de trial us bin prayin' fuh a miracle an' Mistah Archdale show we dis' stain glass windah an' he say it might bin a message ob hope fuh yuh. Him bin right. Yuh hab come back tuh we."

Maria walks over to Porgy and touches his arm. "Gib me de baby tuh hol' an' follow me." Porgy, curious, gets up from the pew and follows her through the crowd.

"Wheah us goin'?"

"Come on, Porgy. Us hab tuh git upstair tuh de gallery pews." She leads him slowly along the central aisle to the stairs next to the altar. As they move further along, the sounds of the choir become louder and more joyous with each step. On his crutches, he uses every ounce of his energy as they begin to ascend the staircase to the balcony.

At the entrance to the gallery, Maria whispers, "Us heah." Porgy moves closer to Maria and sees a woman sitting in one of the pews. In the dim light of the chapel, he is unable to make out any of her features until she turns around. Suddenly he realizes who it is and yells out her name. Bess runs into his arms, they hug one another, and then a flood of questions begins.

"How en de worl' did yuh git heah? How long hab yuh bin heah? Did muh frien's bring yuh?"

"I came tuh Charleston by muhself, an' Maria tol' me 'bout de trial. Calm down, Porgy. Us kin talk latah. I be answer all yuh questions en a minute." They are so excited to be together again that all the questions and answers are just chatter between hugs and kisses.

Maria hands Bess the baby. "De trial be ober an' Porgy be free now." Pointing behind her she says, "I be right back der. Us hab tuh hurry."

Bess kisses Jonah. "Mommy miss yuh, young boy. Mommy be so sorry. I be nebbuh goin' away again." Bess turns to Porgy. "I nebbuh leabe ag'in." Taking hold of Porgy's hand, she helps him over to the stairs. "Come on, Porgy. I hab some clothes pack' an' some money. Us hab tuh git out ob heah."

Thrown off-guard, Porgy says, "Wait. Wait. Wuh happ'n Bess? Why do us hab tuh leabe heah so fast? I be a free man now. Dey say someone kill Sportin' Life, so us kin go back tuh Harlem wid Jonah an' staa't up ag'in, jis' like us plan."

Bess starts crying as she rocks Jonah. "I war de one dat kill Sportin' Life, Porgy."

Porgy's eyes grow big, and his body shakes uncontrollably. The news is so startling that he is totally incapable of comprehending what Bess has told him. "Wuh? Wuh yuh talkin' 'bout? Wuh yuh mean yuh kill'um?"

"When yuh lef', I be broken. I hab no one. All ob our frien's en New Yawk lef' fuh Paris. I din't know wuh tuh do . . . I be weak an' Sportin' Life temp' me back on de happy dus'. At his apa'tment, I foun' a lettah on his desk t'ankin' he fuh gibin' de detective de sworn statemen' dat yuh hab kill Crown. I wan' tuh leabe tuh git tuh Charleston an' tell de trial dat Sportin' Life lie.

"I war git ready tuh go when him foun' out I read de lettah, and him try tuh kill me tuh keep me f'om turnin' he in fuh lyin'. Him war stranglin' me, an' I t'awt I war gonna die. An' fuh a second, I be goin' tuh leh he kill me, an' leh me float intah de darkness. But somethin' came ober me. Muh strengk. Muh lub fuh yuh. Muh dreams. Our son. I knew I hab tuh fight an' I stab he en de neck wid a lettah openah. Him died, Porgy. Sportin' Life die right der on de floor, at muh feet, en his office."

Porgy is shaken by what Bess tells him. "But, Bess, how did yuh git back tuh Charleston?"

"I tek some money an' clothes. I got on a train dat tek me heah an' I walk tuh Maria. Her bin hidin' me en Catfish Row. I be sho' de police be lookin' fuh me by now. I war goin' tuh show up fuh yuh at de trial ef Simon need me tuh, eben do' I would end up gittin' 'rrested. I be glad I din't hab tuh do dat. Us hab tuh go right now, Porgy, befo' dey fin' me."

Shocked and excited at the same time, he asks, "Wheah be us goin' tuh go?"

Bess looks at him, smiles, excitement in her voice, "Paris."

Porgy is confused. "Paris, France?"

"Yes. De police won' fin' me der. All our frien's f'om New Yawk be now en Paris. Yuh heah dem talkin' when dey say Paris be a thrivin' place fuh Negroes. Bettah den heah. I know us kin mek it der, Porgy. I know us kin. Josephine tol' me tuh fin' she ef I ebbuh got tuh Paris. It be a new staa't. Away f'om dis Jim Crow place. An' I won' go tuh jail. I nebbuh wan' tuh be away f'om yuh ag'in."

Maria has been listening from the pews overlooking the altar. "Peter hab yuh suitcases en de waggin, ready tuh tek yuh tuh de ship en de ha'bah. Us hab tuh git yuh out t'rough de back door." She escorts Porgy and Bess down the staircase and then out of the church.

Bess grabs Porgy's hand "No mattah wuh happ'n, I lub yuh."

Porgy kisses Bess. "I lub yuh too." They turn back and wave to Maria in gratitude as they head out the door, on their way to their new life in Paris.

The End